THE
BOOK
OF
ZARA

KENNETH ALAN MOE

The Book of Zara

also including

The Third Song of Creation

HERETICS IN OCCUPIED EDEN

BOOK SIX

Kenneth alan moe

STRANGE ANGEL PRESS
Phoenix, Arizona

Copyright © 2016
Kenneth Alan Moe

Cover, interior design and cover photos by Ethan Moe
Cover painting is "The Head of Echo (Study)" by John William Waterhouse

First Printing

ISBN: 978-0692597620

Dedicated to All Intellectual Women
and the sapiosexuals who love them.

*Of genius they make no account, for they say that
everyone is a genius, more or less.*
Samuel Butler (*Erewhon*)

*The mind is its own place, and in itself
Can make a heav'n of hell, a hell of heav'n.*
John Milton (*Paradise Lost*)

*The human body is too precious to be altered
whimsically by any religion that comes along.*
James A. Michener (*The Source*)

Nakedness is the most democratic of all institutions.
Thorne Smith

CONTENTS

I
FLYING CLOUDS

O to realize space!
The plenteousness of all, that there are no bounds,
To emerge and be of the sky, of the sun and moon
and flying clouds, as one with them.

Walt Whitman (A Song of Joys)

Your slim gilt soul walks between passion and
poetry.

Oscar Wilde

All I ask is the chance to build new worlds.

Thornton Wilder

CHAPTER ONE
THE DEATH OF KEY

These thoughts, memories, reflections, and analyses I dedicate with deep humility to Chief Librarian Key, extraordinary teacher, dear friend, and namesake of my first child. As my beloved Merven mentor lay dying in the Australian winter of 2017, Key asked me to write an autobiographical essay for placement in the Merven Library. Key's robustly brown skin had paled from months of remaining inside due to ill health.

Ignoring his request, I said, "You need to get out into the sun. That will go a long way toward healing."

"I do yearn for the feel on sun on my skin," Key replied. "But the truth is, I am near death. What strength I have left is better preserved here in my nest inside Uluru."

I started to protest, but Key took my hand and said, "Do not deny what I know to be so, and please do not pray for my healing. I wish to embrace my transition into the realm beyond. And in the brief time left to me, I wish to gain your assurance that you will record the story of your life for posterity."

"Why me?" I said. "Surely your autobiography is more valuable than mine may turn out to be."

"My span is sufficiently documented. Do not fret over that. Only remember that even now your life has cultural significance for both the Merven and the human species," Key said. "It is likely that it will gain greater significance in the coming decades. You must promise me you will document it for my peace of mind if for no other reason. It need not be an exhaustive account. We already have much biographical material relating to you. What we do not have, however, are your thoughts and feelings about your experiences of living intimately with our two species. How has your thinking evolved? Write something that will surprise us and be sure to include at least a touch of whimsy. We Merven do like to laugh. I think it would be wise for you to complete your autobiography before you attain seventy years."

"Am I likely to die around that time?" I asked, shaken by the specified age.

"Not at all," Key said, "but many interesting things in your life and deep insights will have occurred by then. What novel experiences you have after that age should be recorded in a second volume, of course, which I hope would be produced once you reach an age counted in triple digits."

"This is because of that conversation we had a decade ago, isn't it?" I asked. "When you loosed that metaphorical thunderbolt in my life."

"I cannot deny that plays a part, but only a part. I should have made this request even if we had never had that conversation," Key said.

Without hesitation I promised to undertake the task and volunteered to write versions in the English and Merven languages. What I did not know at that mournful time was that this promise would lead me to the most unusual love of my life.

When Key's earthly span ended, I was emotionally devastated, far more than I had anticipated. The tears that flowed freely upon receiving the news were not surprising, but I was astounded that I experienced bouts of weeping at unexpected moments for several months.

Early in the spring of that year (fall in the northern hemisphere, but this happened in Australia) when I was nearly forty, I visited the Merven library at Uluru to learn what biographical information about me was already stored there. My intention was to use this source as a starting point for writing my life story and to add materials, documents, photographs, and other items to this collection over the years, thus making the ultimate task of producing the autobiography that much easier. I would not need to duplicate what was already there, but what had accumulated there could serve to jog my memory.

I was still grieving the loss of my dear friend and also anxious about meeting Key's successor as Chief Librarian, Polyglot. Anxious is the correct word here, covering the meanings of eager, impatient, as well as somewhat fearful. All these emotions arose from Sojourner's report to me that Polyglot was the offspring from Sojourner's love affair on a visit to Lhasa, Tibet in the 19th century. I was happy for Sojourner and eager to meet the mysterious progeny whose existence I had known about for years but only through vague references. Would I be disappointed with Polyglot in comparison with Key? Or would Polyglot feel like a member of my extended family, as Sojourner did?

When the meeting did take place, none of my guesses proved correct, but rather I was completely surprised at how I reacted to Polyglot and how I was transformed as a result of this particular visit to Uluru. I will say more about this further into the narrative.

Yet another motivation to visit the library was to learn about the process of electing the Chief Librarian. Pilgrim had given me an outline of the process, but I wanted to know background information about the candidates and why Ployglot had been the ultimate choice.

Since most of the readers of this text will be Merven, I will not describe in detail what I learned about Merven elections. But for the few English readers, here is a condensed version without the necessary intrigue and gossip about the personalities involved.

Chief Librarians are elected to serve for life. When the position becomes vacant, every Merven enclave around the world has the right to nominate a candidate for successor. Most enclaves do, and so the first round of voting includes hundreds of possibilities. The second round includes only the top forty-nine in the vote totals. The third round consists of those receiving the seven highest number of votes. The winner must have a simple majority of ballots cast, and though it is possible that further rounds of voting may occur after the final seven have been determined, historically this has never happened. By the time only seven remain in contention, one has always emerged as the clear favorite. Polyglot was at the top of the count in every round. All this occurs in a single day with all voting done telepathically.

One of my human traits, different from the typically Merven mental pattern, is to think and organize events in chronological order. With me this has been practically an obsession. Anachronisms in books, films, and plays cause me howling indignation, unless they involve time travel. A comment H. G. Wells made in *The Time Machine* resonates with me: "Our ancestors had no great tolerance for anachronisms." Recently, I saw a film set in the autumn before Gulf War I. A character listened to a song broadcast via radio, tapping her feet to the beat. The song was supposed to foreshadow a plot detail, but it significantly diminished my enjoyment of the otherwise well-made movie, because that song had not been recorded much less released for *radio* play at the time specified in that scene. The screenwriter should have used a different song! It would have made no sense to place the action a year later, when the song had been available to the public for six months, because that would have been after the war. For youngsters reading this, they really played songs on the radio in those days!

Had this occurred when I was much younger, I would have walked out in disgust. But the Merven sensibility about such things has permeated by mind, and so now I only take note of such errors and try to relax about it.

Merven do not perceive time as linear, with a starting point and strictly sequential elements elapsing to the present and projecting into the future but rather as an increasingly complex and growing present reality, with aspects and scenes within its scope that may be arranged in one's consciousness as one wishes.

This is prelude to my confession that thus far in this narrative I have already abandoned my own chronological discipline, so I will now shift to the beginning of my life and in due course come to tell of what developed from my first meeting with Polyglot.

What follows, then, is a peripatetic account of my life so far.

CHAPTER TWO
FLASHES OF AWARENESS

Unfortunately, I must rely on family stories to reconstruct the first year of my life. I would like to tell you my experiences of being born and my earliest impressions of the environment I was born into. Alas, as deeply as I have plumbed the unconscious realms of my brain in search of information, I have not been able to retrieve much. All I have are flashes of awareness that somehow made the transition from my short to long-term memory. They are all connected with places -crib, playpen, bathtub- and all have specific smells associated with them. The pleasing scent of baby powder and the acrid fragrance of a dirty diaper hamper still register strongly in my brain and set me to remembrance of the early months of my life.

If you know anything about my noteworthy family, you may have gained certain impressions about me, and I won't dispute the accuracy of third person accounts of my behavior. However, since this is the story from my perspective, it may differ significantly from what you have already heard or read. Keep in mind that my mother was in love with the metaphysical poet John Donne when she was a teenager, and my father was similarly smitten with Emily Dickinson. Essentially, they found what they were looking for in each other, which explains their tendency to wax poetic about me, romanticizing my behavior.

Nevertheless, I'll start with things I do not remember but have been handed down as family lore, and that bear the stamp of authenticity. My parents report that I began saying words, such as dada and mama at six months. A week later, my vocabulary had progressed to include more than fifty nouns. At six and a half months, I added verbs and adjectives to my vocabulary and began speaking in complete sentences. They were simple sentences, to be sure. "Zara hungry." "Zara sleepy." "Zara want bath." "Mary fix bottle." Mary is my aunt, who served as my nanny.

As time passed, my mastery of language increased geometrically. "Zara see daddy kiss mommy." "Zara want daddy kiss." "I want mommy's milk." "Change my diaper." "Rub my feet, please."

My mom tells the story of a late spring evening when I was eight months old. My parents had invited family friends Darla and Yonah Nabi to dinner. Darla is a rabbi and Yonah a publisher. At any rate, while Mom and Darla were in the kitchen preparing the meal, my dad was watching me in the living room while talking to Yonah.

I interrupted their conversation with the words, "Daddy, I'm hungry."

And Yonah nearly fell off the couch. But Dad just got up and went for Mom to come and breast feed me. Then I went to sleep.

After dinner, my portable crib was at the end of the sofa, and the sound of Mom's laughter woke me. "Mommy laughs," I said. "She tells funny story."

"My stars!" Darla said. "I've never heard an infant speak like that at eight months."

Then I rolled over and sat up. "OK guys, time for foot rubs! Me first!"

That's how they introduced the rabbi and her husband to reflexology. Foot rubs and also massage therapy have been part of my life since infancy.

I was born in Prescott, Arizona on October 7, 1977. My parents, Terry Person Morgan and Evan Cloud Morgan, are people gifted with extrasensory abilities as well as high intelligence, and I inherited these capacities perhaps in double doses. Dad was a college history professor at Anasazi College and Mom pastor of a Calvinist church when I was born, but within a few years they became co-pastors of a naturist congregation, the Sedona Natural Christian Church. So I grew up running around naked more often than wearing clothes.

My early years in Prescott and then Sedona, where we soon moved, were filled with joy, as I was surrounded with loving adults and older children. My mother told me many times over the years that they knew I was intellectually gifted by the time I was six months old.

When I was only a few weeks old, my aunt Mary called my mom with a proposition. She was ensconced in a loft in Greenwich Village, trying to make a living as a painter, but the life of a starving artist was not as romantic as reported. In reality, she had a comfortable income from her father's trust fund but was lonely. She offered to be a live-in nanny for me in exchange for room and board and the use of the studio in our house for her artwork. The house was a rambling Territorial structure that my parents called Strange Haven.

Mom loved the idea. Doing full-time ministry and caring for me would be complicated, even with my dad's flexible schedule, so having her sister in the house would be a blessing. Aunt Mary moved into Strange Haven the day before Mom returned to work from her maternity leave.

With three adults tending to my needs, each of them had time to attend to their particular callings. Mary set up a crib in the warm and sunny studio and painted while I slept. She delighted in the clothing optional ethos of Strange Haven and did most of her artwork in the nude. She told me later that I was her favorite model in those days. I still have a painting she did of me as a nude infant. The great thing about it is its anatomical preciseness.

The Board of Elders of First Calvinist Church set Sunday November twenty-seventh as the date for my baptism. Mom preached a sermon that day in which she described the sacramental practices of early Christians. "In those days," she said, "people desiring membership in the church stepped forward naked and after baptism by immersion were clothed in white robes."

When the time came for me to receive the sacrament, Dad carried me, his naked daughter, to the font. Mary, Grandpa Lloyd, and Grandma Nissa stood beside him. An elder read the baptismal questions, which Mom and Dad answered on my behalf. Then Mom took me in her arms and announced the baptismal formula used by that denomination. As she spoke, I felt water soaking my head. I have no recollection of anything anyone said during the rite, but this is one of those occasions where a flash of memory has been imprinted in my brain. The image shows a large hand splashing water on my face in a gigantic room full of people who are staring at me. Apparently they approve of this, because my mother's hand scoops up more water and lets it flow over my bare skin several additional times.

When I interviewed Mom about this event, to be certain I had this chapter correct, she said she placed her hand on my head and prayed for God's blessing in my life and then anointed me with oil, making the sign of the cross with her finger on my forehead. During the entire rite, according to family lore, I calmly cooed with pleasure. Mary handed Dad a towel to dry me, and Nissa brought forth a white gown, which had been Dad's when he was baptized.

Aunt Cedar Cradle said, "I saw a violet aura around Zara's body during the baptism."

"You see auras around everyone, Cedar Cradle," Dad said.

"Well, everybody has one," Cedar Cradle said, "but not violet. That's a sign of intellect and psychic power."

Violet has always appealed to me. There is something alluring and satisfying in this shade, whether in clothing patterns or paintings. When I was five, the wall in my bedroom parallel to my bed was painted violet at my request. I did not know this story about my baptism and the violet aura until I was in my thirties, but it helped me understand my unusual preference for that color.

Another special talent emerged in the summer before I turned one. My parents and nanny wanted to add a pet to the household but couldn't agree on cat or dog. The vote was two for a cat and one for a dog, but in their typical conciliatory fashion, they compromised and brought home from the animal shelter a black and white Australian shepherd, a shorthaired white cat with black markings, and a shorthaired black cat with white markings, all three males. Mom named the dog Preacher, Dad named the black cat Poet, and Mary named the white cat Painter. All were affectionate creatures who loved to be petted, although Poet became a skittish introvert whenever strangers visited.

Very quickly, it became evident that the animals favored one human over all the others in the household: me. Intuitively I understood their languages, and they obeyed my instructions. Even the cats obeyed when I ordered them down from someone's lap, for example, or to come snuggle with me on the quilt on the floor. On more than one occasion, I fell asleep on the quilt with Preacher, Poet, and Painter wrapped in a circle around my body.

Shortly after my first birthday, I proudly greeted my dad with an announcement when he arrived home one evening. "Daddy, I'm potty trained!"

"Congratulations Zara! That's pretty fast, isn't it?" he said.

"It's amazing, really," said Mary. "She wanted to know why older children don't wear diapers, and I explained about the muscle control. She said, 'I can do that' and did."

"No more diapers for me," I proclaimed.

"You're such a joy," Dad said, lifting me up into his arms. "Let's dance a little before dinner." He put a Curtis Lee recording of "Pretty Little Angel Eyes" on the stereo and bounded around the room holding me close to his chest. I was deliriously happy to be whirled about in his strong embrace, and I was aroused by his scent. I was in love with my dad at that age, but since the texture and smell of my mom's breasts also roused me, it is fair to say that I was in love with her too.

One day my mom came home from a frustrating day at work, complaining about a mean-spirited member of her congregation. I don't remember her but from family lore, I gather that Mrs. Bowdler was a highly frustrated woman whose only happiness came from making other people suffer as much as she had.

At any rate, trying to evoke a bit of compassion for the woman, my dad said, "Maybe Mr. Bowdler doesn't rub her feet often enough."

"I'll bet it's more than her feet that never gets rubbed," Mary quipped.

"Let's give Mrs. Bowdler a foot rub," said I brightly.

Mary laughed, but mom and dad exchanged anxious looks. They were thinking that it was only a matter of time before I would repeat something in church that would complicate mom's life as a pastor and perhaps put her position in jeopardy. It's fair to say that a significant number of church members would not have been pleased to hear that their pastor and her family ran around naked when not attending to church matters. A puritanical streak ran through the Calvinist Church in those days. An image of puritans streaking popped into mind as soon as I had written the previous sentence. I had intended no pun, but the thought made me smile.

Mary told me later that she, mom, and dad had agreed that they needed to have a talk with me about family privacy. But it seemed absurd to have such an abstract conversation with a one year-old, so they postponed it until I was old enough. To date, it has not happened, so I suspect it never will.

As life evolved, however, I did not reveal any family intimacies in church. In fact, I talked very little outside our home. Even as a toddler, I had an intuitive sense that my home life, which I dearly loved, was a private matter not to be shared with the wider world.

Not long after my second birthday but before we moved to Sedona in early 1980, something happened that may be the most distinct memory I have actually retained from infancy. I was in the studio, playing on the floor while Mary was sketching. The doorknob on the closet door caught my attention and I wandered over to it. Though I had no sense of the age of things at that time, I have learned since that it was an antique brass bulb, original to the house. Its shape and patina attracted my curiosity.

Upon grasping the fascinating metal globe, I felt a shudder throughout my body and a vision of two children, a girl and a boy, entered my mind. In retrospect, I would judge them to be on the brink of puberty, and I understood them to be siblings, very likely twins. Both were sad, because one of them had to move, leaving the house forever. It wasn't clear why this had to happen or which one had to go. But some vague authority figure had informed them that there was only room for a boy or a girl, and they had to decide which. They were determined not to choose, and I sensed defiance in them.

As I grew older, I probably mentally elaborated upon the vision, filling in the blanks to explain what I had seen and felt. Yet with the adult concepts scraped away, my description here is consistent with what happened when I touched the brass doorknob.

Remembrance of the experience flooded my consciousness from time to time over the next two decades, and eventually I came to interpret it as a sign, encouraging me never to accept vague authority about matters of identity.

CHAPTER THREE
SIGNS

Late one April afternoon when I was two and a half, I was on the roof of the converted resort that served as the church my parents led, as well as our residence. My parents were there along with Uncle Firstlaugh, and Aunt Cedar Cradle and their children, Tzek and Wakhan. It was a pleasant interlude as we enjoyed a spectacular view of bright red rocks and clear blue sky.

Uncle Firstlaugh pointed to the east and shouted, "Look! An eagle! That's a good sign."

"It's not a bald," said Cedar Cradle. "It looks like a golden."

I spotted the bird soaring high in the sky but misheard my uncle's identification of the creature, although I clearly heard my aunt say the word golden, which in my young mind did not connote wealth but holiness. "Come down here, angel! I'll make you a nest!" I called out. This is how the communal church facility where we lived came to be known as Angel Nest.

Eagles notwithstanding, my favorite song from early childhood was "The Teddy Bears' Picnic" by an English singer named Henry Hall. I learned later that this was very popular among English children during World War II. Songs about animals have always appealed to me. The Carpenters recording of "Bless the Beasts and the Children" is another of my early favorites. I later saw the film and read the novel it was based on written by one of my dad's college professors, Glendon Swarthout.

For my fourth birthday, Dad made me a cassette tape compilation of songs from his extensive record collection, which included discs from as

13

far back as 1912 through the 1970s. He picked songs he thought I would like, including those mentioned above, and (among others) "Be Kind to Your Web-footed Friends," a Mitch Miller sing-along novelty (set to the tune of "Stars and Stripes Forever"), "Don't Let the Rain Come Down," sung by the Serendipity Singers, Pete Seeger's version of "Little Boxes," and "Morningtown Ride" performed by the Seekers. The latter two songs were written by Malvina Reynolds, a noted crusader for social justice as well as a fine folk musician. Dad chose well. I listened to that tape over and over for years.

Long before I started kindergarten, they knew I had also inherited their extrasensory abilities plus at least one they did not have, innate skill at communicating with other mammals. One of my earliest memories, that remains vividly fixed in my mind, is going on a hike with my parents on my third birthday. We climbed Sterling Pass out of Oak Creek Canyon into a wilderness area that my dad had explored years earlier. He took us through a hidden fissure in a rock wall that opened into a secluded valley. There was a pool surrounded by a golden-hued rock shelf that I spotted immediately and ran toward. My parents caught up with me to keep me from splashing into it. It was well that they did so, as I soon discovered that the water was icy cold.

The sun was warm, however, and my mom suggested we take off our clothes to bask in its glow. As soon as we had settled our naked bodies onto the smooth sandstone shelf above the pool, a mountain lion ambled onto the ledge right toward us. Though I had never seen such a creature, I was not afraid, and neither were my parents. The lion came up to my dad and sniffed one of his armpits and then my mom's face before playfully nuzzling my forehead. Then the lion settled down in front of me to be petted. As I ran my hand across his back, he purred.

"I didn't know cats this big purred," said my dad.

"Apparently they do," my mom said. "Either that or Zara has extraordinary persuasive power."

"It likes to purr," I said. "I'm not making it do anything strange."

Mom got up to walk around, and we heard a voice coming out of a cave on the other side of the pool. Then Sojourner (whose name we did not then know) emerged from the cave and said, "Nobody seems to be afraid of anything anymore. What ever happened to awe?"

Dad addressed Sojourner as Old One, whereupon Sojourner said hello to each of us, including the mountain lion. Intuitively, I understood the lion language. Dad then asked if Sojourner was influencing the lion's tame behavior, but Sojourner said that I was doing it.

"No, I'm not," I said indignantly. "I'm just being friendly."

"Nevertheless, you are communicating telepathically with the lion," Sojourner said.

Since we did not know Sojourner's name at the time, it seemed the logical thing for me to ask for it.

"Let me save that for another time. In my language the name would mean nothing to you."

As much as I tried to discover the name through telepathic inquiry, all I could perceive then, apart from Old One, was the nonsense image of wandering guest, which I dismissed as not germane. Only years later did I recognize how close I had come to the true name.

A strong desire to touch Sojourner's breasts arose in me, which I communicated silently to Sojourner. It must have appeared to be impulsive to my parents when I did so. Out loud I said, "You look like both mommy and daddy." The term intersex was not then in my vocabulary. My parents looked concerned about my fondling efforts, but Sojourner told them it was alright.

My mom said, "I worry about her inordinate curiosity. I don't want her to get in trouble violating other people's boundaries."

Sojourner responded, "Zara will always be exceedingly curious about the world. There will come a time in her personal evolution when you will not be able to protect her. This is likely to come much sooner than you would prefer, but if it is any consolation, you need not worry about her harming other people. And for the record, she asked permission to touch my breasts and I gave it."

"So you two are carrying on telepathic conversations right in front of us," Dad said.

"It is so," Sojourner replied. "And I know that all three of you are curious about my body. Come and touch anywhere you like." Sojourner reclined supine on the sandstone shelf.

I put my hands on Sojourner's face and said, "You have a big head."

Mom, Dad, and Sojourner laughed at this. Sojourner explained, "That's what your mother called me when she was a little girl."

"Great minds think alike," Mom said with a grin.

I caressed Sojourner's body and felt a sensation of mild electricity pulsing into my hands. Mom asked if Old One would like to touch us in a similar way, to which Sojourner said. "That is kind of you to offer, and it would provide me with heightened memories of you to do so."

Sojourner tended first to my mom and dad, and I could tell from their grins and coos that they were enjoying the energy-laden contact of Sojourner's fingers with their skin. While this was happening, I climbed on the lion's back and pulled his ears, which made him purr again. Then it was my turn. I lay back on top of my mom, and Sojourner used a finger to trace the lines of my face and body, skipping over my genitalia.

Speaking to my mom, Sojourner said, "Zara sent me a message to touch between her legs, and I told her that grownups should not touch children that way."

I said, "I understand. I won't let a bad person touch me there. But you're not a bad person. I can tell."

"Bless you, Zara, but I will not touch that part of you. In my society as it is in human society, it is a serious transgression for adults to fondle children's sexual organs."

"OK for now. When I'm grown?" I responded.

"If you wish then," said Sojourner.

There was no doubt in my prescient mind. "I *will* wish!" I declared.

The mountain lion rolled over and began kneading the air with his paws. "He wants to be touched too. He wants a belly rub," I said. Sojourner obliged the feline's desire.

The most intense memory of that encounter comes from touching and being touched by Sojourner. The energy in Sojourner's caress thrilled me, whether it was Merven fingers upon human skin or my small human fingers upon Merven skin. The sensation was electric. This occasion brought my first conscious knowledge of sexual desire. Though it did not happen, I wanted Sojourner to caress me in a sexual way.

One winter day when I was four, I wanted to go outside and play in the snow. Mom said I could as soon as she located my snowsuit and boots, which would take a few minutes. When she went in search of my winter apparel, I dashed outside naked and romped in the expanse of frozen whiteness. The cold had no appreciable effect on me. As I lay down to make a snow angel, Mom came running outside with my clothes and boots. Apparently she had seen me leave the nest and hastened out, for she was as naked as I.

My first thought was that she was angry with me, but she looked at the shape my body had made in the snow and laughed. Throwing down the things in her arms, she yelled, "Stop! Don't move your arms or legs. You're three-quarters of the way to making a peace symbol." She helped me carefully rise and together we tramped out a circle around my outline and completed the vertical element in the design.

Then she said, "Aren't you cold? I'm freezing."

I said, "Not especially."

She put her hand on my back and was surprised at how warm my skin was. I didn't know it at the time, but this was a significant genetic indicator that would profoundly affect the course of my life.

Next, Dad rushed out with a camera and instructed Mom and me to stand beside our symbolic representation to record the image for posterity. He was laughing too. By then I was beginning to feel cold and Mom was turning blue, so we all went inside. Mom made hot chocolate for us, and she and Dad told me the history of the peace symbol and the demonstrations against the war in Indochina.

As I sipped hot chocolate and listened to them talk, I felt deep love for them as well as profoundly loved by them. This incident is a characteristic example of the quality of my childhood home life.

Another exceedingly fond memory is going on floating (out-of-body) expeditions with my parents and the other people who lived with us at Angel Nest. This made me feel that I was part of a truly intimate extended family. I would liken my first five years to living full-time in Eden. Then I discovered what life was like beyond the protective gates of paradise.

About a year after the trip to the Lion Basin, I was listening to one of my dad's old Kingston Trio records and fell in love with "Wimoweh" also known as "The Lion Sleeps Tonight." Immediately this became pleasantly associated in my mind with the mountain lion I had met in the Basin. Generally, I prefer the Kingston Trio version to the pop version by the Tokens, although I have never found funny the remark about lion meat tonight in the set-up to the song on the "Hungry i" album. Lions are naturally carnivores, but humans are not. I don't think we are even omnivores but that some of our ancestors started eating meat to supplement their need for protein and the bad habit caught on.

In July, three months before my fifth birthday, I overheard my parents talking about their out-of-body experiences. Naturally, I wanted to do that too. "Teach me to float," I insisted.

I remember my parents looking at one another in that characteristic way they do, conducting a detailed but wordless conversation. Once the idea had gained access to my brain, I was impatient about learning the technique, but when they do their wordless thing, there's no point in interrupting.

After what was probably a few seconds but felt like ten minutes, my dad said, "OK, come with us to the bedroom."

I placed my little body supine on the giant bed and listened intently to the instructions my parents provided. After hearing the instructions once and with no questions, I said, "Let me try, now." I closed my eyes and entered into a period of slow, deep breathing. For about five minutes nothing happened, but all at once my mom noticed a change in my face. I've since learned that a blank stare is an indication that one has left one's physical body.

I distinctly remember Mom saying, "She's gone! On her first try! I'm jealous."

Mom and Dad lay back, one on each side of me, and within a minute also popped out of their bodies.

"Zara, where are you?" Dad transmitted telepathically.

"Here, Daddy!" I had already left the bedroom and was hovering near the ceiling of the studio. They surrounded me with their spirits.

"Where would you like to go, dear?" Mom asked. "What would you like to see?"

"Let's go see that eagle I thought was an angel," I said.

We sailed off in search of the majestic bird. Though we flew beside several hawks that day, we failed to find any eagles. Nevertheless, I had great fun exploring the skies around Sedona.

When we returned to our bodies, Mom said, "Zara, this is a special gift and you must use it wisely."

"I know, Mommy. You and Daddy will show me," I dutifully answered.

"Promise us you won't do this by yourself until we tell you it's OK to solo," said Dad.

I hesitated to make such a promise, having already begun to contemplate floating again soon -by myself. "I...I...want..."

"I was a little older than you the first time I floated," said Dad, "but I didn't float outside my room until I was a teenager."

I started to argue but restrained myself.

"We understand your desire to explore," said Mom, "but there are dangers in being out of your body too long or flying too far away."

"Is it dangerous because you meet dead people?" I asked with a touch of eagerness.

"In three decades of traveling without my body, I've never encountered any," said Dad. "I suppose it's possible, but they'd have to have died *very* recently, within seconds or minutes at the most. I suppose if you floated around hospitals you might see them."

"Let's compromise on soloing," said Mom. "You may leave your body by yourself if you promise to stay within the borders of Angel Nest. If you want to go further, one of us or Aunt Cedar Cradle or Uncle Firstlaugh must go with you until we decide you're ready to go alone."

"That's cool," I said. "But I didn't know Aunt CC and Uncle F could float too. What about Tzek and Wakhan?"

"No, but I suspect there will soon be great agitation in that regard," said Dad.

And of course there was. I shared a bedroom with Tzek and Wakhan and wasted no time telling my adoptive cousins about the experience of floating. Firstlaugh and Cedar Cradle thereupon taught their children how to leave their bodies, and we seven souls spent the rest of July exploring Oak Creek Canyon and the purported vortex sites around Sedona, without taking our bodies along.

A regular Saturday morning ritual developed around floating. Instead of watching cartoons on television, we three children stretched out on the carpet in our bedroom, nestled in between our parents, and popped out of our bodies to explore the world.

One Saturday, as we mentally convened in the studio before sailing off to examine the ancient Anasazi cliff dwellings known as Montezuma Castle, the adults sensed another presence hovering in the area.

"Who are you?" Cedar Cradle asked.

Silence.

"The presence is benign," said Mom to her soul-family. She then focused attention on the alien soul and said, "Don't be frightened, whoever you are. We're friendly."

"It's moving away from us," Firstlaugh said. "But I don't pick up any fear. It's more a feeling of shyness, or perhaps embarrassment."

"Please come back," signaled Mom. "We've never met anyone else while floating out of our bodies."

"Are you dead?" I asked.

It turned out to be Huxley Askeladd, the daughter of one of the couples living with us at Angel Nest. Clearly, she was not dead. So, we added yet another floater to the group. As time passed, the number of floaters among us increased dramatically.

On New Year's Eve 1982, I again had the privilege of seeing Sojourner, although we did not yet know that name. It was our annual family reunion at Angel Nest, and people had been coming in all day. Late in the evening, the people who had been scattered around the room gathered in tight semicircles around the fireplace, mouths agape at the sudden appearance of a gravid intersexual who had materialized seemingly out of nowhere.

I ran up and exuberantly embraced the Old One. "I remember you!" I said excitedly. "Do you remember me and the mountain lion?"

"Yes, Zara, I remember you most fondly. The lion sends his regards."

This made me beam with joy. I wished I could have taken the lion home as a pet, but, realistically, there would not have been any place for the lion to roam freely. It would have been cruel to keep him at Angel Nest, although I did not know that at the time. The consolation prize was learning that that lion remembered the encounter with me.

A few minutes later, we finally learned Sojourner's name and no longer had to rely on the descriptors Old One and Big Head, which for an unknown reason made me very happy.

CHAPTER FOUR
PROBLEMS IN SCHOOL

Misbehaving in class became a recurring theme during the early years of my public school career. It is not as though I was guilty of actual misbehavior, but this is the label that was metaphorically pasted on my forehead by professional educators. The basic problem was that by second grade I was already reading at a high school level and was thus bored with the instruction. Mom and Dad had discussed this with my teachers and the school principal on several occasions but none of these highly educated adults could reach agreement on how to handle the situation. The educators pronounced the problem one of socialization rather than academics. For a time, Mom and Dad considered sending me to a private school but postponed making that decision, because apart from boredom in the classroom, I was quite pleased with the intellectual and social richness of my life.

During his childhood and teen years, my dad experienced a number of prescient dreams. Family lore has it that he had a dream about the assassination of President Kennedy months before it happened. Knowing this about my father caused me to pay attention to my dreams. Some time in the spring of 1985, I had a peculiar dream not long before waking up, which stayed in my consciousness after rising. I walked into the bathroom, where Wakhan was brushing her teeth. As she continued to create minty froth in her mouth, I sat on the toilet and let loose a pent up stream of urine.

"I had an unusual dream before sunrise this morning," I said.

"Whaaabou?" Wakhan said.

"I would describe it as a seriocomic nightmare. The church was surrounded by soldiers in combat fatigues -both men and women soldiers. For some reason never made clear, they had declared war on us, but instead of shooting bullets they were bombing us Angel Nesters with balloons filled with religious slogans. Then two Irish warriors, a man and a woman, managed to breach the gate riding on a tank that looked like a bread truck, but once they got inside the walls, they fell to their knees and surrendered."

Her mouth now rinsed, Wakhan said, "Hmmm? I wonder what that means?

"I wish I knew. The dream imagery seemed particularly laden with energy. It must be significant," I said. I wrote the dream in a journal, in case it later turned out to prescient in some way.

Right after Labor Day, the prescient nature of part of the dream became clear. A consortium of fundamentalist Christian churches initiated a picket of our church, claiming that we were somehow fraudulently usurping the Eden that God had taken away from humankind. They carried signs with various ignorant and bigoted expressions of Christianity. My parents hired an attorney named Sigrid Yves to assist them in responding to the situation. I met Sigrid when I interrupted a conference my parents were having with her in the kitchen of our home. They had dressed for the occasion, in shorts and tee shirts.

I came bounding into the kitchen naked, as was my usual state of undress, and addressed my parents, saying, "Excuse me for intruding on your legal conference, but word is out that you're planning a counseling session with the kids to prepare us for fallout from the anti-naturist protests outside the church. When and where do you want us to gather?"

"Seven thirty around the fireplace, honey," Dad said. "And, Zara, this is Sigrid Yves. She's going to help us draft a response to the picketers."

I shook hands with the attorney. "I'm Zara Person Morgan. It's good to meet you."

"It's good to meet you too," said Sigrid. Without premeditation she added, "Zara, would you mind if I sat in on the counseling session?"

"I certainly hope you will," I said. "My parents are bright people, as are the other residents here, but none is a lawyer, and to tell the truth, I don't think they know all that much about the limits and implications of the First Amendment."

"Why don't you spread the word about the meeting, Sweetie, and we'll meet you under the triptych at seven thirty," said Mom.

I bounded out of the room, flushed with knowledge that I had an important message to deliver.

At the meeting, the children present were advised that there may be bullying and teasing at school as a result of the publicity surrounding the picket. Some of my Angel Nest family did indeed experience teasing and threats from classmates. Not I.

In my case, the trouble came from my teacher, Miss Labia Stone, who had been continuously unhappy with me because I could read, write, and think well beyond my years. Miss Stone already knew I came from a naturist family, and she disapproved, deeming the lifestyle unnatural and immoral, so she used the publicity surrounding the picketing as an excuse to make my life even more difficult. She ordered me to move my desk to a back corner of the room and instructed me to remain silent during class. I was not allowed to ask questions or participate in the lessons, as if I wanted to.

"Since you're so advanced, Zara, apparently there's nothing I can teach you," Miss Stone said curtly. "So you might as well sit by yourself and think about fourth grade and not interfere with my important work of educating the rest of the class."

"Why don't you just move me to fourth grade then?" I asked. "I know other kids who have skipped grades."

"Because you are not mature enough for fourth grade," she snapped back. "Now sit quietly where I told you."

"Aye aye, Miss Rock Lips," I muttered quietly under my breath. To my mind, this represented an improvement, but moving my desk to a completely separate place would have increased the quality of sitting by myself.

The picket of our church collapsed when an escaped criminal shot my paternal grandfather. Though sustaining a critical wound, Grandpa Lloyd recovered. But during the chaos surrounding the shooting, the rest of my prescient dream was fulfilled, as a married couple of Irish ancestry, who had been demonstrators, sought asylum from the cult they were part of by riding a bread truck into the church campus. This made me anxious about dreaming for a time, but mainly served to keep me alert to memorable dreams that might in any way be prescient. Thankfully, such dreams would prove to be rare, occurring years apart.

Not long after that, I broached the subject of alternative schooling with my parents. "You both have graduate degrees. Let me drop out of school and you can teach me more than anyone at my rinky dink school could begin to conceive."

"And where will we find the time to prepare lesson plans and spend six or seven hours a day providing you instruction?" Dad asked.

"You mean *how* will you find the time," I replied. "Unless, that is, you have discovered a physical locus for time."

"If this is the way you behave with your teacher," said Mom, "I can understand her frustration. I know it must be exceedingly frustrating for you to be in a class where you are so far ahead of your age peers, but a little discretion would help ease the tension."

"It's not just my age peers," I said. "Miss Stone is not a person acquainted with the life of the mind, if you get my drift."

"Zara, she's a third grade teacher, not a college professor!" my dad sputtered. "What do you expect?"

"I don't expect to be bored out of my skull," I said. "It's unfair to expect someone my age to sit patiently in such a stultifying environment created by someone who has failed to evolve beyond her apparent Neanderthal ancestry."

"What would you like to do with your class time?" Mom asked, ignoring what I thought a creative and clever description worthy of note. "If you could structure your day at school, what would that look like?"

"Well, to be honest, I like the organized games, recess, social activities, music, and art," I said. "I don't think I'd change those, except maybe to add some time for reflection and analysis of the musical pieces we learn and a chance to discuss what we intend to convey with our drawings and watercolors. The real problem is Miss Stone's insipid instruction in language arts and the silly books she reads to the class. If I could have a quiet corner somewhere to read, write, and reflect on ideas, that would be great. That is, if I could choose my own subjects. If I could work on challenging puzzles from time to time, that would be good too. Maybe breaking secret codes would be interesting, or doing a self-study of other languages."

"We'll talk to the principal soon, to see if we can negotiate something like that for you," Dad said.

This represented progress, and I hugged my parents. "Thank you Daddy! Thank you Mommy! I feel so much better now."

The consultation with Dot Dewey, my school principal, went better than Mom and Dad had anticipated, but the negotiated outcome was less than what they had hoped for. Labia Stone had already isolated me from the rest of the class, but it was isolation in place. My desk was at the end of the last row, but I was still included in the regular classroom configuration. If they would not move me up to fourth grade, then I wanted to be in some other room by myself. The proposal that I be allowed to read whatever I wanted at my desk met with approval, although this would not be fully honored. However, Miss Stone continued to maintain the guiding issue was not my intellect but my need for peer socialization. Under no circumstances would she allow me to work independently outside the classroom and the principal sustained this position. Thus a quiet corner for reading, writing, and reflection was ruled out, because Labia Stone had a loud, nasal voice, and the students were inclined to noisy outbursts when given the opportunity to speak. But my desk was moved farther back and sideways, creating a sense of discontinuity with the rest of the class.

I accepted the compromise as an improvement over the status quo and settled into a routine at school in which I concentrated on tuning out the classroom distractions as much as possible. The first day of my new educational freedom, I brought J. R. R. Tolkien's **The Hobbit**, and when I finished that, I worked through his **Lord of the Rings** trilogy. Next I brought a modern translation of Geoffrey Chaucer's **Canterbury Tales** that showed the Middle English text on the verso page and the newer text on the recto page. I read both sides, taking delight at being able to observe the evolution of verb endings and spelling changes in my native language.

I also made my way through a series of science fiction books that I found in my dad's library: **The Foundation Trilogy** by Isaac Asimov, **Dune** by Frank Herbert, **The Martian Chronicles** by Ray Bradbury, and **Childhood's End** by Arthur C. Clarke.

I was further smitten with the mystical work of Samuel Taylor Coleridge. For several weeks, the unfinished poem "Kubla Khan" fascinated me, and during recess I wandered about reciting it. It drove

Miss Stone and my classmates crazy to hear me endlessly repeat, "In Xanadu did Kubla Khan a stately pleasure dome decree."

When I brought in Thorne Smith's *The Glorious Pool*, which came from my mom's library, Miss Stone confiscated it, saying it was obscene and inappropriate for a child. The fantasy farce contained innocent line drawings of nude people. This is when she made the comment about nudism being unnatural and immoral. Thus the agreement to let me read whatever I chose was summarily abandoned.

"Sometimes I wonder about your questionable taste in reading material," she said.

I looked her in the eyes and said, *"De gustibus non est disputandum."*

"Don't you sass me in foreign languages," she responded.

"I would never sass such a *soi-disant* educator as yourself," I said with my head lowered in apparent obeisance. Actually, I did that to hide the onset of a grin.

"I'll accept that as an apology," she said.

It took a lot of effort for me to suppress a guffaw. At any rate, she wouldn't even let me take *The Glorious Pool* back home with me at the end of the day but insisted on mailing it to my mother with a stern warning about providing pornography to a child. Mom's reaction upon receiving the book in the mail was to advise me to read it at home and not take anything to school that would provide an excuse for Labia Stone to present me as incorrigible to the principal.

As I entered the classroom the next day, I noticed that the janitor had put my desk back into alignment with the others. In a moment of whimsy, I looked at Miss Stone and said, "It looks like the corner for the *Asprushya* has been abolished. Am I to rejoin the class now?"

Miss Stone said, "What did you say?"

"My desk has been moved," I replied.

"Well, the janitor didn't know any better," she explained. "But what did you call your corner? It sounds like unacceptable vocabulary."

"Asprushya," I said again. "And to be honest, it does have obscene connotations."

"Well, you'll just have to explain that to the principal," she said in a huff.

"OK. I'll explain to her that you did not know about the Untouchables in India, how they are ostracized and the obscene way they are treated. No doubt she will then wonder about the limitations of your education." I laughed and turned around and made my way to the principal's office. In the end, I was disappointed that though Mrs. Dewey had heard of the Untouchables, she also did not know the Hindi word for them. I was made to sit in detention for an hour. When I returned to the classroom, my desk had been repositioned to its isolated corner.

In the bad old days before the conference that led to permission for me to read and study in my separate corner, Miss Stone held me after class one day and told me I was frightening the other children. This did nothing for my self-esteem until I recognized that she was revealing her own fears not those of my classmates. After I learned she was afraid of me, I confess I did everything I could think of to rattle her in class. But that behavior soon grew tiresome, and I did not like myself when I acted badly out of spite. When the principal arranged for me to have a separate corner of the classroom to pursue whatever academic subject I wanted, I generally left Miss Stone to carry on without interruption, although I may have slipped occasionally.

CHAPTER FIVE
SCOFF

On a hot Sunday afternoon in August 1986, following a drenching monsoon, I was lounging in my bedroom, passing time by working the New York Times crossword puzzle while listening to my radio, when a news bulletin came on about the collapse of a church building near Cottonwood. The church was called Sacred Chapel of Fundamental Faith (SCOFF). The report noted that the edifice had been built by its members rather than by a licensed contractor. During the rainstorm abetted by strong winds, the roof had caved in, causing the first floor to crash into the basement, where the church youth group was meeting. Seven young people were in the basement at the time of collapse, and their fates were unknown. There were no injuries or fatalities among the people on the main floor.

Immediately I ran into the family room and told my parents about the disaster. My dad said, "That was one of the congregations involved in the Crusade against us last year. As I recall, they wanted *our* walls to crumble. The Battle of Jericho all over again. Such irony."

"Well, they may be stupid, but they don't deserve to die because of it," I said. "We should help them. Get dressed and drive me to that church."

"How can we help?" my mom asked.

"Well, it's obvious, isn't it?" I replied curtly.

In short order, we were on our way to the collapsed building. When we arrived, Dad parked down the street, and I stretched out in the back seat and soon floated out of my body. At the church, chaos reigned, as people ran around wailing and shouting for help, while a crew of rescue workers pulled rubble away from the area around the front door. I traveled through the wreckage into the basement and found the seven kids covered in dust and huddled into a space in the far corner where the floor above had not fallen completely through. Some had bruises and a few had broken bones, but all were alive -and terrified, because the concrete above them made ominous scraping sounds as it shifted.

Immediately, I returned to the car and re-entered my body, then dashed over to the rescue crew and said, "They're all alive and in that corner," pointing to the location where I knew them to be. "Start pulling out rubble at that end. And hurry, because I don't know how long the pocket of air will last."

The pastor, Titus Unraed, was working with the rescue crew, and he glowered at me and with an accusatory voice said, "Who are you, and how could you possibly know that?"

Clearly, I did not want to tell the truth about floating, so I said the first thing that popped into my head. "I'm the daughter of the Natural Christian Church pastors, whom you picketed last year, and **God** told me where the children are. Now get going!"

"Get out of here you evil child!" the pastor yelled.

But the other workers had already started digging where I had told them. Within a few minutes, they heard voices below, and within half an hour the youth group had been rescued. One of them was the fifteen year-old son Pastor Unraed, whose name I later learned was Timothy.

By this time, my parents had joined the scene. The pastor appeared to be confused and perhaps a little humbled by the rescue. He said, not to my parents but to no one in particular, "Why would God do this to us?"

My dad butted in by saying, "God had nothing to do with it. You did this to yourselves. You constructed a building using amateur labor. Given that, disaster was nearly inevitable."

"But why would God send an immoral heretic to save true Christians?" Unraed continued.

My mom said, "Putting aside for the moment your mistaken comment about heretics, I don't think God is bound in any way by the artificial models of religion we humans build."

This was too much for the pastor to process mentally, and he walked away shaking his head.

On the way home that day, my dad said my use of floating to rescue people raised an ethical and moral question for people who can travel out-of-body. My mom then named the question. Is one who has the gift of floating ethically or morally obligated to use that gift to save people from jeopardy?

"My sense is that if a floater were in proximity to such a situation, then use of the skill would be an ethical obligation," I said.

"What if doing so would necessitate revealing one has been out-of-body?" Mom asked.

"That's similar to the question of Merven intervention," said Dad. "Sojourner told me Merven avoid getting directly involved in human suffering and life threatening situations, lest they make matters worse. There are usually unforeseen consequences from helping. But in this case, Zara, I am certain that you did the right thing."

A week later, the pastor sent me a letter of thanks and said his understanding of God had grown a bit because of the event. He enclosed a note signed by all the youth group members also thanking me. It is my observation that personal experience is what changes minds, and without the near tragedy occurring, this pastor would have continued to cling to his small vision of a punitive God. A few weeks later, he telephoned my dad and said that he had been doing a lot of praying and thinking about the episode and wanted to come to the NCC to thank me in front of the congregation and also to apologize for his participation in the Crusade. Timothy wanted to come too, on behalf of the youth group.

Dad agreed right away.

When Titus and Timothy came to our church, they kept their clothes on and seemed quite ill at ease in front of hundreds of naked people, but they stood there with me naked beside them and each said his piece. I was embarrassed at the spontaneous applause that greeted their words, especially since Pastor Unraed continued to believe that God had spoken to me, and I wasn't going to tell the truth about floating to the entire congregation. The ethical binds that floating and other paranormal skills can put us in were concrete for me now.

Three months after the building collapse, the family of a girl who suffered a broken arm, concussion, and post-traumatic stress sued

SCOFF for some outlandish sum. Because of the manner of its construction, no insurance company would provide coverage for the church, so there were no insurance funds available for rebuilding or for liability. The church was also unincorporated, and as a result, the pastor had to declare personal bankruptcy. Ironically, the father of the injured girl was one of the volunteers who had put up the roof that collapsed.

At the time I did not know that the SCOFF pastor and my dad had begun meeting privately to discuss theology, but Dad later told me that Titus had been growing in his understanding of the nature of God. After he declared bankruptcy, his congregation folded, his wife left him, and he told Dad that he had nothing more to lose and wanted to start over by joining the NCC. It seemed fitting to him that he do this without clothing to learn if people would perceive the presence of Christ in his nakedness.

He brought Timothy with him the first time he came to worship, initially choosing the contemporary textile service. He wasn't quite as ready to bare all as he had told my dad. Eventually, Titus and Timothy did make the transition to nude worship. Titus left the ministry and got a job as an underwriter for an independent insurance agency, where he evaluated applications for fire insurance.

Rescuing the youth group by floating provided me the impetus to widen my out-of-body travel. I had agreed to restrict my solo explorations to the confines of Angel Nest, but now felt suffocated by this arbitrary limit. And so, without consulting my parents, I began to float farther afield. The first few expeditions I made were harmless, floating around Sedona and the southern end of Oak Creek Canyon. It felt good to stretch the wings of my soul.

One day early in the fall, as I sat bored at my desk in school, the idea came to me to float during recess as a way of re-energizing myself. When the bell rang, I went into the girls' bathroom and locked myself in a stall. Usually, I lay supine when preparing to float, but this was impossible in a bathroom stall. Still, I found that I could manage the task seated on a toilet.

My plan was to float to the teachers' lounge and see if I could do anything to make them think the place was haunted, like ruffling papers or knocking paper cups of coffee off tables. It was juvenile, I confess, but at the time it seemed like fun.

But when I came to the teachers' lounge, I found it empty. There would be no audience for my pranks. So, I headed off to the principal's office, thinking that I might find something fun to do there.

Unfortunately, as I was swooping around the office, the fire alarm went off. This was not something I had done. Since fire drills were usually conducted during class hours and not recess, I assumed that the fire must be real and set off exploring the campus in search of it. Maybe I could again use my floating skill to rescue people.

But it was only a drill. And when I was not accounted for by my homeroom teacher, a search was begun to locate me. A classmate said she'd seen me in the girls' bathroom, so two teachers were dispatched there. At that moment, I didn't know they were searching for me, but when I saw my class assembled in its regular fire drill location, I deduced they would try to find me.

I zoomed back inside in time to see the two teachers enter the bathroom. Pushing through the body of one of them, I zipped into the stall and into my body in time to hear the one I'd zoomed through give a whoop at the sensation of a soul passing through her and the other calling my name.

"Zara, are you in here?" she said with a genuine note of concern in her voice.

I feigned the sounds of waking up, opened the door, and said, "Am I late for class? I fell asleep."

"On the toilet?" one teacher said.

"I…I was…meditating," I answered.

"That's not the intended purpose of a toilet, but that would explain why you're fully dressed," said the other one. "I can't think of a place less suited to meditation. I suggest you save such activities for home."

Fortunately, my reputation at the school was such that neither teacher doubted my story. In retrospect, I shuddered to think what would have happened if they had found my body without me in it. No doubt they would have called an ambulance and my parents would have been contacted. If I had been at the other end of the campus, it would have been difficult for me to get back to my body in a timely manner. And how would I have explained it if I had popped back into my body in the ambulance.

This was a close call, and I was lucky to have escaped embarrassing complications. I vowed to be more careful about when and where I stored my body while floating. I continued to explore the region out-of-body, but only when I had enough time and my body was in a safe place free from public intrusion.

CHAPTER SIX
THE INVITATION

Before the start of the third annual Sky-clad Summer Academy sponsored by my church in June 1988, I received an invitation from Sojourner via a message planted in my brain.

"Hey Mom," I said to the first family member I encountered, "I just heard from Sojourner. We and the Begays have been invited to visit a Merven enclave."

"That sounds like fun, Zara. When and where?" she responded.

"No particular time, but as soon as we can arrange the trip. As to where, I have only partial directions. I suspect we will be met along the way and escorted to the actual place. We need to hike into Havasupai tribal land."

"That's at the bottom of the Grand Canyon!" Mom exclaimed.

"Technically, it's in Havasu Canyon, which runs south from the Grand Canyon," I said. "It's Indian land, not part of the National Park. At any rate, we need to get ourselves to Hualapai Hilltop and then start hiking the Supai Trail into the canyon. I presume Sojourner will meet us somewhere along the trail."

"Your father has talked many times about wanting to hike that trail," said Mom. "I'm sure he'll be delighted by the prospect, Sojourner or not."

On a warm, cloudless day soon thereafter, our extended family set out in search of the Merven habitat. Uncle Firstlaugh, Dad, Tzek, Tseyi, and Whitman -the males of the family- rode in one station wagon, while the females -Mom, Aunt Cedar Cradle, Wakhan, Darrow, and I- were in the other. At Seligman, we picked up old Route 66 and followed it in a northwesterly arc for thirty miles until reaching the Hualapai Reservation Route 18, which ran sixty miles in a northeasterly direction toward the rim of the canyon, until we found the trailhead.

"Supai Village is about eight miles downhill from here," Dad announced as we gathered our gear and locked the cars.

The four adults and Tzek made arrangements to rotate piggybacking Tseyi, Darrow, and Whitman over the course of the trek.

About five miles into the canyon, I said, "Stop. I think I recognize this place. We need to look for a side trail."

"I don't see anything," said Dad. "There's only the main trail ahead."

"Ah! There it is!" I proclaimed.

No one saw what I saw.

"Look! Right there," I said. "See the well worn path across that sandstone slab."

They all saw the flat stone but perceived no pathway.

"OK, you all are going to have to proceed on faith," I announced. "I know now where we're going. Everyone follow me."

They did. Presently we came to the foot of a high, smooth sandstone wall.

"No getting over that," said Firstlaugh, "unless we float."

"Have faith, Uncle F," I said. "An entrance is around here somewhere."

I climbed onto a shelf that looked like a giant slice of petrified brown cheese. Immediately the shelf began to tilt slowly downward at the end closest to the rock wall, revealing a pit and stone steps leading into a wide passageway under the rock.

The underground passage was brightly lit and tall enough that Dad, with Darrow riding on his shoulders, could walk upright with room to spare. It extended a quarter mile through sandstone, opening on the other side into a green and gold valley. A crystal clear creek ran through the plain. Cottonwood trees and grassland flanked the stream. In the distance was a waterfall, and as we neared it, everyone became entranced by the turquoise pool at its base.

"That water is the color of Sojourner's eyes," said Mom. "So beautiful."

"Thank you for the compliment, Terp," said Sojourner, suddenly materializing before them. "And thank you, Zara, for being such a good navigator. And to all of you, welcome to Viaticum. This is my home."

"Does Pilgrim live here too?" I asked.

"Yes, and Quester," said Sojourner. "And you shall meet them both very soon."

"Your entrance is cool," I said. "You must have fun using it."

"We don't need it," Sojourner replied. "We have other ways of getting in and out. It's here for our occasional human guests."

As our entourage followed Sojourner along a wooden sidewalk, Dad said, "By my reckoning, Havasu Falls is about seven miles away, but the waterfall here looks very much like photos I've seen of it. We haven't slipped into some kind of geological space warp have we? Or happened upon an exquisite short cut?"

"No to both your questions," said Sojourner. "Ours is not the well-known cascade. This valley is real, but unknown to most humans. The Havasupai elders know about this place, of course, and are good friends with the Merven, but they don't tell tales to tourists."

Sojourner steered the humans onto a flagstone path that led to a house made of sandstone. The structure had six sides, no two of which were the same length. The entryway was a diamond shaped opening with no door attached. The roof was a flat slab slightly higher on one side so rain would drain off the other side.

The inside walls were lined with cedar, mahogany, teak, and oak. Brightly patterned area rugs covered portions of the hardwood floor of the large gathering room. There were, however, no couches or chairs.

"Please, sit down and rest," said Sojourner. "My soul-mate and child will be here very soon."

"Sojourner, since you're not wearing clothes," said Mom, "would it be appropriate for us to undress also?"

"By all means," said Sojourner. "Oh where are my manners? Please, feel free to disrobe as you wish. You may pile your things in that corner."

As the humans were removing their garments, Pilgrim stepped through the doorless entry carrying Quester. Pilgrim stood six feet six inches tall and had the triangular face, large eyes, and small mouth that characterized the Merven species. Quester was the size of a normal five year-old human. They also were naked.

Introductions made and cold drinks served, everyone spread out on rugs for conversation. Quester joined Tseyi, Whitman, and Darrow in a corner of the room, where they spontaneously invented games that did not require intelligible speech.

"How many Merven live in this valley?" Cedar Cradle asked.

"When all are home, more than three thousand," said Pilgrim. "Most of us do a lot of traveling, though, so it's rare for the whole enclave population to be here at the same time."

Mom said, "The first time I met you, Sojourner, you were wearing a purple robe, and Cloud and I found some kind of canvas garment in your desert shack we presume you had worn previously. But every other time we've been together you've been naked. What's the story?"

"Context," laughed Sojourner. "Ordinarily, Merven do not wear clothing. But when we are likely to be seen by humans, we don something they can relate to. We adapt to the culture around us."

"A purple robe?" Mom asked. "As a five year-old I had no context for that."

"You were a special case, Terp," Sojourner said. "You had no context for seeing me naked, either. Indeed, that would have been quite troubling to you at the time. The truth is, I suspected that you would someday respond to the symbolism of Christian liturgy, and I wanted you to make connections between meeting me and your spiritual journey."

"Was that a clue that you are holy or in some way divine?" Mom asked.

"Definitely not," Sojourner answered. "I merely wanted to suggest that my purpose in your life was benign and beyond the normal prerogatives of your parents. There's also an element of whimsy in my choice of clothes. I wore a saffron robe in Viet Nam when I nudged Den away from a booby trap. I wore a medieval Jewish gabardine robe in Greenwich Village during the New York blackout, when you and Cloud first met. Human costuming is a great game among Merven. It's the closest thing we have to a competitive sport."

"Where else do Merven live?" asked Tzek.

"We have enclaves all over the planet," said Pilgrim. "As you would know the places, we have cities in Tibet, Botswana, the Andes Mountains, the Gobi Desert, the Red Center of Australia, Iceland, Borneo, and Antarctica. There are smaller settlements inside the largest human cities on every continent."

"So you hide in plain sight among densely populated homo sapiens," noted Dad.

"I suppose we do," said Pilgrim, "but I never use that term for humans. It's a matter of personal integrity. It seems to me the height of hubris to call your species *sapiens,* for wisdom has not characterized human behavior throughout history."

"Strong words," said Dad. "As much as I would like to dispute them, I have to agree with you. Humankind does not have a proud record of living wisely."

"I beg your pardon for speaking unkindly of a species I spend my life assisting," said Pilgrim, "but it grieves me deeply to see people continually hurt one another century after century."

"Pilgrim is more emotionally expressive than I am," Sojourner said. "It's a trait I find irresistible."

"It grieves me too," said Dad, "more than I have words to express. Are Merven more humane to one another than we humans are among ourselves?"

"I wouldn't use the word humane, either, in the context of interpersonal kindness," said Pilgrim. "Merven tend to act a great deal more mervenely than humans act humanely. We have a few bad actors among us, and a few unhappy souls, but for the most part, we avoid manipulating one another and live quite peaceably."

Sojourner changed the subject. "Would you like to see the rest of the house?"

The humans followed Sojourner into a bedroom, which was simply decorated with straw mats and small pillows on the floor. A floor to ceiling shelf across one wall held thousands of books, magazines, photographs, scrolls, maps, phonograph records, tape recordings, compact discs, films, puzzles, games, and newspapers.

"Bedtime reading," said Sojourner.

"Some of these I recognize as human works," said Mom. She pulled a linen-bound volume from the shelf. "But I don't recognize the symbols on this at all. Is this what the Merven language looks like?"

"It is," said Pilgrim. "Take a look at the page layout."

Mom opened the book and found that words on each page were distributed in a circular maze. "Where does one start reading?" she asked.

"On odd numbered pages, the reader starts in the center of the maze and follows the sentences to the outside. On even numbered pages the text begins at the bottom right of the circle and one reads into the maze."

"Intriguing," said Firstlaugh. "Mazes are important to some Indian traditions."

"Not all our books are arranged this way," Pilgrim explained. "It's a way to avoid boredom and have a little fun. You see, even though we are scattered all over the planet, unlike humans, we have only one language. There are small regional variations in speech, but hardly enough to constitute different dialects. And the written language is the same the world over. So, we play games with formats. Some publications start at the back and read from right to left and bottom to top, while some start at the front and read from left to right as with English. Mystery novels often start somewhere in the middle and the first task of the reader is to figure out the numbering system. The pages are not sequential, so part of the fun is discovering the order of the pages along with solving the case. I once read a fiendishly clever mystery story that actually began on the first page. It took me a while to figure that out."

"I don't see any equipment to play your records and show your movies," said Cedar Cradle.

"All that is in the library," said Sojourner. "Let me show you."

They followed Sojourner into the next room. At one end of the library was a studio crammed with all manner of audio-visual equipment. The rest of the large room was filled with shelves full of reading, listening, and watching material.

"We have a moderate sized collection," said Pilgrim. "Some Merven families have much larger ones, but size is not very important, because we freely trade with one another."

"How many items in your library?" asked Dad.

"About one hundred thousand and growing every day," said Sojourner. "We have to keep up with what's going on with humans. When we run out of storage room, we donate a big chunk to the central Merven library."

"Where is that?" asked Mom.

"Oh," said Sojourner, "you nearly entered it on your honeymoon. It's inside the subsurface portion of Uluru in Australia. You and Cloud floated under the rock and came very close to the front door of the place."

"Wow," Mom said. "I wish we'd known."

"You weren't ready to know back then," said Sojourner.

"I'd like to see the bathroom," I said.

"Do you need to use it?" asked Pilgrim. "Or are you simply interested in seeing what it looks like?"

"Both," I answered.

"It's the next room," said Sojourner. "You go on ahead and call us when you're finished. Let's see if you can figure out how to use the facilities."

Intrigued by the challenge, I went to the room, peed, wiped, washed my hands, and was back two minutes later. "It's just like a human toilet."

"Actually, it is a human toilet," said Sojourner. "Human manufacturing is superior to ours in many respects, and we see no need to reinvent perfectly usable products."

"The bathtub is really cool," I said. "Come and see."

Everyone rose and followed me.

The tub was carved from stone, with wide graduated steps leading to a central area that covered about a hundred square feet and sloped from a depth of two feet to three feet in the deepest part.

"May I try the water?" I asked.

"Certainly," said Sojourner. "A bath might be refreshing for all you hikers. Be our guests." Sojourner flipped a switch on the wall, and colored lights at the bottom of the tub turned the crystal clear water into a liquid rainbow.

Tzek and I hurried into the water.

"Oooh, it's warm and tingly," I cried.

"The water is treated with a cleansing agent that protects the skin and energizes muscles," said Sojourner. "You all really ought to try it."

The next half hour passed with the five Morgans, the five Begays, and the three Merven luxuriating and at times splashing in the large bathing pool. Then we stepped into the drying room, where warm breezes enfolded each of us, carrying the wetness away without need of towels.

"You must be getting hungry," said Pilgrim after everyone returned to the gathering room. "We have a meal planned, but I need to go to the market for a few things. I'd like to invite you all to come with me, but it would be unseemly for ten humans to be trailing through the place. Merven aren't used to tourists. Maybe Tzek and Zara would like to accompany me, though. Two young ones shouldn't stir up much ado."

CHAPTER SEVEN
LANGUAGE, MUSIC, AND SEX

In the open-air produce market, Tzek focused his attention on identifying fruits and vegetables and asking Pilgrim about the few items he did not recognize, while I listened to the chattering of Merven shoppers all around. At first the clicks, screeches, squeaks, snorts, hisses, barks, and pops seemed an ocean of chaotic noise, but as my mind absorbed the sounds, I began to discern patterns.

On the walk back from the market, I said, "[click, plock] *zjeeek* means hello doesn't it?"

"Very perceptive, Zara," said Pilgrim. "Actually, it means I acknowledge and honor your presence, which is how Merven say hello."

"It's like *aloha,* isn't it?" I said. "It means hello and goodbye."

"Yes, it is used that way," Pilgrim said. "What else have you picked up in your brief visit to the market?"

"Judging from the discreet pointing that was going on," I said, "I suspect *teeez* [snort] *keee* means human being."

"Right again!" said Pilgrim. "You have quite an ear for languages."

"What's the word for Merven?" I asked.

"*Jpb dthhzj* [pop] *keee,*" said Pilgrim.

I was able to repeat the sounds without difficulty.

Pilgrim laughed. "That's absolutely wonderful! I have never before heard our language spoken with an American English accent. But it's an ever so slight accent. You have a good ear and rare gift, Zara, and I'd like

42

to give you lessons in the Merven language. Would you be interested in that?"

"If you've been retrieving messages from my mind, you know I am," I replied. "When can we start?"

"Let's eat first, and then we can talk about language lessons," Pilgrim said.

Throughout the vegetarian meal, Pilgrim, Sojourner, and Quester spoke various Merven words and phrases, and the humans tried with limited success to imitate the sounds. This engendered much laughter all around, as some unsuccessful attempts produced words with very different meanings. For example, Sojourner spoke the Merven phrase meaning 'welcome to our home,' and Mom's attempt to parrot it back produced the Merven sounds meaning 'welcome toenail magnet.'

Dad, Mom, Firstlaugh, and Cedar Cradle each had some skill at pronouncing the Merven language but became tongue-tied more often than not. However, I reproduced the difficult sounds with very little effort.

"Zara is a natural," said Pilgrim. "She's invited me to visit Angel Nest from time to time for language tutoring. I hope that meets with your approval, Terp and Cloud."

"You know it does," Dad said. "All three of you are welcome any time. Of course, our newer residents don't know about the Merven, but we can orient them when we get home. Given what they've already taken in stride, they won't be surprised."

"I am really excited about this, Mom and Dad!" I said. "This is the first educational thing in a long time that fully captures my imagination."

"I'm glad you've found your compelling interest at so young an age," said Mom.

"What's Merven for God?" I asked.

"That's an easy one," said Sojourner. "It's **Kaaadth.**"

All the humans were able to reproduce the sound without difficulty.

"This is one of the rare Merven words that shares a common linguistic root with a human word," said Pilgrim. "Some Merven scholars claim it evolved from a Sanskrit word for mystery, following a course of sound changes similar to the Old Norse pattern that led to your English word for God. The more common understanding, however, is that the Sanskrit term was borrowed from the older Merven tongue. Which came first, the Merven or the Sanskrit is an age-old debate among our scholars."

"What's the Merven word for naturist?" I continued.

"There isn't one," explained Sojourner. "But we have its opposite. [Snort, pop] *teeez* [hiss] *hooola* means a clothing compulsive person or body cover fetishist."

I repeated the term and said, "Very useful. Now, how do you say hell?"

"Actually, Zara, hell is not a Merven concept," said Sojourner. "We have no word of our own for it, and the only time we use it is in discussing human affairs. So we borrow the word for hell in the language of the particular humans we are talking about. If speaking of humans in general and the subject of hell comes up, a typical Merven would say the word in some obscure human language. We are prone to whimsy that way."

"Speaking of whimsy," Pilgrim said, "a worship event is in the gathering stage in the enclave circle. Humans would be particularly welcome -if you'd care to observe."

"Absolutely!" said Mom. "But what does whimsy have to do with it?"

"Our worship is largely spontaneous," explained Sojourner. "We tend to gather to express feelings of transcendent connectedness in moments of opportunity, when things seem to come together in just the right configuration. It's what the Greeks called *kairos,* a moment in time full of possibility, pregnant time, if you will, as opposed to *chronos,* which is linear, measured time like hours, days, and years."

The ten humans joined their hosts in a short walk to a circular field at the center of the settlement. More than two hundred vibrant Merven of varying ages stood in the fine white sand that covered the field. Many held hands in small circles, others had their arms around neighbors' shoulders, while some embraced one another. No one spoke.

As the human-Merven entourage approached, a pathway through the congregation fanned open, and Pilgrim led us to a space in the middle, where the shorter humans stood hidden in the shade of the much taller beings.

Instrumental music that seemed to rise from beneath the ground broke the silence. Dad said later he thought he detected drums, flutes, and violins. The song set all the human spines tingling. Mom's mind perceived a series of sounds that built toward what she recognized as a melody. But just as she comprehended the fascinating pattern and anticipated the next notes, the music shifted in a different direction, leaving a sense of incompleteness in her psyche. We humans were entranced by the song, carried along by its promise of melodic resolution that quivered on the verge but never quite arrived.

Unexpectedly, from a human perspective, the music stopped. And before any of us could finish the piece in our minds, a soprano voice somewhere on the perimeter of the circle proclaimed in prose, "[click, plock] *zjeeek Kaaadth* [click, sigh] *teez* [snort] *keee* Zara [low pitched sigh, rising pitched sigh, pop] *teeez* [snort] keee [click-click]." One at a time, other voices repeated the words.

In a lower than normal voice that provided harmony to the higher pitched phrasing of the consecutive chorus, Sojourner translated, "We humbly greet you, O mysterious and generous God. We gather to acknowledge our deep gratitude for the presence among us of the human being Zara and the gift of language she has inherited as a result of your love. Thank you also for the gifts you have given to the other members of her family who are sojourning with us today. Amen."

"That seems like a lot crammed into a few words," whispered Dad.

"Some of the meaning is derived from the intonation of particular words," Sojourner explained in a normal voice. "A single word takes on additional meanings with changes in inflection. You may have recognized the word for God. The way it was pronounced denoted a reverent greeting. Pronouncing the word in a different way might refer to an action of God or the essence of God or a dozen other things relating to God in actuality or in concept."

The music returned briefly, followed by renewed silence. After an interval of several minutes, without audible direction, the crowd began to disperse, as if everyone had decided independently but at the same instant that the service was over. Following human custom, a score of Merven situated near the humans lingered to shake hands with them and express sentiments of welcome.

Back at the house, we ate again and made arrangements to stay the night. Sojourner set out sleeping mats and pillows on the gathering room floor, and Quester settled in to sleep with the three youngest humans.

After this, the rest returned to the bathing pool to relax and continue conversations.

"Are there any references to Merven in human literature?" asked Firstlaugh.

"Many," answered Pilgrim. "Reports of encounters with giants, Yeti, Sasquatch, and the like are often simply mistaken sightings of Merven. Merven are also mentioned in your Bible. Genesis 6:4 identifies us as sons of God, which is somewhat amusing, because we are simultaneously daughters of God. It was reported that our species produced children with human women, and unfortunately this is true. Alas, this was a failed experiment that was begun with the best of intentions.

"The Genesis account also calls us Nephilim, which I take exception to. It means those who resulted from abnormal or premature births. Ouch! Something the Bible got right, however, is that we are taller than humans."

"Don't be too critical of the text," Sojourner said to Pilgrim. "You know as well as I do that the writers and editors of Genesis had never seen any Merven. They were simply chronicling ancient legends that had survived orally for centuries. It's not unusual for sensational information to be embellished and distorted as it travels from mouth to mouth. And it would be more accurate to say we were much taller than humans in those ancient days. In recent years, they have been catching up with us." Sojourner turned toward Dad and Firstlaugh. "Some of your basketball players are taller than adult Merven. If this evolutionary trend continues, all sorts of mischievous probabilities may unfold. Incidentally, there are also references to us in the thirteenth chapter of Numbers and the first chapter of Deuteronomy."

"Do Merven write commentaries on books of the Bible?" asked Mom.

"Many such works have been produced," said Sojourner, "although at present we have none in our library here. We do have a Para-biblical document you would find of particular interest, however. Chief Librarian Key translated a 4th century Greek manuscript into Merven, Hindi, Chinese, Spanish, and English. The English version is in our bedroom. It's related to the Gospels of John and Thomas."

"I'd very much like to see that," said Dad.

"Perhaps we should adjourn to the library," Pilgrim said. "It is not prudent to peruse reading material in the bath."

Soon all were dry and settled on cushions.

Sojourner handed a slim pamphlet to Mom, who read the title aloud. "*Original Nakedness, or Naked from the Beginning.* Intriguing."

"As I indicated, this is a translation of a fourth century manuscript," Sojourner explained. "However, Merven scholars believe it to be a copy of a late first century document, contemporary with the Gospel of John. In content, vocabulary and style it is similar to John."

"Our scholars also believe it to be a source document for the Gnostic Gospel of Thomas," added Pilgrim. "Chief Librarian Key has custody of the actual manuscript, which seems to have been created in haste. The letter strokes appear hurried."

"What might account for that?" Dad asked.

"Our scholars speculate that the first century document was deemed heretical and set to be destroyed, but someone opposed to such action secretly copied it. Actively suppressing heresy as well as hiding suspect manuscripts were common in that era."

Mom scanned the text. "This looks like a compilation of excerpts and miscellaneous pericopes."

"Read a little of it to us," said Cedar Cradle.

Mom cleared her throat and used her preacher voice. "'The Word became flesh and dwelled among us, and we have beheld its naked glory, glory as the eternal image of God, male and female in one flesh.' There's a break here and another excerpt. 'After the guests tasted the good wine Jesus made, they all (with Jesus and his disciples) removed their garments and formed a great circle where they danced naked without shame...This first sign in Cana of Galilee revealed glory in him and in his disciples, and in those who believed in him.' Another break.

"'After Jesus had raised Lazarus from the dead and bade him walk naked in the road to his home, Jesus and his disciples visited Lazarus and his sisters Martha and Mary in Bethany. Lazarus knew that Jesus and his disciples were accustomed to setting aside their robes when dining in secret, and he decreed that members of his household do likewise whenever Jesus visited.' Break.

"'I have yet many things to say to you, which you must bear into the future. When I am with you in private, you lay aside your garments like children in the garden. As from the beginning, in nakedness you pray and sing and sup together, male and female without shame. I say to you a time will come when men will punish you for your lack of shame. Do not be afraid and do not believe them, for truly their hearts are filled with fear of your innocence and joy. Let not your hearts be troubled, for after the time of trial, a new day will dawn when you will no longer disrobe in secret but trample your garments beneath your feet even in the marketplace.'"

Mom paused. "There's more, but that's a taste for now."

"Wow! May we borrow this to study?" Dad asked.

"You may read it here, but we cannot permit you to borrow it," said Sojourner.

"Conservative churches would go ballistic over this," said Firstlaugh.

"No, they would simply say it was one more in a long list of heretical documents that circulated in the early centuries of the Christian era," said Pilgrim.

"Of course," Dad agreed. "I'm not tempted to publish it, but I do want to study it in depth."

"Someday, perhaps, you shall have that opportunity," Sojourner said.

"Can we change the subject?" Tzek said, looking at Sojourner, who nodded. "I've heard people call you the Old One. How long do Merven live?"

"A normal life span is in the range of 350 to 375 years. A few reach 400, and a small number die prematurely, mostly from accidents. But let me answer the question in your mind that you are too polite to ask. I am 212 years old. Pilgrim is a mere child of 199."

"It must be hard to become so intimately involved with humans given our much shorter life expectancies," said Cedar Cradle.

"It is," said Pilgrim. "And it takes an especially heavy emotional toll when people die prematurely. My carping about human foibles is simply a defense mechanism to help me cope with the tragedies of senseless violence and murder within your species."

"One of Pilgrim's early assignments was Abraham Lincoln," Sojourner said. "His assassination still weighs on Pilgrim's soul."

"I warned him in a dream not to go Ford's Theater," Pilgrim said. "I did not know what Booth was planning, but I was suspicious. Something evil was in the air. But dear Abe had a death wish. He longed for release from the huge demands that had fallen to him. He was such a sad man. I loved him so."

"Did you watch over President Kennedy too?" Mom asked.

"No. Someone else had responsibility for him," Pilgrim said. "The thing to bear in mind, though, is that not every human listens to Merven advice. Not everyone is open to intuitive communication, and some who are open frequently ignore it. We Merven never second-guess one another when tragedies occur. We know that probability is as likely to favor a mistake as a success. And we have to be very careful about over-intruding into human events. Blatant interference on behalf of one person could result in great suffering for others."

"What's the name of that song that was played during worship?" Mom asked.

"It doesn't have a name," said Sojourner. "At least not yet. The musicians composed it as they played. It was a spontaneous tribute to God for the blessings revealed this day. If enough Merven like it, they may ask the musicians to recreate it, and then someone will give it a name."

"It had an aura of exploration about it," said Dad. "As if the musicians were searching multiple pathways through a forest of notes and tones."

"And though they moved through beautiful territory, they never found the exact path they sought," said Cedar Cradle, "so they decided to stay in the forest and search another day."

"I have a strong sense we will hear this new song much in the future," said Pilgrim. "Therefore, I now name it 'Zara's Gift.'"

I blushed.

"That's a beautiful name," said Wakhan. "It's the first Merven music I've ever heard, and I think it's great. Do Merven like human music?"

"An unqualified yes," said Pilgrim. "Some human songs of the rock genre appeal to many Merven, ironically because either subconsciously or through sheer happenstance, phrases from the Merven language have been incorporated into otherwise ordinary lyrics. Of course, in context these isolated words make no sense, but that's the charm, I suppose."

"For example," said Sojourner, "There's a recent song -and we think of anything since the First World War as new- called 'Papa-Oom-Mow-Mow' that repeats the Merven sentence 'pray for many broccoli massages.' And there's one called 'Walkin' My Cat Named Dog' that nicely illumines the Merven conceptual ethos. A Merven inspired it, of course, although not the elided g."

"I'm partial to ballads," said Pilgrim. "Whenever I hear 'Someone to Watch Over Me' by the magnificently creative George and Ira Gershwin, it reminds me of my life's calling and my cynicism temporarily dissolves. The Al Dubin and Harry Warren song 'I'll String Along with You' always brings a smile to my face. Both numbers are laced with tender Merven-human irony."

"I savor songs about artists," said Sojourner. "Many humans I watch over are artists of one kind or another.

"The only song about an artist I can think of offhand is the Van Gogh tribute 'Vincent' by Don McLean," said Dad.

"That's one of my favorites, but you would recognize more than immediately come to mind," Sojourner responded. "The Stephen Sondheim musical **Sunday in the Park with George**, about the painter Georges Seurat, has a wonderful song about artistic methods called 'Putting It Together.'

"Artists also work in other fields, such as literature, the stage, music, and dance. I particularly enjoy the Lennon and McCartney piece 'Paperback Writer,' and 'What I Did for Love' from the dance musical *A Chorus Line*. The quintessential actors' song is the Irving Berlin number from *Annie Get Your Gun*, 'There's No Business Like Show Business.'"

"I know all those," Said Dad, "But I never made the thematic connection."

"Songs about musical artists abound, of course," Sojourner continued. "It's not surprising they would write and sing about their own art. Al Jolson revealed the singer's psyche with 'Let Me Sing and I'm Happy.' But I'm partial to Dan Fogelberg's 'Leader of the Band' and Kris Kristofferson's 'If You Don't Like Hank Williams.' Also, 'Johnny B. Goode' by Chuck Berry and 'Killing Me Softly with His Song' by Roberta Flack. Surely now you can think of others."

"Billy Joel's 'Piano Man' immediately comes to mind," said Mom.

"And 'Homeward Bound' by Simon and Garfunkel," added Cedar Cradle.

"How about 'Seventy Six Trombones' from **The Music Man?**" Firstlaugh added.

"Right on all counts," said Sojourner with a laugh. "And I would add a personal favorite from the 1930s. Edythe Wright did the vocal on a

Tommy Dorsey arrangement of 'The Music Goes 'Round and Around' that is rich in musicians' idioms."

Wakhan's question about music led to a longer answer than she had wanted, so she now changed the subject. "Are you two married?"

"Merven don't have wedding ceremonies, the way they do in many human cultures," Sojourner said. "We choose to be life partners. Certain creatures, as you say in English, mate for life. They don't marry in a formal or public ritual; they simply decide to stay together. That's how it is with Merven. Usually, but not always, we mate for life. Merven are inclined to leave a little room for flexibility in relationships."

"Since we are raised in an ethos drenched with responsibility for oneself and in covenant with others," Pilgrim continued, "we don't need societal permission to bond romantically or its pressure to keep us together."

"What are your rules about sex?" Wakhan asked next.

"This is a sensitive subject among certain human societies," said Sojourner. "Merven sexual ethics are simple for us but, I think, very hard for humans. Generally speaking, any sexually arousing or orgasmic behavior is considered good if it occurs between or among peers and does not include pain, compulsion, psychological degradation, or any kind of violence to the body or spirit.

"In the case of children, peers are other children of similar age. It is never acceptable for adults to have sex with children. But it often happens, for example, that a quartet or quintet of ten and eleven year-old Merven will spend an afternoon pleasurably exploring one another's bodies. I believe you call it playing doctor. We consider this normal and encourage it in groups.

"Adults are free to engage in erotic play in mutually agreeable situations, in constellations of one, two, or more, as seems good at the moment, subject to the constraints I mentioned earlier."

Though I was not experienced in such matters and thus remained silent, I thought the Merven attitude toward sex seemed sensible and reasonable.

"That would be a hard sell in most human societies," said Dad.

"That's because human societies are often formed around fear and urges to control people," said Pilgrim. "Humans tend to bind sex and jealousy in the same package. Sojourner can tell you that I sometimes refer to your species as **homo invidus** -jealous man. I find it difficult to fathom the strong urge you have to manipulate one another. That so often leads to the very violence you're trying to protect against."

"In moments of frustration, Pilgrim also refers to humans as **homo avarus**," said Sojourner. "Greedy man. Of course, that's only a way of covering pain. Pilgrim's the most soft-hearted being I know."

Pilgrim's violet eyes looked into Sojourner's turquoise eyes and radiated profound affection. "[plock, screech] **nbzjeeeb** [sigh]."

"I love you too, dear," Sojourner whispered in reply.

"Where'd the Merven originate?" asked Tzek. "Savage thinks another planet."

"We evolved from the same branch of primates as you," said Pilgrim. "Our origins reside in a mystery 200,000 years old. It has to do with a creature you call **Homo heidelbergensis,** our mutual ancestor who appeared about 800,000 years ago. Six hundred thousand years later, **Homo heidelbergensis** began to evolve into three distinct species. The one you call Neanderthal did not survive. Your species flourished, numbering now in the billions. Merven have succeeded also but with a much smaller population. Our scientists say Merven evolved first and played a role in the emergence of your species. It's clear we have a symbiotic relationship. Merven and humans need each other."

"That's the scientific answer," said Sojourner. "We also have a creation myth that adds layers of mystery and heroism to the academic dry bones of archaeology and evolutionary science."

"But we do not speak of sacred subjects outside our own society," Pilgrim hastened to add.

"Perhaps we may speak of mythic things to certain humans in years to come," said Sojourner.

Dad said, "I've learned to be patient with enigmatic Merven pronouncements. Myths can wait. But I don't think of evolution as a dry subject. Exploring the origins of species is fascinating."

"Indeed," said Pilgrim. "Yet the tasks of evolution are never ending and require constant tending. It can become tedious from time to time."

"How does evolution require tending?" Mom asked.

Sojourner smiled and said, "I believe my spouse was indulging in poetic license."

CHAPTER EIGHT
COMING OF AGE

After the visit to the Merven community, in light of the discussion about music, my dad gave me complete access to his record collection. From a next-door neighbor, he had inherited a large collection of 78 rpms dating back to the teens in the last century. In addition, he had his own stacks of 45s and 33s. I discovered some wonderful musical treasures among the discs, especially from the 20s to the 40s. Among my favorites: "Yes! We Have No Bananas" by jingle-voiced Billy Jones (1923); "Let's Misbehave" suggestively sung by Irving Aaronson (1928); "Puh-leeze! Mr. Hemingway" by innocent sounding Elsie Carlisle (1932); "Let's All Be Fairies" performed by the Durham Dance Band (1933); and "The Hut-Sut Song" by the bemused King Sisters (1941). At the time I was not able to understand the spine chilling "La Vie en Rose" that was layered with the grieving voice of Edith Piaf (1946), but it haunted me with its beauty. Though I was not yet a teenager, I had more interest in the musical treasures of the past than the pop and rock music of the present, though that would change somewhat in high school as I developed a taste for alternative rock.

Immersing myself in music from eras long before I was born had a catalytic effect, I think, on a second prescient dream that came to me three years after the first one about the fundamentalist picket of our church. One of my favorite songs from the flapper era, "Let's Misbehave," was swirling around in my head one night, becoming incorporated into a dream. An Army colonel, who claimed to know my father, was telling me about his misbehaving. He had been married and divorced five times, he said, but now he was living in sin. There was not much else to the dream.

Months later, in the new year, such a man, a former Army chaplain, showed up in my dad's office, and they resumed a friendship that had begun when my dad was in the Army two decades earlier. When he talked about the meeting with Crimond Greenpasture at dinner, I realized the prescient nature of that dream and was grateful it was not about a tragic event. In time, Crimond became part of our family.

Dad said he had told Crimond about Angel Nest, including how it came to be named. For most of that year, I had been harboring a sense of embarrassment about my error that resulted in naming our home. On a previous occasion when a family member told a stranger that story in my presence, it suddenly occurred to me that this was a way of memorializing my mistake and reminding everyone of it. I was sure that people hearing it for the first time must be silently laughing at my stupidity. It never occurred to me that anyone could find it endearing.

So I scrutinized the faces of people when Dad or Mom or someone else told the tale, discovering in the process that the only person who thought less of me for mishearing the word eagle was myself. As my adolescence unfolded, I was surprised to learn that people liked me more for my mistakes than for being correct. Even so, I was not then and am still unable to make a deliberate error, even when speaking.

By March 1989, Pilgrim's periodic tutoring visits to Angel Nest were producing results far beyond initial expectations. I was already more fluent in the Merven tongue than any other human in memory and perhaps in history. Of course, not many humans had tried to learn the language - perhaps seventy or eighty over the last five or six millennia, Pilgrim thought.

"[click, plock] *zjeeek*," I said as Pilgrim materialized in the gathering room. "[bark] *leee jpbaaa* [snort, screech, plock, sigh]."

"I'm sorry you've been impatient for my return," said Pilgrim in English. "I've been busy in Australia."

"*zszeee jpb dthhzj* [pop] *keee*," I said.

"She wants me to speak only in Merven," Pilgrim said to Mom, who was relaxing in a rocking chair near to where I was stationed on the floor surrounded by books and maps. "I don't want to be impolite in the presence of a non-speaker."

"That's quite alright," said Mom. "Your purpose is to teach Zara not me."

"I'll translate into English," I declared. "That way Pilgrim can correct me if I get it wrong."

"*jpbaaa* [click, plock] *ooodth* [sigh]," said Pilgrim.

"[grunt, sigh]," I responded. "Mom, Pilgrim finds this room a pleasant and beautiful place and enjoys being here," she translated. "And I said that I find it that way myself."

"[rising sigh]," said Pilgrim.

"According to Pilgrim, my translation was excellent," I reported and blushed.

"Well, I think I'll go see Vala about a curriculum question," said Mom.

As soon as she had left the room, I said, "[plock, sigh, plock, grunt] *baaazaaa* [sigh, buzz] *tzooob*."

"[buzz, sigh, plock]," replied Pilgrim.

"But why won't you teach me some Merven dirty words?" I demanded.

"Because," Pilgrim continued in English, "we have very few such words, and they are not appropriate for an eleven year-old child."

"I may be eleven, but I am not a child!" I responded.

"Intellectually you are correct, but you have a great deal of emotional growth ahead of you," Pilgrim said. "Let's compromise. I'll teach you one taboo phrase, if you promise not to use it in the presence of other Merven."

"[grunt]," I nodded.

Now it was Pilgrim's turn to blush. "[plock] *tgeee* [screech] *leeekb*."

"[plock] *tgeee* [screech] *leeekb*," I repeated. "Clearly it has something to do with sexual relations but I can't discern in what way."

Pilgrim blushed again. "I have never before said that phrase aloud, much less heard it from the lips of a youngster. But I have heard it spoken by a few oldsters in frustrating situations, and I must confess I have **thought** about using it from time to time. It is a strong suggestion - a demand, really- concerning the anatomically unlikely act of self-impregnation. There are very unpleasant overtones connected with its use."

"I get it. I promise I won't use it around Merven, but I may say it to myself if some human messes with me" I said.

As it happened, I was able to use that expression in a suitable manner a few weeks later. While I carried my tray to a table in the lunchroom at school, a boy noted for bullying said loud enough for everyone in the area to hear, "Here comes smart-ass Zara. She's so smart she's an ass!" He stuck out his leg to trip me, but I was too agile for his clumsy game. After I got past his table, I turned back and repeated the taboo Merven words and added, "But I'm sure you've already done so many times."

His uncomprehending stare was a priceless gift to me.

On my twelfth birthday, October 7, 1989, among other things, Mom and Dad gave me a pair of khaki shorts and a white vee-neck tee shirt.

"This adult Angel Nest uniform is a symbol of your coming of age," said Dad.

Coincidentally, my first period had arrived a few days earlier.

"This means that you may float by yourself whenever and wherever you choose," said Mom.

"It means I can float by myself without guilt," I replied. "I've been doing it on my own for years."

"We would be disappointed if you hadn't" said Dad. "We tacitly gave you permission to float by yourself about six years ago."

"But you didn't bother to tell me explicitly," I said. "Your instructions tethered me to Angel Nest. So I had to feel guilty about sneaking out of my body on the outside."

"I hereby absolve you of all out-of-body related guilt," Mom said.

"Well, to be honest," I said, "I didn't feel *that* guilty. I figured you knew I was doing it and would say something if you really objected."

"You figured correctly. A word of advice, though," Dad added. "Some Angel Nesters, who shall go unnamed, have used floating as a means of gathering intelligence on the activities of certain groups or individuals."

"Like the fundamentalists crusading against the NCC?" I asked.

"That's one example," Dad continued. "The point I'd like to make, however, is that gathering intelligence *per se* is not a bad thing. But I would advise you not to use floating as a means of tormenting, teasing, or otherwise disrupting people."

"I wish you hadn't said that. I have been mulling over ways floating could help me embarrass some of the girls at school who regularly make fun of my vocabulary. They make disparaging remarks about intellectuals being responsible for all the problems in society. They say I think too much for my own good; that my brain is going to explode. One of the girls in my science class calls me Miss Pointy Head, which she picked up somewhere as an apt metaphor for an intellectual. This, of course makes absolutely no sense, because a pointy head would have little room for a brain and would thus work much better as a metaphor for a dunce. The consensus bottom line of this pack of girls is that I'll never attract a man by being smart."

"Don't believe that for a minute," Mom said. "I got that same message in high school, but it was completely wrong."

"I know, and that's why I have the mental capacity I do. Genes from equally brainy Mom and Dad," I said. "And for the record, it's way too early for me to be worried about attracting a boyfriend." In my mind I added, "or girlfriend."

"My advice about not harassing people while out-of-body is just that, advice," said Dad. "We'll leave it to your judgment."

"A sense of ethics about floating has already evolved in my mind," I said. "I won't do anything that is criminal or even approaching illegal. But I imagine in self-defense, I wouldn't put much stock in ethical niceties."

"Your dad and I once used floating to produce evidence against a child molester, though we had entered his apartment without permission. With your sensibilities, the field is wide open for creative activities," said Mom.

"While we're on the subject of coming of age," I said, "I've developed the idea that when they reach mental maturity people should be allowed to rename themselves if they want. Parents do the best they can naming their children, but not knowing who they will grow to be, they often choose names that eventually don't fit."

Dad leaned forward with a look of fascination on his face and said, "What would you name yourself, then?"

"I've thought about it a lot, and couldn't come up with anything better," I replied. "I would stay with Zara Person Morgan. You two got it exactly right when naming me."

Mom beamed and Dad grinned.

"Would you care to offer nominal comments on your siblings or anyone else?" Mom asked.

"Yes, I think all the Angel Nest parents did well in the naming department," I said. "My theory is being open to intuition has served this community well."

I detested group projects, in large part because other kids did not want me in their groups. No one was willing to work with me. Apparently I was too threatening. The sad part of that is that I could have helped other students get high grades on their projects. My seventh grade teacher assigned us geography projects, allowing us to self-divide into teams of two or three. We were to give a presentation or demonstration to the whole class. Once again, I was left out and had to do a project by myself. For this particular subject, I decided on flash over substance.

The trios and duets stood before the class and did show and tell, for example about the products of one country or another. One exhibited a scale model of a section of the Empire State Building made with Legos. To be honest, all of the projects were good and some were even interesting.

When it came time for my solo act, I placed a large piece of tag board on an easel and proceeded to draw freehand an accurate outline of the United States, using a black marking pen. Then, starting with the states bordering the outline, I drew in the shapes of all fifty states, obviously placing Alaska and Hawaii in insets. That done, I marked the locations of and labeled all state capitols with a red marker, and added in the largest city of each state in blue. Where largest and capitol were the same, I circled the red capitol in blue. The resulting map was correct as to shape and scale. Some of the small states needed to be labeled outside their lines on the side of the board.

Though few of the students liked me, they applauded when I was done. Apparently, entertainment is endearing. This was one of the few moments in my elementary school career in which I was happy and which I still savor. Unfortunately, the teacher graded me down because I had done it alone.

<><><>

In the spring of my eighth grade year, I entered the school spelling bee and easily won. Thus I would be going to the district bee and if successful to the state competition. I had a dream of reaching the national spelling bee. Early in the contest, the presenter gave me the word dialog.

I said, "There are two acceptable spellings of this word in American English. D-I-A-L-O-G and D-I-A-L-O-G-U-E."

He paused for a few seconds and then, with a slight smirk, said, "Correct."

No challenge was made to my answer at that time. After I had won, however, the presenter huddled with the principal and several teachers. A few minutes later he announced that I was disqualified for giving two spellings of dialog. The runner up, a son of one of the teachers, was declared the winner.

This stung. It felt like a deliberate act to keep me from competing. I won't call it a plot, because I doubt they had the wits to plan for this eventuality. But I still believe that certain teachers did not want me to represent the school in this or any other endeavor. One of the teachers involved in the discussion that resulted in my disqualification had been trying to have me diagnosed as autistic. Here was an example of my cooperating with the program and yet forces beyond my control denied me a genuine accomplishment.

I sent a letter of protest to the school board but received no reply for weeks. In the mean time, the district bee took place and the replacement winner in my school bee bombed out in the first round. After it was no longer possible for me to advance in the tournament, the school board instructed the principal to issue me a certificate as winner of the school bee, while at the same time affirming that the runner up had also won.

It's not difficult to understand why I couldn't wait to get out of grade school. My dad told me that high school was a chance to start over and that the classes were better. I hoped that was true but did not want to get my hopes up.

To that time, I had adopted various methods of coping with stress and disappointment. After the spelling bee episode, I engaged in two activities to ameliorate the pain. One was crossword puzzles. I'd been solving them for years, the harder the better. The New York Times

Sunday puzzle was one of the easier ones that I regularly worked on. Of course, it wasn't that difficult. I preferred the Saturday Times puzzle, because it was the hardest of the week.

But now I decided on a disciplined system for completing them. I would go through the across clues completely, filling in the answers I knew. Then I would go through the down clues doing the same, returning again to the across clues seriatim. I was very strict about not filling in any down words while going through the across ones and vice versa. For some reason, the rigidity of this discipline satisfied an emotional need to exercise control over the chaos in my life.

The other coping mechanism was a furious season of masturbation. Whenever I found sufficient solitude, I would masturbate, three or four times a day on some occasions. This did provide a level of emotional relief, but no real satisfaction. I felt no guilt about doing this but there was no particular joy in it either. Halfway through the summer I was so thoroughly sated and sore that I quit.

At dinner one chilly evening in January 1992, I reported that Preacher, the family's Australian Shepherd dog, had told me he was tired and ready to die in peace. The cats, Painter and Poet, had expressed similar sentiments, I added. Though my announcement was met with protestations of disbelief and denial, within a week, each pet in turn was found dead in different isolated nooks around the property.

CHAPTER NINE
BARELY GRADUATING

Encounters with social prejudice and conflict appeared for me as soon as I entered public school. Rejection came not only from my age peers but also from teachers who did not know how to or did not want to deal with my extraordinary educational needs. In addition to this, my family practiced naturism, which at the time was contrary to the norms of the larger community. It would not have been surprising, therefore, for me to have suffered teasing or negative feedback because of the naturism, but except for rare occasions, this did not happen. Nearly all my social suffering in elementary and high school was due to my intellectual capacity along with my refusal to descend to the level of the curriculum in order to get along. I was ostracized, which is almost a literary cliché, for smart kids. The only thing I lacked for looking like a classic brainy nerd was glasses.

To be honest, I also suffered at not finding any intellectual peers in my age cohort with whom to bond socially. My dating life in high school was close to nonexistent. But I cannot say that I was lonely, for family and friends at home, among whom we all shared great mutual affection, surrounded me. My intellect was consistently appreciated at home.

The norm in middle and high school is that girls will have non-romantic girlfriends and boys will have the male equivalent. The closest I came to having a gal pal in those years was Wakhan Begay. She and I were very close, but her parents were my parents' closest friends, and the Begays were essentially family. We lived together at Angel Nest, and

Wakhan and I shared a bedroom. She was my *de facto* sister, although I tended to use the language of cousin to categorize the relationship.

However our bond may be described, Wakhan was the only person near my age (a year-and-a-half older) with whom I did things. Both introverts, we were comfortable with one another. She and I would go to movies together and go out for ice cream. After she got a driver's license, we cruised the area in her car, and shopped for grooming and hygiene supplies, clothes, music recordings, and books. Mostly books. Neither of us fit the stereotypical mold of teenage girls, as we shunned all but basic makeup and had simple tastes concerning our limited wardrobes.

It was an honor to be Wakhan's maid of honor at her wedding in 2005. Naturally, it was a naturist ceremony, with my parents officiating. She married Camelot Wickham, who is mixed race, Anglo and Maori. According to her dad, since she married outside the tribe, no incest taboos were involved. Camelot's parents actually belonged to the Calvinist church in Prescott when my mom was pastor there, but they switched to the NCC in Sedona after mom traded denominations.

In school, my mind involuntarily saw things that were well beyond the scope of the curriculum, and all too often beyond the ken of the teachers. I was not trying to show off or straining to find peculiar notions. They simply appeared in my mind. My speaking up about what I perceived did not endear me to the faculty, for even if teachers understood the point or insight I was addressing, they experienced my words as disrupting the lesson plan and disturbing the fragile minds of the other students. In one form or another, I repeatedly received the message that I was troubling my classmates with things that were beyond their comprehension. Several teachers sought to have me diagnosed as autistic, but thankfully competent medical personnel refused to go along with that strategy.

Bullies teased me in high school, because I was both smart and physically attractive. Some teasing can be jocular and essentially well meaning. This was mean-spirited and ignorant. One boy specifically told me that girls were not allowed to be both smart and beautiful; therefore, I must be either stupid or ugly. Since I had a nice *bod*, he said, it must be stupid, because I couldn't get along with teachers or classmates. He called me a nudist freak who just didn't fit in with normal people.

My nemesis in those years was a student whose name, thankfully, I have forgotten. I could stir up the chemicals in my brain to retrieve it, but it would serve no useful purpose. His family were members of a poor excuse for a fundamentalist church, and he had bought the doctrinal line completely. One of the hallmarks of the church was denial of anything relating to evolution. For alphabetical reasons, this boy seemed to be seated adjacent to me in many classes and without invitation took upon himself to talk at me before the bell. One day he told me that he did not approve of smart girls.

"Girls have no need of education beyond about eighth grade," he said. "It's in the Bible."

This comment hooked me, and so despite the better wisdom not to respond, I said, "I don't remember any reference to eighth grade in the Bible. Where exactly in the Bible is that found? Give me chapter and verse."

"I don't know the exact place," he confessed. "But I can recite the verse. It's only three words. 'Children, kitchen, church.' That's the biblical role for women."

"I know that aphorism," I said. "It's not from the Bible; it came from Kaiser Wilhelm II of Germany. In German it is '**Kinder, Küche, Kirche.**' It was his vision of the proper place of women in German society."

"Well, it's in the spirit of the Bible," he maintained.

"Interesting assertion," I continued. "Do you know who took up the Kaiser's slogan? Hitler and his Nazi minions. They used it as justification for treating women as inferior."

"Are you calling me a Nazi?" he said.

"What do you think?" I asked. "You're the one spouting Third Reich philosophy. But it doesn't matter, because in any case you are without doubt a misogynist."

"Whatever that is, I'm not it," he retorted.

I chose not to point out to him that he had no grounds for denial if he did not know what it was he claimed not to be. Instead, I escalated the issue. "Of course the Kaiser and Hitler failed to understand the meaning of those three words. The first word, **Kinder**, expresses the notion that women should be in charge of children. Wouldn't you agree?"

"Yes," he said.

"And the second word, **Küche**, indicates that women should be in charge of the kitchen. Right?"

"Absolutely," he said.

"Thus to be consistent, the third word, *Kirche*, must mean that women should be in charge of the church. Rightfully, the priests and pastors should be female."

His face turned gray and then quickly red. "No! That's not right. God doesn't allow women to speak in church, so they couldn't possibly be preachers."

"We're not talking about God but the philosophy of Wilhelm and Adolf, which you so much admire. We're talking about what meaning the words logically convey."

Just then the teacher walked in and the bell rang. Before directing his attention to the teacher, he bent close and whispered, "You're going to hell."

Those inclined to think in stereotypes may assume that as a so-called nerd brain, I did not do well at athletic endeavors. Ironically, I succeeded more consistently at sports than in any other dimension of school life. I lettered in tennis and track. My fortes were singles tennis and cross-country track. I was very good at long distance running, glorying in the solitude of a lengthy run. Outside of school, I entered six or eight Ten-K races a year, regularly clocking in under forty minutes. All of the coaches were kind and encouraging to me, unlike a number of the academic teachers.

For my daily maintenance runs, I would often make circuits around the interior of the church campus, where I could run naked. But that got boring after a while, and I would have to don shorts and tee shirt to set out across the countryside. Whenever he saw me leaving for a run, my dad would say, "Run like the wind." This inevitably led to that song from *Dirty Dancing*, "She's Like the Wind," playing in my mind. Thinking about that now causes fond memories of my dad in those days. I am as prone to bouts of nostalgia as anyone.

Someone once asked me why I became a runner. Without reflecting on it, I responded, "My mom dances, my dad hikes, and I run." At the time it seemed an apt description of my role in the family constellation.

In the spring of my senior year, many female students anguished about getting dates for the prom. Not me. Mostly, I was indifferent to the event. Then one day after a cross-country run, I was walking behind the bleachers to cool down and heard voices around the corner. I stopped to turn and go the opposite direction but was hooked by the conversation, so I stayed quietly in place. Thinking they were alone, a member of the boys' cross-country team asked a girl on my team to go to the prom with him.

Ricky Valenzuela was a nerd with thick glasses, and like me, a good distance runner. The girl he asked had been friendly to him, although in my judgment, had not shown any social interest in him. Unconfirmed word on campus was that her mother was a member of the Daughters of the American Revolution. Whether this was true, she did exhibit blue blood manners. From the gasp she made, I assumed that the prom invitation was a shock, and after a quick recovery she said no. "It's not that I don't like you," she added, "but my parents would never allow it."

Ricky's dad was a roofer and his mom a hotel maid. Though he was born in the United States, his parents came here without documents, although they later received amnesty during the Reagan administration.

Ricky stood in place while the DAR girl strode away. I paused about ten seconds and then without premeditation stepped around the corner and feigned surprise that anyone was there.

"Oh, Ricky! I'm glad I ran into you," I said. "I've been thinking about the prom and how unlikely it is that anyone would ask me, so I thought I'd take things into my own hands and do the asking. Would you be willing to escort me to the dance?"

Now it was his turn to be surprised. "I...uh...I...sure," he stammered and then broke into a huge grin.

At home, I had a chat with Mom about what I'd done, and she was pleased.

"I waited in vain for an invitation," she said. "I was distraught that no one asked me, but in those days, girls did not ask boys."

"It's not a big deal for me," I said. "I wasn't pining away to go, but I couldn't stand to see Ricky dismissed that way. He's one of the top kids in class."

So, for the first and only time in my life, I wore a formal gown. The search for the prom dress felt like an ordeal, because I have little patience for such endeavors. At last, however, I found a lilac gown that fit me. It was designed to be worn without a bra, which suited me well. The downside was that it had a built-in padded bosom to compensate for bralessness. This made me looked stacked, an effect I didn't care for, but Ricky loved it. He had trouble keeping his eyes off my chest all night.

The big surprise for me was that people noticed that I had deigned to attend a social activity with a date, no less. I was used to being a low priority object of gossip about my intellectual antics, but this was new. In short order, "Ricky and Zara" became a major item of social gossip. We were both teased mercilessly. One coed found it hilarious that "brains of a different color" were dating. The strange part of that, given my tan, was that our skin tones nearly matched, with Ricky slightly lighter than I.

It had never been my intention to develop a romantic relationship with Ricky. The prom was a one-off event as far as I was concerned. But I enjoyed his company. Being a nerd, he had a trove of interesting things to talk about. He was a huge **Doctor Who** fan. And so we did go out on a few dates after the prom, and we did do some strenuous necking, but nothing below the neck. I also invited him to go skinny-dipping in the pool at Angel Nest. He was nonplussed that my family thought this was perfectly respectable.

Ricky received a full scholarship to the University of Arizona, so after graduation, our paths diverged.

The collection of my biographical materials in the Merven library includes copies of all my report cards from elementary and high school. How these were obtained I have no idea, but apparently I am not the only sentient being obsessed with particular subjects. These report cards reveal a mixed academic record, about which I care not a fig. For the record, however, I am quite fond of figs, so perhaps a residual hurt at the unfairness of being found scholastically deficient can be found in my memory. I can remember times when I felt stung by receiving an F on a test only because I knew the subject better than the teacher. To be honest, my feelings of being unfairly graded were intense at the time, but generally I managed to keep them under control because I did not want the unjust judges to know they had hurt me. That would be to give them power over me.

True-false tests were an exception to this sense of aggrievement, because I truly enjoyed demolishing those phony constructs and taking the consequences. I think I failed every true-false test I ever took, because I could find ways in which even the ostensibly true answers (the ones the teacher counted as true) had exceptions that made them ultimately false. There was a streak of stubbornness in me then that led me to answer false to all questions and to include annotations as to why they failed to be true.

I especially exasperated my economics teacher by marking false to every question on the true-false final exam and providing annotation as to why none of the answers could possibly be true given the imprecise way the questions were phrased. "There are too many exceptions to statements that may be ostensibly true," I wrote at the bottom of the examination. "I could drive a new Mack truck through some of these exceptions without having to worry about scraping the sides against any strong words." I asserted that it must be full of trick questions designed to teach students how to think critically but he disagreed with my provocative assertion. My real problem with the economics course was that the curriculum taught overly simplistic concepts that failed to describe adequately the reality of international commerce and monetary policies.

This test nearly kept me from graduating, but the principal prevailed on the teacher to award me a D for the course rather than an F, so that they could be rid of me. As a matter of principle, I had been prepared to go all the way to the school board to demonstrate that I had in fact scored 100% on the test, whereas most of my fellow students had failed it. Having given up my intellectual pretense that the economics teacher was a wily trickster, I came to the new conclusion that he was being willfully stupid about the test. But I let it go, because the D grade meant I did not have to fight the school board or go to summer school to repeat the stupid course.

My problem with algebra was that I could produce the correct answer without the tedious steps of showing how I got there. My journey from problem to solution in mathematics was typically via intuition. I tried to explain this to one teacher by likening my algebraic method to traveling through an astronomical wormhole. I bypassed the miles of empty space to reach the right destination (right answer) because my mind had automatically made the necessary shortcuts. I told her to give me a problem to solve that had not appeared in our textbook to demonstrate my intuitive ability. She did so, and after fiddling with it in my mind, I was able to solve it correctly without pencil on paper. This did not get me a better grade, although the teacher did acknowledge that she no longer suspected me of cheating.

My report cards tended to be characterized by As and Ds. These disparate grades were not related to the content of the particular courses, for I mastered the material easily in all cases. Rather, I received high marks or low depending on the personality traits of particular teachers. Those who were self-confident, autonomous, and self-aware consistently praised my work. But my intellect and behavior threatened and frustrated some other teachers. In retrospect, I acknowledge that this was partly my own doing, for in those days I assumed that most people with college educations were as bright as I, and therefore they were simply being pigheaded when they refused to grasp the ideas and principles that were obvious and elementary to me. I exempted a few of my grammar school teachers from this assumption.

Yet there were bright spots along the way. From sixth grade onward, at least one teacher each year affirmed and encouraged my intellectual growth. One year it was the science teacher, another year it was the art teacher, and several years English teachers provided me a sunny isle in a murky plebeian sea. I romped through German, Spanish, and Hindi in high school, the last course arranged through an adjunct faculty agreement with Anasazi College.

I graduated from high school in the spring of 1995 –barely.

At commencement, one of my perennial tormenters, of the America first, anti-intellectual persuasion, sat to my right. He turned to me and said, "If you're so smart, why aren't you graduating with honors? Some say you're a genius, so why aren't you valedictorian?"

The question stung, because I had asked myself that same question. What was it about me that kept me from conforming to the norms of the system and thereby succeeding in it? In a way, I believed that I *had* earned academic honors and that my poor grade average was the result of unjust teachers and a flawed educational system. But I wasn't going to say that to this bully.

So I said, "Unlike you, whose life has already peaked in high school, my course is on an upward trajectory. And what you apparently have failed to grasp in your plebian brain is that geniuses, Albert Einstein being a prime example, rarely do well in school systems that are designed for average and mediocre students."

"Yeah, whatever," he said.

The day I escaped from high school was very happy indeed, and since then I have never engaged in the typical nostalgia for those supposedly best years of one's life. They were clearly not my best years, and I was ecstatic to leave them behind. As the decades have passed, I have been very faithful about getting home for Angel Nest reunions, yet I have never attended a high school class reunion. I continue to receive invitations for alumni events, I suspect because in terms of formal educational achievement and professional attainment, I am the star of the class. But I stubbornly refuse to go.

Of course, my poor grade point average did not prevent me from getting into college. I scored a perfect 1600 on the Scholastic Aptitude Test, and my father was still teaching part-time at my chosen institution. Anasazi College accepted me and had no problem with my declared major: "wherever my curiosity travels."

Nevertheless, I fell into depression soon after graduation. I should have been elated to have high school behind me, but a feeling of numbness overtook me and I wanted to sleep most of the time. There seemed to be no point to continuing with anything. Nothing felt fun.

Dad noticed and asked me what was wrong.

"I don't know," I said. "Nothing seems interesting anymore."

"Classic depression," he said. "I know the signs all too well. The first thing is not to be afraid of it. Periods of depression can be useful sources for creativity."

By this point, Mom had entered the room, and she said, "Yes, all that internal focus can be ultimately beneficial, but not if the depression is prolonged. If you're still feeling down in a week, I'd be glad to do a healing service for you…if you're comfortable with that."

"Thanks, Mom," I said. "I'd like that very much."

When Pilgrim came to visit a few days later, the fog permeating my brain had not improved. Pilgrim's advice was to eliminate meat from my diet. For years, I had been reducing my consumption of beef, pork, chicken, and turkey, so that I was only eating these meats at social events such as picnics and potluck suppers. So from then on, I became a modified vegetarian. I still ate some dairy and fish. I saw no immediate benefit from this change of diet but over time, I felt more energetic.

The following week, Mom conducted a service of prayer and laying-on of hands, but it did not alleviate my depression. Since my mother has a well-known gift for healing mental and emotional disorders, I mentioned this in my regular correspondence with Key.

Key's reply explained why. My mom has never been able to heal herself, and Key explained that she and I are too close, genetically and emotionally. Her gift can be used only on unrelated people.

As the weeks of summer unfolded, my condition did not improve. One afternoon, my dad came up to me as I was dozing in a chair in the family room and said, "There's something we'd like to try for your depression."

"I'm willing to try almost anything," I said.

"Stay where you are," he instructed.

He summoned assorted Angel Nest residents who happened to be there at that moment and had them lie on the floor across from me. In addition to Dad, there were Wakhan, Encantadora, Mary, Darshan, Huxley, and Cedar Cradle. They popped out of their bodies and as a group floated into the space occupied by my corporeal body. Instantly I felt a huge boost of energy and joy. They remained inside me for a while and then departed one by one. Dad was the last to leave.

"Wow!" I cried after they had returned to their bodies. "I feel great!"

"I don't know why I didn't think of this earlier," Dad said.

Cedar Cradle added, "The effects of this may not last, so take advantage of the high to start doing something productive."

Huxley said, "Whenever I'm feeling down, I do a self-inventory looking for something whimsical to do, something I'd thought about but never done."

"That's a wonderful idea," I said. "The problem is that all my notions of whimsy are buried in my psyche at the moment, and I can't get access to them."

Aunt Cedar Cradle was right. The energy and afterglow of the group floating into my body had faded completely by that evening. Still, the next day I felt generally better, and when classes started, I dove into college studies with renewed strength.

About a week before the start of my college classes, I was relaxing in the common room at Angel Nest, perusing an old issue of FKK, the German naturism magazine. All my life I've had a tendency to inhabit certain photographs, mostly of people. That is, I lose myself, my conscious identity in them. This particular time, I turned a page and beheld a willowy young woman standing in a confident posture with her hands on her hips, and I was promptly absorbed into her image. Her eyes and mouth looked like mine, as did the way she held her facial features for the camera. Except for the fact that she had blonde hair all over, she could have been a double for me. It felt like I *was* this woman.

On a different occasion, I was reading another German naturist publication, Sonnenfreunde, when the same thing happened in response to a photo. This time it was a slender young man. Except for the abundant black hair on his head, chest and below, he illustrated what I would look like as a male. The photo entranced me and I fell into it with all my mind.

I've had similar kinds of experiences when looking at physical objects, usually antique ones, going as far back as age two. My name for this phenomenon is tapping into the Universal Consciousness. If there is a more technically accurate name, I don't know it, but in any case, I am prone to mystical adventures arising out of ordinary circumstances.

When visiting an herb shop in Sedona, my eyes were drawn to an antique mortar and pestle, and I was transported into another realm. I stood in the midst of a leafy forest that I somehow knew was in the northwest of England. And I danced naked around a majestic oak tree. Nothing in that was out of character. I had danced naked around oak trees in Oak Creek Canyon. A likely explanation is that I associated herbs with pagan healing rituals and pagans with Celtic England. It was the trance with its sharply intimate sensation that is noteworthy, I think.

None of this is surprising, however, because both my parents are prone to mystic fits and other ecstasies. It runs in the family.

II
NO COWARD SOUL

No coward soul is mine
No trembler in the world's storm-troubled sphere.
Emily Bronte

All prophets are more or less fussy.
Samuel Butler (*Erewhon*)

If you can't get rid of the skeleton in your closet,
you'd best teach it to dance.
George Bernard Shaw

CHAPTER TEN
COMING OUT

As to physical appearance, my dad has told me I have the face and body of a Pre-Raphaelite model but with a tan. He advised me to look up paintings by Edward Burne-Jones and John Waterhouse to confirm his comment. He was right, including the ethereal quality to my face. As to the rest of my appearance, I am 5' 9" tall and slender, with blue eyes and fine, straight brunette hair, which I usually wear shoulder length but have experimented with various lengths and styles. As to personal grooming, I tend toward the natural but not consistently so. I use very little makeup most of the time. I confess to shaving my armpits and legs but often go for long periods without doing so. I have never used a razor on my pubic hair, although I have from time to time used a pair of mustache scissors to neaten the thatch.

Throughout my life, I have had a very limited wardrobe. At any given period my closet and dresser might contain couple of pairs of jeans, several pairs of khaki shorts, a few simple skirts and dresses for everyday use, a small assortment of blouses, and a large inventory of tee shirts and tank tops, plus multiple pairs of lightweight running shorts. Socks for all occasions generally fill an entire dresser drawer, but I have never worn nylons or pantyhose. One aspect of my development that has not evolved is a sense of fashion. Those who care about such things might classify my wardrobe as traditional nerd. Generally, I have not worn undergarments, especially a bra, although I do wear panties during my period and sometimes on other occasions if I feel like it. Bras are bad for women's breasts, and I've never even had one on. I take seriously the research showing links between wearing bras and breast cancer. Being a naturist, I've seen the red lines on many women after they've removed their bras, and these could indicate blocking lymphatic drainage, which corrals carcinogens in breast tissue.

In addition to a bra, another item that I have never owned nor worn is a bathing suit. The only swim parties I've been invited to have been hosted by naturists, so I've never had a need for such covering. It must feel uncomfortable, I imagine, to swim wearing clothing.

Generally, I have owned more footwear than clothes, with multiple pairs of hiking boots, various sandals, high quality running shoes, and one pair of pumps. And I have more hats than footwear. Since family members have not had occasion to buy me clothes for birthday and Christmas gifts, they have fallen into the habit of finding unusual hats for me. Apart from the dress-up kind, I like hats. By dress-up, I mean what my mother calls hats women used to wear to church (non-naturist, of course). My prize hats are a pith helmet and a conical straw peasant hat from Viet Nam, given to me by my Vietnamese brother Den.

I recognized at age eleven that I am bisexual. To be clear, I am truly bisexual and not homosexual trying to cover or heterosexual wanting to seem exotic. As long as I can remember having feelings of sexual attraction, I have experienced them powerfully for certain people of all human sexes as well as for intersexual Merven. Over the years, I have met people who do not believe bisexuality exists. A few have been so doctrinaire about it as to declare than having any same-sex attraction is equivalent to being exclusively gay or lesbian. This is balderdash. The existence of bisexuality was clearly documented in the work of Dr. Charles Kinsey in the 1950s. People can pontificate all they want about sexual attractions, but none of that changes the fact that I am genuinely attracted to women and men equally. Both engender in me powerful feelings of fascination and lust.

Although I knew about the breadth of my sexual feelings as I approached adolescence, apart from masturbation, I did not engage in sexual activity until I was in college. This was due entirely to the circumstance that I had not met any real person who sufficiently excited my sexual desire until then. So I made do with erotic scenarios involving Mr. Spock of **Star Trek** and Barbarella of the film of the same name. Had I met someone of either sex with the mental capacity and physical appearance to attract me, if encouraged, I believe I would not have hesitated to pursue sexual relations with that person. I fantasized a lot about having sex with a Merven but didn't know any except Sojourner, Pilgrim, and Quester who were part of my family. I did not fantasize about them, because that would feel like an urge for incest, which notwithstanding an infantile sexual attraction involving Sojourner, I did not have.

I lived in an intimate community among people for whom I felt great affection, especially Wakhan and Tzek Begay, whom I loved dearly. They were roughly in my age cohort, and it could have been tempting to explore sexuality with either or both of them, but even thinking about that also felt like incest. No one explicitly taught me that incest is bad, but from my first exposure to the concept I have had an innate aversion to it. Later in my life, this aversion would be severely tested.

The concept of virginity, and more specifically the ending of that state, is problematic for me. First, I reject the use of the verb lose with respect to virginity. I prefer to say that I ended rather than lost my virginity. But a second issue remains. What counts as an end to virginity? Loss of one's hymen? I lost that at age ten riding a horse, bouncing exuberantly on the saddle. Sexual acts with another person? Orgasm induced by another person? The common view is that penetration of the vagina does the deed. But penetration by what? Fingers? Tongue? Dildo? Tampax? I experienced all four of these inside me before an actual penis. I have come to think of having multiple ends to my virginity, each one a fond memory.

When I was twenty, in my junior year in college, I asked for time alone with my parents to tell them something important about me. My motivation for telling them was that I was neck deep in trying to manage a *ménage a troi*, and was feeling so much stress that I thought it would show in my general comportment. Also, I wanted it out in order to reduce the emotional burden I was carrying.

They sat on a couch and I sat facing them in a rocking chair. I was not nervous about coming out to them, but there must have been a sense of melodrama surrounding the scene, because they looked tense and serious and remained silent until I spoke.

I said, "Relax, Mom and Dad. I simply want to let you know that I am bisexual. I think you have a right to know this about your elder daughter."

The atmosphere lightened immediately.

Mom said with a twinkle in her voice, "I am so relieved. I thought you were going to say you've become a Republican."

We all laughed heartily at that. Then I said, "Would you still love me if I were a Republican?"

Dad said, "Certainly, but we know you so intimately that the news of such a conversion would lead us to question your sanity. We'd want a second opinion."

Mom said, "Yes dear, we would continue to love you the entire time that you were locked up in a psychiatric ward."

I said, "I knew you wouldn't have any issue with my being homosexual, but I wondered if the bi part would cause you even a tweak of concern."

Then Mom said, "Zara dear, we've known about or at least strongly suspected your sexual orientation for a long time. Years, actually. But it's good that it's now in the open so we can converse appropriately about it if the subject arises."

"How did you know? What specifically tipped you off?" I asked.

"Your eyes," Dad said. "We saw your eyes dilate in response to faces you found appealing, and I noticed years ago that your eyes reacted equally to images of attractive males and females."

"That phenomenon occurs in artists, regardless of their sexual orientation," I said.

"True," said Dad. "But we also noticed your behavior in settings where sexual tension was evident, and your face and gestures revealed positive attractions to both males and females."

Then I said, "Only faces? What about attraction to bodies?"

"Yes," said Mom. "Bodies too. But faces are more compelling. It was Helen of Troy's face that launched a thousand ships, not her breasts or legs."

Dad added, "No matter how beautiful, physically fit, well-proportioned, or appealing a person's body may be, you won't develop a healthy intimacy unless you find that person's face appealing in some way. Faces don't need to be classically beautiful to be attractive. They can be quite plain, but in most cases some feature or another, lips, eyes, cheeks, smile, will attract interest."

Mom said, "Focusing on facial features is not superficial, as some would argue, nor is it sexist, unless done to the exclusion of personality and intellect. A face reveals much about a person's life history and health and even more about one's soul. You have a particularly compelling physiognomy, Zara, and I've seen many people gaze at you."

I blushed in acknowledgment of her last remark and then said, "Yes, and I gravitate to interesting faces. As Dad noted, I've done my share of gazing. Some faces that society judges ugly I find fascinatingly beautiful. But none of this discloses my bisexuality."

"It manifests the artist in you," said Mom. "Nevertheless, your bisexuality does not surprise us."

"You are free to tell anyone you wish to about this conversation," I said. "Henceforth I am openly bi. And since I'm out now, do either of you have any advice or counsel for me?"

Dad said, "It would be redundant to say be yourself, because you have been honestly so your entire life. I suspect that if it hasn't already, your orientation will on occasion prove to be both a gift and a burden."

How right he was. Bisexuality is a gift that makes life more complex and relationship choices fraught with complications. For me, complexity is generally a delightful condition, certainly adding interest to everyday activities. But one cannot be responsible for the feelings of others, and I learned from experience that in a relational constellation involving three human people (two others and me), I was the only one not jealous. To my great joy, however, jealousy has never arisen in any of my relationships with Merven.

Now here I am getting ahead of the story again. So much for the careful chronology that I neurotically desire and need. This digression is clearly a result of the Merven language (and thus Merven behavior) influencing my thinking patterns. Ah well, I am old enough now that I must let go of childhood obsessions, and if I wander in the narrative, so be it. Since this work is intended primarily for a Merven audience, it makes sense to let the telling of it bounce around in time in a manner likely to bring its readers pleasant satisfaction.

Anasazi College provided a wonderful environment for me. The movement back and forth between home and classroom felt to me like moving between Eden and Elysium. My course work was entirely interesting and challenging, the faculty members I studied with were fully supportive and encouraging, and there were so many fascinating students that the romantic, emotive aspects of my personality blossomed.

In my freshman year I developed an erotic attachment to a sophomore woman, Prisca Hastings, and we enjoyed spectacular sexual explorations. In private, I referred to our physically enthusiastic sex sessions as the Battle of Hastings, which made Prisca feistier. My sophomore year, I enjoyed an equally strong sexual relationship with a male freshman, Kelmscott Heath. I suppose it is trite to describe these as liberating experiences, but for me that is what they were.

The combination of intellectual and sexual refreshment was exhilarating, and I wanted those days to go on forever. Then came a reality check in my junior year. I rekindled the relationship with Prisca and then attempted to sustain a *ménage a trois* with her and Kelmscott. For a brief period it was exciting for all three of us. The bedroom games we played were splendid. But all too soon, Prisca began acting insecure and jealous, continually seeking my assurances that I really loved her more than Kelmscott. I could not in truth admit to that. Although I was very fond of them both, I did not love either one and was not even fonder of one more than the other. Prisca's clinginess increased, which Kelmscott picked up on, leading to a diminution of his ability to perform, which then led to her criticizing him for lack of élan.

Kelmscott, embarrassed and angry, left the relationship, but then Prisca blamed me for the departure and stormed out, accusing me of loving him more and thus taking his side. Sometimes I do not understand women, but lurking in the future was even more reason to find Prisca perplexing. The *ménage* should have worked, in my estimation, because all three of us were intellectually brilliant, physically attractive, open-minded, and adventuresome. But now it was no longer fun. I brooded for a while then licked my ego wounds and got on with life.

In the aftermath of that experience, I had another vivid dream in which I was visiting Denmark, but climate change had turned it into a tropical paradise. While shopping for mangos in the open-air market, I met a porn star, who immediately fell in love with me. I found her extremely attractive, both physically and emotionally. I suspected the dream was the result of my emotional turmoil at trying to sustain an unstable sexual threesome. Clearly, if Denmark was a tropical isle, the world had turned upside down. I documented this in my journal, but had no intuitive sense that it was in any way prescient. Still, the dream stayed with me, coming to mind every year or so before settling back into my subconscious.

CHAPTER ELEVEN
COURSES AND CLOSURE

My favorite professor at Anasazi was professor of English Chaucer Dickinson. I took more courses and independent studies with her than any other faculty member. For the spring semester in1996, she facilitated an independent study for me to examine the sexual euphemisms and double entendres in the works of Geoffrey Chaucer, Will Shakespeare, and in the King James Bible. The professor-student discussions on that subject were filled with hilarity. Both of us roared with laughter as we dramatically recited quaint sexual terms.

The one that induced the greatest laughter was my comment on Ezekiel 16:17, which includes a reference to dildos. They are described as "images of men" made of silver and gold, with which women committed whoredom. "Pretty expensive dildos," I said. "But evidently, Ezekiel did not approve of them. I guess he didn't have the anatomy to savor them properly."

This set Dr. Dickinson into a spasm of uncontrolled laughing, which in turn set me off. We continued that way back and forth for at least fifteen minutes, trading vulgar speculations about what other sex toys Ezekiel might find distasteful.

When we had recovered out senses, I changed the subject to her very successful fantasy novella, *The Timberscape of Memory*. "Your book has done so well, you should write another one. Have you thought about it?"

"I've played with some ideas, "Chaucer said. "At one point I considered writing a modern, female version of *Robinson Crusoe*."

"Great idea! That would be in keeping with your island motif," I said. "Defoe's novel is a classic but his thick prose gets in the way and could use some updating. And a female protagonist is exactly what's needed. You should do that."

"Yes, but I have a problem with it. Every time I've tried to outline the story, it turns into a depressing tale of descent into madness. The effects of years of isolation would not be pleasant to describe," she said.

"That's your extroversion asserting itself. My first thought when you mentioned the subject was a sojourn in paradise. Such wonderful solitude," I replied.

"The idea makes me shudder," Chaucer said.

"Then that's why you need to write it, to explore your fears," I said.

"I'll give it some more thought," she replied. "But I wonder if our professor-student relationship has just been reversed."

"Oh, I hope not," I said. But from that point on, we were on a first name basis.

She never wrote the book. At least, I never saw it in print. For all I know, she may have written a draft but decided not to publish.

The following spring, I did another independent study with Chaucer, exploring my premise that the English language existed in a form recognizable to speakers of Middle English prior to the Anglo-Saxon invasion and that therefore Anglo-Saxon is not the source of Middle English but simply an external influence on it arising from the circumstances of Angles and Saxons ruling much of the country. I made a sufficiently strong case for the idea that Chaucer gave it some credence and urged me to write a book about it. Alas, as with her failure to write a female *Robinson Crusoe*, I never got around to writing a book about the origins of English.

While in college, I decided to experiment with dead people. That is, I arranged to test my hypothesis that while floating, I would be able to perceive the soul of anyone who died in proximity to where I was floating. If demonstrated, this would provide substantial evidence, if not proof, of the continued existence of the soul after physical death. If successful in such a perception, my plan was to try to interact with the departing one and follow the soul as far and as long as I could without endangering my own continued living existence.

A motel room near the Flagstaff Medical Center provided a safe place to store my body while I hovered around the ceiling of its Emergency Department. The inevitable moment arrived when a severely injured patient did not survive, and I watched the area above the new corpse for signs of a departing soul.

For an instant, I thought I sensed the presence of another non-bodied entity in the room, but the sense evaporated before I could be sure I had actually felt it. Maybe it was an apprehension of my own anticipation or perhaps only a nurse's sigh.

And so I bided time, and in due course, another patient died on an operating table, and I focused all my attention on the area above the body, seeking any indication of the presence of another soul. All I perceived this time was an invisible, immaterial, and seemingly insulated wall of benign mystery between the one who had just died and me.

Naturally, I was disappointed. For a while I waited for more passings but eventually flew back to my body and went home. I never tried this again, and this is the first time I have ever revealed that experiment.

My most productive independent study proposal came in the fall of 1997. This was done jointly with English professor Bookman Donne (another of my favorites) and Chaucer Dickinson.

"I'd like input and guidance from both male and female perspectives. You see, I had a particularly vivid dream about a myth of creation in the Bible. Actually, there are two myths woven together, one in the first chapter of Genesis and the other in the second chapter," I explained.

"I am very familiar with those competing chapters," Professor Donne said.

"So am I," Chaucer echoed.

"Excellent!" I said. "The vision that came to me in a dream was a third creation myth. What I propose to do is write a mythic poem of a thousand lines, with guidance from the two of you as I work on each section. It will extend from the creation of humans to the end of the age. I have an outline that I'll include in the written proposal for the IS," I said.

After studying my outline, they agreed to the independent study to review and critique my work that ultimately resulted in **The Third Song of Creation, a Myth in Five Seasons**. I was elated that my professors spent more time affirming my writing than offering editorial advice.

The first issue I took to them was about food. I wanted the early humans in my poem to be vegetarian, skipping the hunter-gatherer stage.

Dr. Donne said, "It's your vision and myth, Zara. You can make them be and do whatever you want. The issue is whether what you describe, in this case a vegetarian society, will hold together internally in the poem."

"Thanks, Dr. Donne. That's very helpful," I said. "I was more concerned with verisimilitude and historicity. I'm not worried about internal cohesion."

"Since you and Chaucer are on a first names basis, I think it will make our conferences less stuffy if you call me Bookman," he said.

"Thanks, Bookman," I said without a pause.

Both Bookman and Chaucer were members of the congregation my parents led, so I saw then in that naturist context all the time. But I did not want to impose that intimacy on this academic context, unless they suggested it. Both now had, so I began to feel as if I were an informal member of the faculty in addition to being a student.

As work on the epic poem unfolded, Chaucer and Bookman offered excellent advice and raised important questions. Commenting on the eroticism in many of the verses, Bookman suggested that I include at least one allusion to the erotic love poetry of the Song of Solomon. I did and then challenged him to find it. It took him all of thirty seconds to do so.

In section XIX, I used the German term **erotisch Nacktkultur**, and Chaucer advised me to replace it with the well-known **Freikorperkultur**, and I agreed that this was a better word choice that carried a wide resonance.

Chaucer also asked me if the angels in the poem represented the Merven in any way. Without thinking, I said, "Definitely not! They are more like the accusing angel of Job, **ha-satan**. I want to depict biblical angels as problematic and complex." But as I thought about it, I admitted that the angel Ebenezer was modeled somewhat on the Merven.

Bookman asked me about autobiographical elements in the work. I said, "There is a little bit of me in Vayu, but only a little. The physical descriptions of Zephyr and Corposant were influenced by the triptych in the Angel Nest family room."

"The one of your parents merging together?" Bookman asked.

"Right," I said. "Aunt Mary painted it, adding hints of wings and feathers on their bodies."

"It's a powerful painting and well worth mining for literary material," Chaucer said.

The experience of writing my own myth along with the sage and appreciative guidance from Chaucer and Bookman boosted my spirits greatly.

Throughout my college years, I had continued to run in Ten-K races in the Sedona area. As the end of my junior year approached, I decided to expand my horizons by registering for the Whiskey Row Marathon in Prescott in May 1998. I hadn't been training for Ten-K runs, because they were so easy, but I knew that a marathon was much more strenuous. Gradually, I increased my weekly mileage to include single days of ten, then fifteen, then twenty miles. Since Whiskey Row is a hilly run at high altitude, I worked on up and down courses and drove to Flagstaff, which is nearly two thousand feet higher than Prescott, for practice.

When the day arrived, the longest I had run in training was twenty miles. So all I had to do now was run twenty miles plus an easy Ten-K. I had been tapering for two weeks before the marathon and felt rested. The best thing about this kind of running is that one competes only with oneself. Whiskey Row is a small marathon that does not attract the international stars who make the rest of us feel inadequate. My only goal was to finish the race.

Along the route, I saw participants slow down to a walk for a while and then begin running again. My internal moral sense was that walking in a marathon was borderline cheating. It might be justified in extreme cases but if I slowed to a walk, I would feel that I had not really run a marathon. Some people stopped briefly to rest before continuing on, and to me this counted as certain cheating.

Though I was close to hitting a wall in the last three miles, I kept a running stride, albeit very slow at times, rather than fall into a walking stride. When I finally collapsed over the finish line, I found that I had clocked a respectable three hours and thirty-nine minutes.

Exhausted does not begin to describe how I felt at the end, but I had done it and could cross that off my list of life accomplishments. I did not know if I would do this again but concluded that if I did, the next one would be on a relatively flat course.

Wakhan graduated from Anasazi in 1998 and decided to go on a graduation trip to Washington State. She asked me to go along for companionship and fun. We took the shuttle down to Sky Harbor and flew into SeaTac International Airport, where we rented a car. I don't remember the make or model, but the trunk was too small for both suitcases, so we stuck mine in the back seat.

Our first stop was to visit Begay family friends who lived on the Yakima Indian Reservation, who pumped us for information about living in a naturist lodge. They repeatedly commented on how weird that was, but nevertheless, they wanted to hear all the details.

Thence we took a look at the ashes of Mount St. Helens and meditated on the raw geologic power of the earth. Our next adventure was a speedboat ride on Puget Sound. During the course of the trip we also went to Mount Ranier National Park. Though tempted, we did not try to climb even part of Mt. Ranier physically, we but did reach the summit out-of-body.

This was a good break from the daily routine of home, but I was glad to be back at Angel Nest, where I could cocoon to recover from the effects of extraversion in unfamiliar places along the journey.

In the fall of my senior year, I did an independent study with psychology professor Stanford R. Shock on the subject of mindsight, a newly coined term for perception while out-of-body. I told Dr. Shock that I had experienced an OBE but did not elaborate on my family history of leaving our bodies to float around the countryside. I wanted to do research to see if other reports matched my experience. Ultimately, the IS was unsatisfying. Most of the research I uncovered was about Near Death Experiences, which I had not had. And my experimentation at the Flagstaff Medical Center, looking for departing souls, did not bring usable results.

I also did an IS with Rabbi Darla Nabi, visiting at her office in Prescott to learn biblical Hebrew. Her congregation shared a sanctuary with the Calvinist church my mom was once pastor of, and she and her husband are part of the Angel Nest family. Another IS my senior year was led by Prasada Pratyaksha, also an Angel Nester. Her field is political science, but since she grew up in India, I approached her about learning Sanskrit. She claimed to know very little about that language but was willing to monitor my self-study. In the end, she said that I had taught her Sanskrit, but I got the credit hours. Truth be told, I would have done the study even if no credit were given.

My final course at Anasazi was an independent study with Bookman Donne in which I examined American and British culture through the lens of J. K. Rowling's *Harry Potter and the Philosopher's Stone*. The marketing department of the American publisher decided American children would reject anything with the word philosopher in it and insisted the title be changed to something more provocative. Thus it became *Harry Potter and the Sorcerer's Stone*, thereby demolishing the original title's connection with alchemy, which the book was about. I dismissed the American publisher as simply stupid but used the event as a vehicle for an ungracious critique of certain educators and the non-literate portion of the American public.

I acknowledged that I had thoroughly enjoyed the unfolding *Potter* series and that I found myself emotionally drawn to the character of Hermione Granger but did not specifically add that I saw a great deal of myself in aspects of the young witch. Hermione's concern for the rules was the exception that did not correspond with any part of me. I wrote, "Though Harry Potter is an appealing archetypal hero, ultimately he cannot become the savior in this epic apart from Hermione. She is the intellectual queen without whom no one and nothing can be saved. Hermione is essential, and without her there is no story to capture our imaginations and hearts."

The thesis length paper I wrote for Bookman became an act of catharsis, in which I verbally exorcised the emotionally painful years that I had sat trapped in dull classrooms. During that time, many of my teachers and even some students had thought of me as an intellectual snob, but in this they misunderstood my fundamental character. My view was at base optimistic and egalitarian, for at the time I believed that nearly all people are mentally capable of profound thinking. Then and now I find it exceedingly frustrating that so many people choose to wallow in shallowness and not use their brains.

Shortly before graduation, Prisca sought me out, saying she had something important to tell me. She had graduated the previous year, so I was surprised to see her on campus. We found an unoccupied shaded patio and sat on benches facing one another.

"What's on your mind?" I said, interested but wary.

"I told my parents," she said, showing a woeful countenance.

"Told them what?" I said. Before she could reply, it dawned on me that she meant she had come out to them. "That you're bi?"

"Not quite. I told them I am lesbian," she said.

"I assumed you were bisexual," I said truthfully.

"No, that was just cover to hang on to you," she explained.

I thought but did not say that it was a poor strategy. "Well, how did your folks react to the news?"

"They freaked out," Prisca said. "We're Roman Catholic, and homosexuality is looked on as a disorder in the Church."

"Another surprise," I said. "Not the disordered ideology part. I knew that, but I didn't know you're Catholic. You never once mentioned it during our relationship."

"I had pretty much abandoned the faith at the time," she explained. "But since you seemed to be quite happy with your faith, I didn't say anything that might bother you."

"Tell me more about your parents freaking out," I said.

"Well, they sent me to see a priest for counseling. I told them that I had already been to confession multiple times about my sins of the flesh. They were somewhat relieved to hear that. Anyway, this priest told me I needed extensive counseling to deal with my impure urges. We began meeting once a week for an hour or two."

"Is this leading to a tale of seduction by a priest?" I asked.

"No, not at all," she fired back. "During our fourth session, he told me that he is gay, but that as a gift to God he has taken vows of celibacy and chastity. He punishes himself every time he starts to fantasize about sex with another priest or a parishioner."

"Sounds like he's into self-loathing," I said, but Prisca ignored my remark.

"The upshot of my counseling was that I foreswore lesbianism, returned to the church, and became a practicing Catholic again. I'm praying about the possibility of a vocation in the church, and as part of that discernment process, I'm cleaning out my spiritual closet, which is why I want to tell this to you," she said.

"You're thinking about becoming a nun?" I asked, at first bemused and then stunned.

"Yes," she answered without hesitation.

"Pardon me for saying this, but wouldn't a convent be a difficult place for someone trying to control her attraction to women?" I asked.

"No offense taken," she said calmly. "The intimate life in a convent includes a lot of emotional support from the other sisters to remain chaste. I've already spoken with several sisters, who have encouraged me to take the step, to offer my life to Christ."

"It's your life, and you need to decide what path you will follow," I said in a neutral voice. "But how does telling me this help clean up your psyche?"

"It allows me to freely accept God's grace for any role I played in luring you into a sexual relationship. To the extent that I did so, I ask your forgiveness," she said. "It also provides me the opportunity to give you some heartfelt advice. Zara, you are a lovely person with a lovely soul, but like me, you have wandered from the path of God's will. With all my heart, I encourage you to abandon your perverse sexual agenda and get straight with God."

Now I was truly stunned. For a long time I sat in silence, unable to formulate a response.

Breaking the silence, she said, "I know you won't be able to do it overnight. I can give you the name of my priest if you want, but I suppose you would rather go to a pastor in your own church."

At last I said, "You have done your duty, Prisca. You are absolved of any guilt you may have been harboring about the state of my eternal soul or your role in putting it in jeopardy. I think you must love me to say these things to me. But my church does not view homosexuality as a disorder, and my parents fully embrace me as a bisexual person."

"I'm sorry if I have offended you," she said.

"The only person you have offended is yourself," I said.

She stood and stiffly offered me her hand. "Goodbye then, Zara."

I took her hand in both of mine, and tears formed in the corners of my eyes. A wave of sadness washed over me. "Goodbye, Prisca."

CHAPTER TWELVE
THE LANGUAGES OF PARADISE

Growing up in the church, as a double PK, one might think I would take either the path of complete acceptance of the religion of my family or the complete rejection of it. I chose neither path. The church of my parents is, admittedly, progressive and non-dogmatic, and I remain comfortable with its ethos. My parents never tried to convince me to believe the things they believe. Indeed, they do not agree between themselves on every aspect of religion but find that kind of agreement unnecessary.

At any rate, this is a prelude to the part of my life in which I decided to go to seminary. My goal was not to become a minister but to immerse in a milieu that I found and still find immensely fascinating. This is a suitable place to note the religious path that I have chosen. I am a spiritual humanist.

Spiritual Humanism allows for the existence of a universal or terrestrial consciousness that humans (and other mammals) may access, connect with, or be influenced by. Some call this universal consciousness God. SH finds value in exploring the scriptures of many religious traditions for wisdom, psychological insights, sociological information, and literary treasures, but not dogma. The approach is metaphorical and not limited to particular sources.

Here is the chain of events leading to my enrolling at Pacific Crossroads Theological Seminary. As previously noted, in 1998, Wakhan received a Bachelor of Arts degree from Anasazi College. Beginning in high school and continuing through college, she assisted my mom with healing services at the church. Like Mom, Wakhan has a gift for healing psychic wounds. There was never any doubt that she would become a pastor, although she had multiple options for education leading to ordination. Her long-standing preference, however, was PCTS in Lahaina, where, coincidentally, she had been conceived.

Mom frequently spoke with great affection about attending PCTS, and when she came home for Christmas, Wakhan raved about her classes. No one was surprised, therefore, when the following year, I, who also had been conceived in Lahaina, joined her at Pacific Crossroads. My ultimate goal was a doctorate in comparative religions or perhaps ancient Semitic languages, and this seemed a good place to begin that process.

Together, Wakhan and I returned home over the holiday break in December 1999. The Angel Nest reunion that year held the promise of being memorable, and the promise was fulfilled.

On New Year's Eve, Pilgrim and Sojourner arrived, along with another Merven whom I did not recognize. They appeared in front of the fireplace at ten that night. Sojourner quickly made introductions. "And arriving in North America only moments ago from Uluru," Sojourner announced with diplomatic gravity, "this, dear friends, is Key, the Chief Librarian of the Main Library of all the Merven -a very important personage. Chief Librarian is a rank among Merven equivalent to your President of the United States."

Key bowed. "I am so glad to be among humans about whom I have read so much. And I am especially keen to meet Zara, with whom I've exchanged a great volume of correspondence over the years, all carefully cataloged and preserved, of course. I am hoping at long last to meet her face to face."

Eagerly I pushed through the crowd to stand before Key, bowing just as Key had, and then embraced the Chief Librarian. "[click, plock] *zjeeek* [bark] *leee*," I said.

"Thank you. I am splendid!" crowed Key, clearly pleased with the hug. "And you? I understand you are studying holy things in Hawaii?"

"Yes, and keeping up with my Merven studies also," I replied. "Thank you for the recent volume, *Comparative Perceptions of God among Dolphins and Whales*. Many of the concepts cannot be expressed in English, but I [sigh] *beeezeee* them in Merven."

It felt wonderful to meet in person, to see the physiognomy of someone I had known only through distant communication. When I was able to have a private conversation with Key, I ventured into a sensitive area. "Years ago, when we visited in Viaticum, Sojourner mentioned the Merven creation myth, and Pilgrim said it was not spoken of in the presence of non-Merven."

"That is the custom," said Key. "But there is no religious taboo against revealing it. And if anyone were entitled to break the custom it would be I. The time has come, I judge, to satisfy your curiosity, Zara. Be discreet, however, in sharing this knowledge with others who may not appreciate our culture as deeply as you do."

Key's eyes rolled inward as if in search of a carefully stored memory, and then the librarian began to speak in somber tones. "In eons past, long before the invention of history, **Kaaadth** anticipated the evolution of human beings, foreseeing that they would be beautiful creatures but unpredictable and inclined to recklessness and self-destruction. But Kaaadth loved the idea of them and loved what they might in time become. Kaaadth did not wish to interfere directly with the emergence of such creatures, lest their spirit of adventure be dampened. They must have complete free will in order to develop to full potential. Yet the Transcendent One did desire to protect these fragile primates when ultimately they emerged as a species.

"So, **Kaaadth** encouraged a mutation among a small number of the ancient order of beings who walked upright on the earth. It was a tiny mutation, but within a dozen or so millennia, the first Merven appeared. And Kaaadth said to these first of our kind, 'Beyond all other sentient creatures on Earth, you have been given the greatest mental capacity. You shall use your brains for the benefit of others. You shall be gentle guardians for the developing human species. You may assist any other creatures according to your desire, but watching over the humans shall be your primary duty.' That, as humans would call it today, Zara, is the Merven mission statement."

"I can see how some humans might not appreciate the myth," I responded. "**Kaaadth** must love you very much to entrust you with the nurture of potentially beautiful creatures like us."

"Oh, Zara, you are not potentially beautiful," said Key. "You are truly beautiful right now. And so are your people."

"Thank you," I said and lightly kissed Key on the cheek. "And while we're on the subject of myths, I'd like to hear your response to a theory

I've been playing around with. It seems to me that some world religions, such as Judaism and Christianity, are at the edge of radical change. True believers, though declining in number, are clinging ever more tenaciously to ancient doctrines, while most other adherents are letting go of literal understandings in favor of religious beliefs more in tune with the facts of science."

"Go on," said Key encouragingly.

"I suspect that by the end of the 21st century Christianity and Judaism will be overtaken by something like spiritual humanism, at least in North America, Europe, Australia, and New Zealand."

"What does this have to do with myth?" Key asked.

"In the Western World creedal Christianity replaced the religions of ancient Greece, Rome, Scandinavia, and Britain, among other places," I said. "The sacred lore about the superceded gods became mythology, but beliefs about the old ways continued to influence the developing practices of Christianity. Myths are extremely powerful. My theory is that when religions die out, they lay down rich layers of mythic material to fertilize the religions that rise in their stead. I believe that spiritual humanism will grow out of the decay of Christianity and Judaism, but the new religion will be nourished and formed by Jewish and Christian mythology."

"Interesting," said Key.

"One more point," I added. "I suspect that in due time spiritual humanism will give way to a more inclusive primate spirituality and eventually to spirituality that embraces all intelligent mammals."

"What about the inclusion of other sentient animal life?" asked Key.

"Hmmm. I don't see that coming in the next millennium," I said.

"It seems you have been integrating Merven thought patterns with human intellectual growth," responded Key. "Nicely done! Now, let me ask another question. How has the experiment with the sacred library progressed?"

"It's used frequently," I answered. "Mostly people go there to meditate or pray and not for study or casual reading. All the books in the sacred library -except one- are available in the regular church library in print or audio format."

"And the exception?" asked Key.

"A book I placed on a special shelf. You know it well, since you wrote it *A History of Merven Library Science*. I'm the only one who can read it, the only human that is. And of course, you're welcome to visit our book shrine any time you'd like. You don't wear jewelry or sandals, so you wouldn't even need to store any possessions in the locker room."

"I would like that very much, Zara, and was hoping for an invitation to meditate in such a room. Though I spend most of my life tending to a library, every time I enter a new one, I get -what's the English phrase?- goose bumps. A library set aside as holy is especially intriguing. I have brought along another volume to place with due reverence in this one -to satisfy your father's wish."

"Aha! **Original Nakedness**," I said.

"Indeed, a facsimile of my translation with Merven on one page and English on the facing page," said Key with glee. "In the meantime, shall we join the others?"

We moved into the kitchen and joined a group of humans and Merven deep in philosophical conversation.

"Would anyone care to go outside for a stroll around the resort?" Key asked.

"It's cold out there, and I don't feel like getting dressed," said Encantadora, which was the exact response Key intended to elicit from any one of the humans.

"But cold doesn't affect the Merven. Why exactly is that?" asked Cloud.

Pilgrim replied, "Breathing and imagining. We practice a technique called **doomoo leeekaadzg**. We can alter our body temperatures to stay warm in frigid environments and cool in sweltering ones. We can go naked anywhere in any season."

"As it happens," added Key, "it is good this subject has arisen. Centuries ago we taught this practice to Tibetan lamas, and it has served them well, allowing them to survive outside for long hours in subzero temperatures. You may enjoy learning that some of them go nude into the Himalayan snow to meditate for long periods of time. The lamas call this **thumo reskiang** in their language."

"That would be a rather useful skill for naturists in the winter," said Encantadora. "Will you teach us how to do it?"

"Key, Pilgrim, and I discussed this very matter on the way here tonight," said Sojourner. "We decided it might prove to be a beneficial skill for you in the future for reasons unrelated to friendly moonlight strolls."

"That certainly sounds ominous," said Sigrid.

"Do not fear," Key said. "All shall be well. Nevertheless before departing Angel Nest this holiday season, we are prepared to teach *doomoo leeekaadzg* to a select number of you, and once you have mastered the art, you can teach others in the same manner as you have taught one another to float."

A light flashed in my brain. I already know how to do that, I thought. I've been doing it since I was about four.

Key looked at me, smiled, and telepathically said, "You have an innate ability to do this to a limited extent, Zara. You're the reason we want to teach others as well. But you do not yet know *how* to do it. With a little instruction, you will be able to master the technique and use it well."

I responded, also telepathically, "I suppose we should keep this conversation to ourselves."

Key answered, "Yes, that would be wise."

I did master the art of *doomoo leeekaadzg* before anyone else in the family, but all of the others caught on without difficulty.

If the years at Anasazi were golden, the ones at Pacific Crossroads Theological Seminary were platinum. I leased the same residence that my parents had stayed in while Mom was pursuing her divinity degree. Apart from the engaging coursework, I managed to make extended visits to see Key in Australia.

Many opportunities for intellectual and sexual stimulation arose on the Island of Maui during my years at PCTS. Indeed, each kind of stimulation often led to the other in circular fashion. A spirited discussion with a classmate about the nature of God resulted on more than one occasion in a spirited romp in bed. Such verbal jousting affects me like an aphrodisiac, and most of my partners, male and female, confessed to similar feelings. And post-coital mumblings have often lured my lovers and me into profound speculations about transcendent things. Living in a small house rather than a dorm made it easier for me to be discreet in my relationships, and I doubt that any seminary faculty or staff knew or guessed my bisexual orientation. Certainly none of my divinity student lovers had any interest in talking with the professors about the kinds of adventures we had at my house.

Early in my time at PCTS, I visited a retired professor named Evangeline Beecher England, who told me she had taught both my parents and thought highly of them. She hoped I would do as well as they. She commented that from her observations of me and reports about me from members of the faculty, that I had indeed been raised well and had become a fine young woman. Though well into her 90s, she was mentally sharp and not as frail as one would expect. She served fresh fruit and vegetable smoothies for lunch which invigorated me considerably.

While living on Maui, I took frequent advantage of the proximity to visit grandma Penny and grandpa Randall who had a home in Waimea on Oahu. On one visit, they took me to the Punchbowl Crater, National Memorial Cemetery of the Pacific. The setting was unexpectedly moving. I kept thinking about all three of my grandfathers, Lloyd, Tom, and Randall, who had served in World War II, and my dad and uncle Firstlaugh, who had served in Viet Nam. They had all survived their wars, but so many veterans who had physically survived had suffered for years thereafter none-the-less. For some reason, the sight of the neat rows of tombstones gave me a sense of the immense costs of war, and I wept.

I continued to maintain a regular running regimen, including occasional barefoot runs on the beach, which felt like cross training. In a typical week, I logged 25 to 30 miles. During my three years at PCTS, I ran two more marathons, one each on Maui and Oahu.

Between graduating from PCTS in the spring of 2002 and starting work on a PhD at Stanford that fall, I visited Key in Uluru. It seemed a necessary pilgrimage as prelude to beginning doctoral studies. One of our conversations at the time related to my musings about the apparent popular preference for dystopian books and films rather than utopian ones, which had always held greater appeal to me.

"Why does struggling against a dystopian system seem to be more interesting than living in utopia?" I said.

"Most humans are easily bored with a peaceful life," Key said. "They prefer the pursuit to the actual state of utopian existence. Utopia is like sex. It is more powerful in the imagination than in real life."

"Sex is also pretty good when you have it in person," I said.

"But if you have it all the time, it cloys," Key noted.

"How can humans come to appreciate utopia better?" I asked.

"For that to happen, humans need an evolutionary change in brain chemistry," Key said.

"And how likely is that?" I said with a skeptical tone.

Key smiled but did not answer.

CHAPTER THIRTEEN
NEW VERSIONS

Having always been a fast worker with regard to something I very much wanted, my years at Stanford, 2002 to 2006, were relatively brief for attainment of a doctoral degree. I can be goal fixated when I choose to be. And yet, it was there that I learned patience and how to manipulate personalities within the system. My PhD advisor, Venet Jones, was excited about the subject of my dissertation, intersexuality and androgyny in ancient Hebrew and Christian writings. Though an exceedingly bright and accomplished scholar, she could conceive of my subject only in the context of her own groundbreaking paradigm, and she pressured me to frame my work with her model.

One thing we agreed on was a sense of amazement that so many sensual and erotic images and descriptions in the scriptures had escaped the censorship of pious redactors and scribes over the centuries. But our visions diverged from that point.

I fully grasped her paradigm and recognized the substantial evidence she provided to support it. However, I did not find it particularly useful for my work. In short, she proposed that the entire range of sexual images and attitudes expressed in the scriptures (including my narrow area) grew from envy of the Canaanite fertility cult and the consequent guilt associated with that feeling. The Jews and early Christians fell into approach/avoidance patterns derived from contact with idol-worshiping peoples, which is why the biblical texts present such confused and contradictory views about sex.

Venet's particular expression of feminism focused on the pathology of the sexual double standard in ancient Hebrew patriarchal society.

"There's no getting around the essential disorder and injustice of a culture in which a man could have sex with as many wives, daughters, concubines, and prostitutes as he could handle, but women could not," she told me. "Women were considered property and their sexuality severely proscribed. The only way a man could get into trouble was by having sex with another man's wife or other female property."

To engage her in the conversation without committing to her paradigm, I said, "The sexual double standard in American culture is a bastard descendant of that ancient patriarchy. Young men are expected to act out sexually, but young women are expected to be either virginal or sluts. I agree that examination of the scriptural texts through a lens of pathology is useful and in the present day context, a feminist critique is vital."

My own sense is that quite apart from any psychological issues, intersexual and androgynous images were naturally present in early Hebrew and subsequent Jewish and Christian communities. Ideas, stories, and depictions of these phenomena were not gained in reaction to Canaanite culture but are naturally and organically present in all human societies and civilizations. They may not represent the majority population, but they appear in the flesh with real people and are transformed into art and literature out of profound motivations.

Nevertheless, I was required to devote a great deal of my dissertation to expounding my advisor's model and integrating her thought into my work. Based on my behavior in elementary and high school, it would have been in character for me to rebel, but because of my deep involvement in the Merven community, I had learned to go with the flow. And to her delight, I was able to expand her psychological model by identifying the ways in which ancient Near Eastern peoples functioned to their detriment by ceding authority and credence to psychotic and paranoid prophets on an equal footing with those prophets who were wise and healthy.

The title of my dissertation is ***The Prevalence and Significance of Intersexual and Androgynous Elements in Canonical, Deutero-canonical, and Non-canonical Jewish and Christian Texts***. The first text I presented in the dissertation was Genesis 1:27. "In the image of God, male and female, God created them." From that beginning, I identified and interpreted hundreds of additional phrases, proverbs, and verses from Judeo-Christian religious writings, all relating to sexual and gender identity.

Although no one on the Stanford faculty knew about it, Chief Librarian Key was a critical source in my research work. My advisor had the impression that I possessed amazing skill at finding arcane scrolls and manuscripts tucked away in obscure libraries, synagogues, churches, and monasteries, and this was generally true. But without Key's copies and notes about where the original documents were stored, I would have missed much important material. Key's assistance was also a factor in the relative speed at which I completed the doctoral requirements.

My years at Stanford formed an era of sexual celibacy for me, although not by design. Partly this happened because I was so enmeshed in my studies and writing, but the bottom line is that I never got laid in California. I've known people who intentionally indulged in periods of celibacy following divorces because it felt therapeutic to them. But in every case, this was only a stage in their healing.

Some spiritual leaders talk about the gift of lifelong celibacy. I don't see it as a gift, and most of the religious celibates I've met weren't happy about it, accepting it as a sacrifice required by the community. The only ones I know who are able to embrace celibacy, abstinence, chastity, or whatever it may be called, in a healthy way are Aces, that is, asexuals. They are far rarer, however, than the population of celibates in religious vocations. From my perspective, the suppression of natural sexual behavior in the name of some religious doctrine is immoral. Nevertheless, I made do with autosexual release during the pursuit of my doctorate.

At any rate, once I had successfully defended my dissertation, as framed by Venet Jones, I fell into another bout of depression. I would soon be conferred with a doctoral degree, and yet I was sad. I flew home for another round of family and friends floating into my body, which gave me a needed boost, but this lasted only a week.

In a flash of recognition, I figured out how to rise out of my funk. I rewrote my officially accepted dissertation the way I had originally intended, and after my degree had been conferred had it commercially published.

Out of academic courtesy, I sent a copy to Venet for response (if any). The new version did include acknowledgment of her support and intellectual contributions, although little of her paradigm remained. After reading the revised version, she texted me and graciously acknowledged that my rewrite is a more coherent product than the one she helped to shape. I want to point out, however, that she chose to text me rather than teleconferencing, which is the usual way we communicated in those days. My supposition is that she found it difficult to look me in the eyes when complimenting me for substantially abandoning her paradigm.

I shall digress at this point to comment on my use of text as a verb in the preceding paragraph. Classically, text is a noun. In my early years I eschewed such transpositions of parts of speech out of a snobbish sense of what constituted elegantly correct English. As I matured, however, I came to accept emotionally what I had long known intellectually that languages do, in fact, evolve. Since text as a verb has persisted in common English for four decades, it is no longer a suspicious neologism. This is merely one example of hundreds I could cite where in my lifetime nouns have been transformed into verbs by popular usage. The weirdest one I ever heard was a musician telling the audience that he loved pianoing for us. That one goes too far, I think.

With regard to the device then used for texting and the unending succession of improved electronic tools, I wish to interpolate a cautionary note. I enjoy the advantages of technology, including the many means of instant communication. I own many of the latest microchip toys and gadgets. But I use them to a limited extent and am not dependent on them. I invest far more time and energy in the technology inherent in my own mind and body and believe the world would be a better place if more humans would do the same.

Now, after four years of diligent research and pleasurable writing, as well as successfully coping with faculty imposed academic constraints and complying with the administrative requirements of the process, I had a PhD from Stanford University. The future was wide open.

For a long time, however, my brilliant scholarship did not open any doors to well-compensated employment, so in exchange for room and board, I worked as an adult education teacher at my parents' church, where I developed a strong following for thought provoking classes on religion and other arcane subjects that members wanted to learn about. Additionally, I taught occasional classes at Anasazi College as an adjunct professor. Through a recommendation from Venet Jones, I also entered into the business of freelance editing, beginning with scholarly articles for journals but eventually (through Aldous Askeladd) editing science fiction and fantasy novels for budding novelists. From these varied efforts, I made a comfortable living.

"Please open your Bibles to the Gospel of Thomas," I instructed the adult Bible study class. "You will find it right after the Gospel of John and before the Gospel of Mary Magdalene."

A man raised his hand. "I can't find it. It's not in my Bible. It goes from John directly to Acts."

"You need either a PCCV or PAV for Thomas to be included," I explained. "For those of you with outdated Bibles, I have printed copies of Thomas. How many need copies?"

Three hands went up. The twenty other class members had the newer editions. One of the three, a new member, asked what PCCV and PAV stood for.

With polite patience learned in my doctoral program, I explained, "PCCV is the Progressive Council of Churches Version and PAV is the recently published Progressive Anglican Version. These are 21st century Bible translations that include four additional books, including our subject for today, Thomas."

"What are the other new ones?" the new member asked.

"One is Deutero-Mark, which is a first century text with much of the same material as Mark but also many verses that may have been edited out of Mark later in that century. It was discovered in a Dead Sea cave. Its major significance is that it contains what most scholars acknowledge are clear references to Jesus' wife. More traditional scholars have found ingenious arguments against the issue of Jesus being married, some of them claiming that the spouse language is simply allegorical.

"Mark 14:8 contains language about a woman anointing Jesus' head with an expensive ointment, and to quell objections to the expense, Jesus said that she was anointing his body for burial. Deutero-Mark has a parallel passage where Jesus said she was preparing the bridegroom for the wedding feast, and has Jesus saying, 'Lo, you are gazing at my bride.'

"You can imagine that many traditionally orthodox Christians would have a hard time accepting this, but D-M has quickly become a favorite among the traditionally non-orthodox crowd. As expected, there was fierce objection to publication of the PCCV, including mass protests and death threats against the publishing house, and most denominations still haven't approved it. But the progressive version is gaining traction among the religious left. I know a pastor in a mainline denomination who uses it for her private devotions, even though her congregation wouldn't approve reading it in worship. Occasionally she sneaks quotes from the PCCV into her sermons, so far without anyone noticing. That speaks volumes about biblical illiteracy among church members.

"Another new book is called Deutero-John, which is similar to Deutero-Mark in that it contains verses that may have been removed from the Gospel of John at some early point, but it also includes language found in the Gospel of Thomas. Deutero-John is known in some quarters as *Original Nakedness.*

"The publication of Deutero-John, even before it was added to the Christian Scripture canon, led to a change in church practice in several denominations, including ours, the Australian Natural Christian Church, and the Community Church of the Liberated. D-J makes manifest that Jesus intended washing one another's feet as a sacramental act for all his disciples to perform. The NCC, ANCC, and CC of L have taken official action, citing both John and D-J as warrants, to recognize foot washing as a Christian sacrament along with communion and baptism. Later this year at their annual meeting, the Northern Reformed Congregational Church will be debating a proposal to add foot washing as a sacrament.

"Those of you with PCCVs will note that the four traditional gospels have been re-arranged, with Matthew and Mark trading places. This is because Mark is the earliest written of the gospels and therefore should come first. As a compromise among scholars, Deutero-Mark and Deutero-John are placed following Luke, although Deutero-Mark's composition is likely earlier than Luke and Deutero-John's is later.

"I've already mentioned the fourth new book, the Gospel of Mary Magdalene. It was first published in incomplete form in the mid 20th century. A complete codex was discovered in this century, making clear the advanced spiritual nature of Mary and the intimate physical relationship she enjoyed with her husband, Jesus."

Once everyone had opened to the Gospel of Thomas, I continued, "Let's take a look, now, at Saying 19. In this verse Jesus refers to the *five* trees in Paradise. Whoever knows these evergreen trees, Thomas affirms, will not taste death. Now, Genesis 2 names only *two*, the tree of life and the tree of knowledge of good and evil. Does anyone want to hazard a guess about which of the five trees Jesus was referring to?"

Danmark Aktebild raised his hand.

"OK, Danmark," I said. "I'm sure you know the answer, so it won't be a guess. Please tell the class."

"According to 3 Baruch, angels planted the Garden of Eden. Legend holds that Michael planted the olive tree, Gabriel the apple, Uriel the nut, Raphael the melon, and Santaniel the vine. Philo, thinking metaphorically, as did the redactors of Genesis with their trees of life and knowledge, named the five as the trees of life, immortality, knowledge, comprehension, and knowing good and evil. Another interpretation is that they stand for the five books of the Torah. The Naassenes, a sect of Christian Gnostics who were active at the end of the first century taught that they represented the five human senses, with the Eden being a metaphor for the human brain. There are, of course, many pentads from the ancient world, which would provide additional apt metaphors."

"Everyone got all that?" I said with a laugh. "Don't worry about remembering the list, although I'm sure Danmark would be glad to refresh your memories. Incidentally, the sect Danmark cited, the Naassenes, were noted for promoting integration of male and female aspects. Their concept of the Son of Man was androgynous. There is some evidence that they connected homosexuality with the androgynous ideal, thus presenting a positive view of homosexuality in contrast to the purportedly negative one set forth by Paul."

"Let me add another side note," said Danmark. "The Naassenes made much of the concept of living waters, from which life sprung in Eden, and which the Christ controlled. The living water is that from which the olive draws its oil and the vine its wine. Jesus tells the woman at the well about living water in John 4, which of course would also be the same water that he turned into wine in John 2."

"Connecting the water-into-wine in John 2 with the living water in John 4 is an intriguing thought, which we ought to explore more fully in another class. But getting back to the five trees, let's take some time now for each of you to develop your own list of five trees representing your understanding of Paradise. You are free to be as creative as you like."

The following week, we continued exploring material related to John the Apostle. At the beginning of class a woman raised her hand and said, "Last year, in her class on the Book of Ruth, your mother said that in the ancient Hebrew culture, feet were a euphemism for genitals."

"That's right," I said.

"So, Jesus was a Hebrew man, right?" she continued.

"Jewish, yes," I said.

"You've made a point of emphasizing the metaphorical nature of John's gospel, subject to wide interpretations. So, I was wondering about this business of him washing the feet of his disciples," she said. "Could that have been a euphemism for washing their genitals?"

I replied, "John is indeed the most esoteric of the gospels and subject to multiple levels of interpretation. I suppose one could push that to include washing feet as a metaphor for sexual activity. In the case you cite, since everyone there was male, it would be homosexual activity. But John's gospel was written originally in Greek, which has a different set of sexual euphemisms. I suspect that in this case, the text was actually washing real, dirt encrusted feet."

"But it could be possible that it's about more than just feet?" she said.

"With John, nearly anything is possible," I said.

CHAPTER FOURTEEN
LEAPING SPECIES

Abandoning the forward progress of my narrative for the moment, I had a significant conversation with Chief Librarian Key while I was still living in Stanford. My PhD process was nearing an end but the fate of my dissertation remained in limbo when Key sat down with me for an intimate talk. Key said, "My dear, it is vitally important that you bear at least one child, more if possible."

"Right away?" I asked with some bemusement. "I'm not finished with my academic hoops. My dissertation may not be accepted. I may need to rework it, necessitating up to another year in Stanford."

"That's purely academic," said Key with a chuckle. "I could not resist saying that. Pardon me. I do not think you need to worry about your dissertation."

"Are you going to lean on the committee telepathically? Perhaps suggest to those who hold my fate in their hands how spectacular my research and writing are..." I noted with amusement in my voice.

"Of course not," Key said. "Your work stands on its merits. They will not need my advice. And as for bearing a child, waiting for a brief period is alright, but this is something that should be done within the next few years."

"That doesn't sound quite as urgent as the tone of your voice," I said, "I am not averse to that prospect, but I am certainly curious why you deem it vital." The matter of not being in a relationship did not occur to me as an obstacle. Intuitively, I knew that Key would not suggest such a course without confidence in my finding a suitable reproductive partner.

Key said, "The particular mutations present in your DNA carry the means to make a much needed contribution to the evolution of your species. You likely represent a catalyst for initiating a tachytelic era."

"You mean speeded-up evolution," I said.

"Yes, it is a natural phenomenon that occasionally a species will undergo a rapid series of evolutionary changes in a compressed period of time. At other times, the rate of change will be brachytelic, that is, slow. An average rate of evolutionary change is called horotelic. We think a time of tachytelic change is about to occur in a segment of the human race and that you have a part to play in it," Key said.

"So, I'm a fast woman. Whoopee! Let the catalytic games begin. The times they are a-changin'," I said and then sang the Bob Dylan line with a suitably raspy twang.

Key smiled indulgently.

"Sojourner and Pilgrim love that song," I said with a shrug to justify the moment of whimsy.

"Yes, to their credit they appreciate much human music," Key replied and then added gravely. "Though it may make me seem stuffy to you, music is not my area of interest and is also off the subject."

Key had always exhibited twinkling eyes in my presence, even when discussing dry academic trivia, so this turn to seriousness caught my attention. Now subdued, I said, "Give me an example of the kind of mutations you're talking about."

A smile returned to Key's face. "Both your parents have the ability to read the memories of one another in certain circumstances. It was an exciting day when Merven scientists were able to confirm that they possessed this particular trait. This was the first strong evidence of the evolutionary trend I refer to."

"I know about that," I said. "They can do it with other people, too, not just between themselves. At first they thought it required a penis and vagina connection, but later they learned that it only required mutual sexual arousal and focused concentration while physically touching. Uncle Firstlaugh and Aunt Cedar Cradle can also do it, and so can Wakhan and I."

"As I am well aware," said Key. "And how many times have you utilized this ability?"

"Quite a few," I replied. "To be honest, though, I have used it more often for obtaining the memories of my partners than for mutual exchange."

"When you engage with partners who are truly your equal, you will want to exchange thoughts rather than simply absorb them one-sidedly," Key said. "The significance of this mutation, however, is that it is similar to the Merven ability to communicate telepathically. This is why it is so important that you procreate."

"Yes, but I'm not the only human being with this mutation," I said.

"Of course not," Key replied. "You also have the innate ability to keep your body warm in frigid conditions. That is an extremely rare trait."

"You taught me how to do that," I said.

"I refined your technique, but you were born with this adaptation," Key responded. "Yet even if it were merely a learned technique, it enhances ones chances of survival and effects changes in one's DNA."

"Which then could be passed along to one's offspring?" I asked.

"Exactly," said Key.

"OK. So, what does all this signify?" I asked.

Key paused until a mildly dramatic silence prevailed and then said, "You well may be the Eve of a new hominid species. I think so. Gifted people from around the world are likely to mate with your offspring. Such partnering offers opportunities to influence the gene pool in ways that would be greatly beneficial to both our species."

"You want me to play a role in Eve-olution?" I quipped.

Key groaned good-naturedly.

"But when you say both our species," I continued, "do you mean that I should conceive a child with a Merven?"

"I intended no such meaning," Key said. "However, your question suggests an interesting dimension to the subject of your offspring. If such a mating should eventuate, the probabilities favor the resulting issue enhancing the desired outcome."

"You're being confoundedly cryptic again, " I responded. "What precisely is this desired outcome?"

Key sighed and explained, "Merven scientists anticipate that the new hominid species, of which you strongly represent a probable precursor, will have much in common with us Merven in terms of mental and physical functioning, for example, the ability to communicate telepathically in a normative and clear manner."

"But I can communicate telepathically with you and other Merven right now. And so can my parents and dozens of other people I know. And although my parents can't do it, I can communicate telepathically with animals," I said.

"You communicate telepathically with Merven because we pass the necessary energy to you. You could not do so clearly otherwise," Key replied. "And though you may be able to absorb vague thoughts from average humans, you are not fully conversant with them, and they have no clue as to mental conversation. As for animals, that is a rare gift that makes it all the more important for you to bear children. This will represent another small advancement toward the new species."

"And yet," I suggested, "these new hominids will be distinct from Merven and human alike."

Key said, "Indeed! Of course, since an incarnate example does not at present demonstrably exist, we cannot say with certainty, but our expectation is that the newly evolved hominids will include a much higher percentage of introverts in the general population. Extroversion is likely to become a minority trait. Additionally, we suspect they will not be intersexual, as are Merven, but remain generally divided into two primary sexes, as are humans. However, some intriguing early data hint that the males and females of this emerging species may well be predominantly bisexual in orientation."

With sophomoric enthusiasm, I responded, "Cool! Have I been counted in that intriguing early data?"

Ignoring my question, Key continued, "From the Merven perspective, the best result would be that over an extended period of time, the new hominids would peacefully displace the violence-prone Homo sapiens, whose species would enter an evolutionary cul-de-sac and die out. The predominance of introversion in the new species would assist this development. Then the new hominids would live side-by-side and cooperatively with Merven in an extended age of peace and prosperity. At some point along the way, such an outcome surely would mean that Merven would no longer need to function as guardian angels for humans."

I laughed. "So, at base you want humans to evolve in order to put the Merven out of a job. This sounds like a long range retirement plan."

"I suspect," Key said with serious intonation, "that it will prove psychologically difficult for Merven to let go of the guardian role. This is not a development that would come easily, and in all likelihood would meet with considerable resistance in many enclaves. Yet in ages hence, with the elimination of substantial demands on our time, Merven would be freed to develop our arts and sciences much more fully. These would be worthy goals."

"Speaking of worthy goals," I said, "How would these new hominids peacefully displace homo sapiens? As belligerent as humans are, I don't see my species going gently into that good night."

Now Key laughed and said, "*You* certainly would not go gently, but there are -dare I say- *humanitarian* ways of assisting what needs to happen. There need be no raging against the dying of the light. The essential problem with humans that evolution needs to solve involves brain chemistry. A large number of humans have brains that are, to use an outdated expression, *wired* to be fearful and reactionary.

"In varying degrees, a majority of humans have this mental wiring, although thankfully a growing number do not. Clearly, however, a large proportion of your species has this trait imprinted strongly into their brain cells. This is an organic feature, which at the dawn of your species, when you lived among other predatory mammals, served a useful purpose. Now, however, it impedes human problem solving ability and hinders the capacity to build cooperative civilizations. People with such brains are naturally suspicious of people who are different and also resistant to new ideas. They are also responsible for most of the violence done by your species."

"So, as humans, we need to select against this kind of brain functioning," I said. "But that will take a very long time to produce good results."

"A long time, yes," said Key. "And yet evolutionary leaps may shorten the requisite interval."

I said, "For the present, is there any way to treat reactionary brain syndrome medically or psychotherapeutically?"

"Well, now you have hit upon something," Key said. "There are certain parallels between brains and immune systems in humans, and for that matter in Merven. Immune systems protect our bodies from harmful substances and infections. But those with allergies have dysfunctional immune systems that cannot tell the difference between harmful and beneficial things and thus over-react by fighting off harmless and even beneficial substances. Reactionary brains function similarly. They have difficulty distinguishing real danger from ordinary circumstances and frequently perceive good ideas and nice people as threats. It is hard for people with such brain chemistry to tell friend from enemy. For this reason, people with reactive brains tend to be attracted to positions of authority despite being ill-suited for actually managing or governing."

"Given that parallel," I responded, "would it be productive to treat people's reactionary brains with methods similar to how we treat allergies?"

"To an extent, yes," said Key. "It is possible to immunize people psychologically so that they do not continually function our of fear in ordinary circumstances. And there are promising pharmaceuticals that may provide organic relief. But evolution provides the most complete answer."

"You still haven't explained how the new hominids could peacefully displace Homo sapiens," I noted.

"Reactive personalities are attracted to others who are like them in appearance and who are afraid of the same particular differences," Key explained. "So, it would prove beneficial to encourage such people to settle in safe, homogeneous, and socially irrelevant enclaves."

"Gated communities?" I exclaimed. "*Segregated* communities?"

"Of a sort," Key said. "Part of what troubles your species is that reactionaries stifle the progress that adventuresome and creative people work hard for. If the fearful ones would self-segregate into gated communities, the way ahead would be more open for the real achievers among you."

"And how do we accomplish that?" I asked.

"As long as they feel safe, it is easy to distract them with games, circuses, movies, popcorn, candy, and chips," Key said. "Drug them with food."

"Oh that's cynical," I said. "One of the things I most appreciate about Merven culture is the lack of cynicism."

"I confess, alas, there are some among us whose manipulations may cross boundaries," Key replied. "But if the fearful brain folk are comfortable enough and sufficiently entertained, they will neither realize nor care that the best of life is happening beyond the pale. Homogeneous gated communities are evolutionary dead ends, but they would not recognize this."

"Yes, but wouldn't they become suspicious of one another within the pale? Wouldn't that characteristic still operate within their brains? Wouldn't they fight among themselves?"

"From time to time," said Key. "And yet if they had access to enough toys, they would not be likely to kill one another. Surely it would not be difficult for the creative ones out in the real world to provide a stream of amusements to placate those on the inside."

I said, "A century ago, naturists organized themselves in essentially gated communities. Would you say that they formed a dead-end culture that amused itself by running around naked?"

"Not at all," Key responded. "Naturists formed cells, egg cells if you will, with permeable walls that let in nourishing ideas and all kinds of interesting people while excluding only predators who would harm the community. And see how these germinating cells have given birth to healthy societies!"

Key's thoughts made me feel uncharacteristically humble but also excited and elated at the prospect of being part of an evolutionary leap for humankind. My sense was not that I was better than everyone else, but rather that my species was wearing out and in need of evolutionary rejuvenation. If I could play a part in resurrecting humankind, even as a new species, then I would do so responsibly.

CHAPTER FIFTEEN
THE TWO KEYS

Key made the proposal that I bear a child at a time when I was not involved in a physical relationship with anyone, male, female, or for that matter Merven, and I was thus inclined to let the idea of getting pregnant remain a distant prospect. In fact, I was enjoying a season of pleasant solitude and would have been reluctant to begin a relationship even if an attractive individual had suddenly appeared. Another comment that Key had made to me in that previous conversation remained in my mind. The things we say no to influence our lives as profoundly as those we say yes to. Things we deny are as consequential as things we accept. I took that to mean that having a child and not having a child would each bring particularities to my life, which could be beneficial or not either way.

I was surprised therefore by a subsequent talk when Key demonstrated a degree of urgency not typical of Merven and counseled me to take action promptly via a sperm donor. My mentor could be very persuasive, and in this case I found myself agreeing to the procedure within ten minutes of first hearing it.

Key selected the anonymous donor, but would not tell me who he was. Key told me only four things. First, the donor did not live at Angel Nest but knew people who did. Second, he was not related in any way to my extended family. That is, any possible genetic relationship between us would be millennia in the past. Third, the donor also had mutations in his DNA similar to mine. And fourth, the donor possessed an IQ comparable to mine.

At the time, my parents were perplexed by my precipitate efforts to conceive a child. I made repeated comments about the late hour of my biological clock and the prudence of getting pregnant while still young, which they accepted but did not, I suspect, entirely believe. I chose not to tell them of Key's assertion about evolving hominids, in large part because I thought it would seem preposterous to describe myself as the Eve of a new species. Little embarrasses me, but that bit of speculation very much did so.

All the staff at the fertility clinic were helpful and encouraging from my first visit there to the actual artificial insemination procedure. Everything went smoothly, and I felt a warm glow of elation when the deed was done.

The day after I had medical confirmation of being pregnant, I received a summons for jury duty. At the courthouse, I was selected for a trial. During *voir dire*, as potential jurors were questioned, the judge explained that this was a case with charges that could result in the death penalty. The attorney for the prosecution asked if any potential juror had scruples about the death penalty, and I raised my hand, the only one to do so.

"I'm Zara Person Morgan, juror number 667. I am opposed to the death penalty on religious and ethical grounds."

"Are you a clergyperson?" he asked.

"No, but I have a divinity degree from an accredited seminary," I replied. "But that's irrelevant. I do not believe the death penalty serves any useful purpose. For the far too many innocent people convicted of capital crimes, it amounts to state sanctioned premeditated murder. For those guilty of egregious crimes, it is a get out of jail free card. Being put to death relieves them of the punishment due to them."

"You claim to be a religious person. What about going to hell?"

"I don't believe in hell, but I do believe that the harshest punishment anyone could receive is to be locked up in prison, to be deprived of liberty for life with no possibility of parole. Solitary confinement for a long life is far worse punishment than a quick death."

"If all your fellow jurors voted for the death penalty, would you be able to set aside your scruples for a unanimous verdict?"

"Of course not! That would make a mockery of the judicial process. Speaking of which, if the trial were about finding the truth and making judgment based on that, I would have no trouble participating. But if it's about each side trying to make its own best case by devious argument, verbal deception, withholding of the truth, and spin, then I would not be able to be an impartial juror. I would have to devote my time to critiquing the incompetence of the various attorneys. If the trial were about legal technicalities rather than principles, then Dickens' famous line from *Oliver Twist* seems apt: "The law is a ass - a idiot."

I was not selected as a juror.

The course of my pregnancy was generally serene. The morning sickness passed quickly and the chemical changes in my body produced pleasant sensations that compensated for the ungainliness of the last month. Most women who have given birth enjoy telling the story of their labor and delivery, and I am no exception. I employed a midwife to assist with the birth and delivered my son in a squatting position. The pain was not as excruciating as I had been led to expect, although it was greater than any I had previously known. The strenuous part of labor lasted three hours. The midwife expressed amazement at how easily this had gone for a first pregnancy, calling it unprecedented in her experience.

Considering the date of fertilization, it is *not* completely coincidental that Key Person Morgan was born on October 7, 2007, my thirtieth birthday. He weighed seven pounds even and was 21 inches long. I had already decided that he would not be circumcised, and this met with the approval of his pediatrician, Dr. Helene Finn, who refused to do or countenance the procedure. Helene was a member of my church, and I felt blessed to have her add my son to her practice. She, of course, said she could not imagine not taking him on.

Members of my family (and this was not at my urging) quickly began calling my son K. P. They said it was to distinguish him from Key the librarian. Dad said, "We certainly don't want to call him Little Key or Keylet or anything like that."

"And I would cringe every time someone said he's a Keeper," added Mom. "On second thought, maybe he'd grow up to play Quidditch, so Keeper would fit."

At first I objected, but the affection they expressed with the K. P. nickname softened my resolve against it. And as he grew, he came to enjoy being known as K. P. My dad once told him that his name was only one letter away from a Wall Street fortune, but by that time, the J. P. Morgan brand had faded into obscurity and so the quip made no sense to young K. P. Morgan.

Within a few weeks of his birth, Mom approached me about baptizing my son. "We recognize that you may prefer anointing rather than make baptismal vows on his behalf, but I want to begin the conversation."

"Actually, I would prefer baptism as long as I could choose the formula," I said. "I could never assent to the language of Father, Son, and Holy Spirit."

"Do you have something in mind?" Mom asked.

"Along the thematic lines of my poem, *The Third Song of Creation*, I was thinking of baptism in the name of Artist, Lover, and Enlightener," I answered.

"Your dad would like that," Mom said.

He did, and the full immersion baptism took place the following Sunday.

Although the Merven Key did not reveal K. P.'s biological father, I assumed I would be able to gather identifying information by examining my son's facial features, hair, and skin color. Alas, I was not able to discern much, because K. P. possesses the ability to change his skin color, eye color, and the color and consistency of his hair at will. Over the years, as I gazed at him, I would see glimpses of what could be Asian or African or Native American ancestry, but other times all I could see was Northern European features.

K. P. did not lack for parental nurture. I loved being a mother, and there were so many male, female, and intersexual adults acting *in loco parentis*, that he hardly knew his father was not present in his life. For all I knew in those childhood years, his biological father could have been present at least part of the time.

Shortly before dying, Key did tell me that K. P.'s biological father had seen and interacted with him on multiple occasions and had a natural affection for the boy. However, he did not know that K. P. was his biological son. Sojourner had planted the idea of becoming a sperm donor in this man's brain, and having once made several seminal deposits, he put the matter out of his mind. I deeply appreciated this information and unsuccessfully pressed for more. However, it seemed important to Key that I not know the name of the donor, which in my mind made his identity all the more mysterious. Was he a married man? Would he be in danger if his paternity were made public? I knew that Key would die without revealing the name, but I suspected that some day I would find out some other way.

For the early years of K. P's life, we lived at Angel Nest with my parents. The job market for college professors was difficult during this period, and my area of specialization was not considered useful even in the whimsical realm of academe. I applied for positions at the University of Michigan and the University of Wisconsin but received no response from either school, not even an acknowledgment of receiving my *curriculum vitae*. The prospect of having to live in such cold places ameliorated the snubs. The universities are excellent, but Wisconsin and Michigan are not high on my list of desirable places to put down roots.

So I worked at the Sedona Natural Christian Church as an adult education specialist and from time to time as an adjunct professor at nearby Anasazi College. I also earned extra money as a freelance proofreader and editor of articles intended for scholarly journals. My dad's friend Aldous Askeladd, a successful science fiction writer, also referred a number of budding science fiction and fantasy writers my way for editing and proofreading expertise. In those days, the documents to be edited were sent to me by email as file attachments, so I did a lot of work staring at a monitor.

My work for the NCC congregation required me to attend worship services there, but I would have done so anyway, because I found them edifying and transcendently mysterious.

The first fantasy writing client Aldous steered my way was Victor Thrall, a tremulous man a few years past twenty, who was engaged in writing down an alternative world that he had mentally created in junior high as a means of coping with a violent family life.

"So, you're chronicling a parocosm," I said the first time we met.

"A what?" he said.

"An imaginary world developed in childhood," I explained. "It's a fine literary tradition. Anne and Emily Bronte imagined a South Pacific island they called Gondal. Tell me about yours."

"Well, it's a hidden valley," he said. "Very beautiful, peaceful, and serene."

"What's distinctive about it?"

"An ancient people live there. They've never heard of alcohol or drugs, and guns have never been invented. The elders examine people who want to have children, and only those deemed mature enough are allowed to procreate. As I said, it's very peaceful there."

"What is the conflict that gives texture to the narrative?" I asked.

"There isn't much, really," he averred. "Some people grumble when they're not allowed to have children, but they eventually come around to see the wisdom in that. That's about it. But there's detailed descriptions of the nice things people do for each other."

"This is a place where you would love to live, I imagine," I said.

"Oh yes," he replied. "I've been mentally living there for years, and now I want to record it for posterity."

"What about sex?" I asked next.

"Well, sex goes on," he said. "Not in graphic detail, but it's implied. I was eleven when I first thought of this place, and I'm trying to keep true to that level of innocence."

"Do you think some people would read this as dystopian?" I asked.

"Why would they do that?" he responded. "It's a beautiful place."

"Population control is a dystopian theme," I explained.

"So is irresponsible parenting," he shot back.

"I'm sure it is well worth saving for posterity," I said, "But novels without conflict are difficult to get published. Let me have a look at your manuscript. I'll make recommendations, and we can discuss ways and means of independent publishing."

Victor's parocosm was moderately winsome, and even without any challenges or obstacles for the protagonist to deal with, the story was worth developing for a young adult audience. Alas, it was so atrociously written that I had marked every page with a dozen or more spelling and grammatical errors, and I was employing a lenient standard. I advised him to put away the manuscript for at least a decade and then rework it.

"Let it lie fallow while your mind continues to ripen and build psychic sinew," I said. "Without doubt, your rewrite will be deeper and wiser."

In a huff, he said, "I'll find a better editor tomorrow."

I never heard from him again, but the book has never been published.

CHAPTER SIXTEEN
SECOND AMENDMENT GROUNDS

It has generally been my habit to stay up to date on local, national, and international news, though I confess aggravation that virtually all the local television news programs begin breathlessly with "Breaking News!" And this is almost always about crashing, burning, or shedding blood in some fashion. I try to check in with cable news channels, but find myself quickly disgusted when they get stuck on one story to the exclusion of everything else that's happening in the world.

At any rate, about this time, a series of reports on the activities of a white supremacist group in Arizona captured my interest. An organization called the Sanctified Christian Underground Militia had claimed credit for burning crosses and painting threatening graffiti on the walls of a synagogue, a mosque, and a Catholic church in Central Arizona. I had an intuitive sense that SCUM might decide to target the Sedona NCC. Perhaps that thought came from remembrance of the picket against our church nearly a quarter century earlier, but it carried the weight of premonition.

According to an FBI spokesperson, SCUM was believed to be stockpiling weapons and ammunition at a compound hidden in the Aquarius Mountains in Mohave County. My thought at reading that tidbit was that nothing could be less Aquarian than building a secret arsenal. Whenever SCUM members vandalized a place, they scattered flyers around the property proclaiming the wisdom of SCUM. Thus we learned that SCUM practiced what it called Second Amendment

Christianity. They claimed that the Second Amendment was inspired by God because slaves and all people of color need to be kept in their place.

I noted mentally that they were partly right. The amendment was not inspired by God, but rather to placate Southern slave owners who wanted a militia to track down runaway slaves and prevent slave uprisings. This historical fact undermines the modern day use of the amendment, in my opinion rendering it obsolete. But I wasn't getting much traction with that argument in Arizona in those days.

We further learned that SCUM revered mass murderer Timothy McVeigh and cult leader David Koresh. Members wore web belts with bayonets attached to emulate Christ. Jesus, they maintained, carried a sword, which he bequeathed to his followers upon his death. They were his true and faithful followers.

All this was fresh in my mind when Kelda Wickham, a member of my adult Sunday school class, approached me after church one Sunday in 2008 and encouraged me to get involved in a matter before the State Legislature. Kelda was (and still is) a vigorous animal rights advocate. She said there was a bill before the legislature strengthening laws against animal cruelty.

"Since you strongly oppose cruelty to animals, and with your silver tongue, Zara, you might be able to convince Senator Messer to support the bill to strengthen provisions of animal cruelty laws," she said. "It's sponsored by a Republican, so it has a chance of passing, but we need every vote we can get."

In my mind, this was clearly a non-partisan issue, although I would have as readily agreed to visit the lawmaker had it not been. At any rate, soon thereafter I paid a call on State Senator Thirel Messer at his district office in Cornville to encourage him to support the bill.

Messer's initial response to me was that the bill interfered with the God-given rights of hunters to kill wildlife any way they wanted to. "I'm a dyed-in-the-bone supporter of the NRA," he said.

My unspoken thought was that the NRA is a society of men with small penises looking for compensation by carrying artificial ones in the form of guns, along with the compliant women who enable them to feel macho.

Messer added, "Laws against animal cruelty are a threat to manliness. God wants men to be men."

From the movement of his eyes, I noted that he was looking at my chest and deducing that I was not wearing a bra. My guess is that he was probably thinking that my lack of an undergarment was communicating a desire for sex and that I must be promiscuous.

He raised his eyes and said, "I could be induced to vote your way on this bill, in exchange for a little...affection. You're quite an attractive animal yourself." He stepped closer and put his hands on my breasts and said, "Ooh, such nice firm tits. My hands say B-cup."

My sense upon seeing him face-to-face was that he was a sleaze ball, so I was not entirely surprised at his proposition, but the physical gesture was unanticipated. Nevertheless, I kept my wits and did not raise my arms or step back but firmly said, "No! Stop that!" Then I sharply kneed his testicles. He screamed in pain and shouted for his private security guard. When the guard rushed in, Messer groaned that I had attacked him when he refused to buy my liberal tripe.

The guard cuffed me and roughly pushed me into the waiting room while Messer called the sheriff's office. I kept my mouth shut. The security guard also noted that I had no bra and felt my breasts and ran his hand down to my delta, making sexual moaning sounds as he did so. With a strong voice I said, "Take your hands off me!"

Two deputies soon arrived, and Messer told them that I had first tried to get him to agree to vote for a bill by seductive means, but when he said no, I attacked him. One of the deputies drove me to the sheriff's office to be booked. The other, I later learned at the trial, stayed with Messer to take a statement.

"I'm going to record this," the deputy taking the statement said.

"I don't like those tape recorders," said Messer. "They can be edited."

"As long as it matches the written statement that I will have you sign, it will be fine," said the deputy.

Messer reluctantly agreed. His signed statement included: "She came in wearing a seductive dress and in a come-hither voice proceeded to seek my vote on an animal protection bill. I explained to her that I opposed that bill on Second Amendment grounds. I am against animal cruelty but this bill goes too far and is unconstitutional. After I explained this to the girl, she got all slinky and sidled up to me and started purring in my ear, saying she could make it worthwhile for me to vote her way. I stepped back and said that won't work, young lady, and then she kneed me in the...groin."

At the sheriff's office, I asked for my attorney and called Sigrid Yves. When Sigrid arrived, I revealed that I was wearing a recording device and had taped the conversation. Sigrid and I played it for the deputies.

I then said, "Clearly, you have detained the wrong person."

Sigrid demanded the arrests of Messer and his guard.

The deputy said he'd take that under advisement and confiscated the recording for evidence. I was immediately released.

After we got outside and into Sigrid's car, I told her that I had made two recordings. The first recorder was my intuitive idea, but it was Sojourner who suggested that if I were concerned about the need to document the meeting, a backup recording would be prudent. I sent Sojourner a thank you message for the tip. Two days later, when Messer and his guard had not been arrested, Sigrid released copies of my back-up recording to Dagmar Solbrent, who as former host of the Arizona Afternoon television program had many contacts in the broadcast news community, and to Duffy Davar, reporter for the Verde Valley Intelligencer.

When the contents of that tape hit the newspaper and TV news, the Sheriff's Office was on the receiving end of public outrage for not arresting the senator and security guard. As a result of the publicity, Messer was forced to resign his seat in the legislature. He and the security guard were thereupon arrested and subsequently stood trial, at which I testified. Both were convicted. The unjust part of this was that they were convicted of making a false statement to a law officer and not sexual assault or even sexual harassment. They received six months probation and had to pay small fines.

I received hate mail from men accusing me of destroying the career of a decent politician guilty of nothing more than "boys will be boys playfulness." I was called a ball-buster, cold bitch, and repeatedly told that I had been asking for it because I was not wearing a bra. One letter from a female said that since I pranced around naked all the time, I had no grounds for pressing charges against a normal man. One said that women who didn't wear bras were anti Second Amendment whores. Some of the mail was much worse than these examples. I am no prude when it comes to sexual language, but I draw a line at violent imagery. The combination of crudely sexual and sadistically violent language in threatening letters grieved and frightened me.

Sigrid Yves reviewed all this hateful correspondence and took all the letters threatening physical harm to the County Sheriff. His office promised to look into the matter but noted that it would not be a high priority.

At least the animal cruelty bill passed without Messer's vote.

In the next election cycle, Messer ran again for his old office and eked out a primary victory against two opponents. He easily won the general election with strong financial support from the NRA. What appalls me is that he won a majority of women's votes.

Voting against one's best interests is common in this country. Doing so to benefit the poor and powerless demonstrates ethical enlightenment and compassion. Doing so to advance the interests of the privileged class is a confession of ignorance.

In the wake of the publicity surrounding the Thirel Messer case, Norwell Edenbrook, Headmaster of the private school on our church campus, approached me during fellowship time after worship. His sandy hair was shaggy in a way that made me want to run my hand through it.

"I greatly admire the way you handled that unpleasant situation," he said.

"Thank you," I replied.

"Actually, I admire you for far more reasons than that," he continued. "Your adult Sunday school classes are first rate."

"I'm flattered," I said. "And I can say the same for your teaching. Your class on the importance of Christians embracing evolution was most engaging."

"For some time now, I've been building up the courage to ask you to dinner," Norwell blurted nervously. "Would you do me the honor?"

This surprised me. I had pictured Norwell as a confident and erudite Englishman, who though reserved, was not shy. There was no question that he was a stellar Headmaster at the Free Light Progressive Academy. At the time, the only intimate relationship I was involved in was breastfeeding K. P. and changing his diapers. The prospect of dinner with Norwell had great appeal, and I said yes.

Thus began what quickly evolved into a passionate sexual interlude. Norwell possessed a highly charged libido as well as great success at bringing me to climax. So intently focused was he on practicing the arts of love that I assumed he had considerable experience with many other women. However, he admitted to only one previous relationship.

One evening, after an especially delicious course of making love, Norwell said, "Zara, I love you. You know that, don't you?"

"Love is such an expansive word, with so many meanings," I replied.

"Now don't get philosophical with me," he said.

"What should I get then?" I asked.

"Serious," he said. "These last few months with you have been wonderful for me and I hope for you as well."

"Wonderful is an apt word." I said. "But I think I would use the word enjoyable."

"Enjoyable it is then," Norwell said. "That's all I needed to hear. Zara will you marry me?"

Once again Norwell Edenbrook surprised me. I had not anticipated this at all, and for a time I said nothing. Then, to fill the silence, I said, "This is certainly a *Jungfreulich Erlebnis*!"

He laughed. "Virginal? After all the passionate sex we've been...*enjoying*? There's another reason I love you so; your great sense of irony."

"Well," I responded, "it is a virginal experience for me to receive a proposal of marriage. No one has ever done that before."

"It's not virginal for me," he said.

"Someone has proposed marriage to you?" I said.

"No, I proposed to a woman in London. That was years ago. When she turned me down, I fled to the States to do graduate work to get over it," he confessed.

The earnest way he said this caused me a momentary surge of affection for him. "There's no shame in losing at love," I said. I almost ruffled his hair but resisted the temptation.

"But you are avoiding the subject," he said, "so I think you're not ready to answer me. Will you at least take some time to consider the matter?"

"You know that I'm bisexual, Norwell. Does that not give you any pause about marrying me?" I said.

"Not in the least," he said. "In point of fact, I would be open to your inviting a woman into our marital bed from time to time, if you'd like that. Anyone you wanted."

Avoiding the word yes, I agreed to think it over. Although I knew right away that I would not marry him, I waited a week before telling him no, so that it would appear that I had given his proposal due consideration.

Norwell was so hurt that he abruptly broke off the relationship. Here was yet another surprise, because I told him I was perfectly willing to continue our intellectual as well as sexual explorations, including experimenting with another woman for a fun threesome. It seemed only reasonable to me that the opportunity to continue the wild jungle sex along with our dynamic academic conversations, without covenantal commitments, would be welcome. Attempting to ease his pain, I said I was not closing the door to the possibility of marriage at some distant time but had no interest in matrimony in the near term. But he didn't see it that way and for a time stopped coming to church to avoid encountering me. Sometimes I have a hard time understanding men.

In response to repeated encouragement to do so, in January 2009, I took the *Jeopardy!* Online screening test. The literary, geography, and wordplay answers were easy. I did not know the answers to a few pop culture, sports, and potent potables questions and assume that my guesses were wrong. Nevertheless, I did well enough to be invited to Southern California for an audition, where I participated in a mock game. Here again, I did not do well with matters of social ephemera, but I did win the game.

Doing a post game self-evaluation, I judged that the segment where I was invited to talk about myself did not go well. It's difficult for me to be truthful without being perceived as cocky. False modesty is something I have never been able to pull off. And chatting for the sake of chatting is a skill I lack. However, the coordinator assured me that I had done well and would be placed in the potential contestant pool for eighteen months. A call to appear on the show never came.

Early in February, I was walking home after teaching a class at Anasazi College on the evolution of the Aramaic language, when a pickup truck swerved by me and made a sudden stop. My first impulse was to raise my fist and curse at the idiot behind the wheel for driving like an asshole. Then the driver and passenger, both large men, jumped out of the truck and charged at me. I turned and ran, but with surprising speed, one of them caught up with me and reached around, slamming his hand over my face. The hand was covered in a cloth soaked in some chemical, and I lost consciousness.

The next thing I remember is a drowsy recognition that I was in a moving vehicle. My body was curled up in the back seat of the cab of the truck. My hands were tied behind my back and my feet at he ankles, but for some reason, I was not gagged or blindfolded. From the sound of the tires, I guessed we were on a dirt road. Trying to remain calm and clear my mind, I tried to consider my options but was too befuddled to come up with any. All I could do was wait until something else happened that I could use for orientation. A few minutes later, the truck stopped and I was roughly pulled from the cab and forced to stand. Snow was coming down fast and a frigid wind whistled through the surrounding woods. Before me was a dilapidated house trailer.

CHAPTER SEVENTEEN
SCUM

"Hey Jesse, she's awake," said a man who appeared to have serious reservations about regular bathing.

"Oh good, Buck. Let's strip her and tie her to that ponderosa," said Jesse.

Blood drained from my face, increasing my wooziness, but then a bolt of fear flashed through my entire body, clearing my mind. I was determined to memorize the faces and physical descriptions of my abductors, in case I had the opportunity to identify them for law enforcement.

That thought gave me no solace, however, because in Yavapai County, I was held in low esteem by officers of the law, owing to the Messer mess. My guess was that I was no longer in Yavapai County, however. Judging by the surrounding forest, I thought it likely to be Coconino County, probably north of I-40.

The one called Buck was a beefy man with a pale, freckled face with red patches on his cheeks from exposure to cold weather. He wore a thick but frayed black sweater. Jesse looked like he worked out with weights. He was a head shorter than Buck, perhaps five feet seven, but even in the frigid weather, he wore a sleeveless denim jacket that showed off his pumped up arms. Both men had buzz cuts and wore camouflage hunting trousers and cowboy boots. Sheathed bayonets swung from their belts.

Buck held me in a vise grip while Jesse pulled off my shoes and socks and then unzipped my jeans and pulled them down.

"Wouldja look at that?" Jesse said. "No undies. Nice snatch, bitch. Now let's see what your tits look like, shall we?"

Buck untied my hands so that Jesse could remove my jacket and rip open my blouse. When I was naked, Jesse walked back to the truck and returned with a pistol, which he pointed at me while Buck renewed his grip on me.

"No funny stuff, now, bitch," Jesse said, directing the barrel of the pistol at my crotch.

Buck tied my arms to my body and shoved me against a large pine tree and pinned me to it with ropes around my neck and waist. Jesse spread my legs apart and separately bound each of my ankles to the tree. Now I was terrified.

"You can go ahead and scream all you want," Jesse said to me. "No one's gonna hear it but Buck and me, and I kinda like the sound a scared, naked bitch makes. It turns me on."

"Why have you kidnapped me?" I spat out with what little force my voice could muster.

"Because you attacked a good friend of ours," Jesse replied. "I don't mind telling you about it. You need to be taught a lesson for what you did."

"I've never attacked anybody," I said. "What friend, and who the hell are you?"

"Yeah you have," said Buck. "We done our homework on you, bitch. You testified at his trial and your picture was on TV. We know where you live. We been watching out for a chance to get you."

"Messer?" I said.

"**Senator** Messer to you," said Jesse. "You got him kicked out of the legislature for a while, but he got the last laugh, because he's back. Now we want to punish you for your lack of respect."

"Did Messer pay you to do this?" I asked.

"Naw, he don't know nothin' about it. It was our leader's idea. He thought it'd be good to branch out a little," said Jesse.

"Leader of what?" I asked.

"Sic-em," said Buck. "You heard of Sic-em, I'm sure. We're in the news all the time."

"I have no idea what you're talking about," I said.

"Sanctified Christian Underground Militia, Sic-em for short, like in attack dog. We're like pit bulls for Jesus," Jesse said. "We're real good at attacking lefties, pope-kissers, kikes, and ragheads."

Now I knew that my premonition had been correct.

"SCUM!" I shouted.

"You're ignorant as well as disrespectful," said Jesse. "It's pronounced Sic-em! Now I want you to say it properly. Say it, bitch!"

I remained silent, so Jesse slapped me hard across the face then grabbed my hair and yanked it back. "Say it, bitch!"

I whispered, "Sic...em." Mentally, I translated my words as sick...them.

"Let's get inside, Jesse. It's cold out here," Buck said.

"Not so fast. I'm thinking of having this bitch warm me up," Jesse said. He looked me in the eyes and whispered, "I bet your pussy is nice and warm even if your tiny tits are cold as a witch's."

"You're not s'posed to do that," Buck said. "The leader told us never to rape a white woman until he had a chance to check her out first. Any other color is OK but not white."

Apparently their leader had adopted a form of the medieval custom of **Droit du Seigneur** whereby the lord of an estate claimed the right to deflower the daughters of his serfs. The lord, or in this case the leader, gets to go first. At that moment, however, I was not thinking about this outrageous and degrading historical custom.

"What he don't know won't hurt him," Jesse said. "We're a long way from HQ up here. And why would I want to stick my dick in something that ain't white? I'm getting hard looking at her tied up like that. I need some relief, man."

I felt like screaming at that point, but worked desperately at keeping my wits. It was the most fertile time of my cycle, and a frigid dread gripped me that I was about to be impregnated by a rapist.

"Let's go inside and discuss your love life, Jesse. I'm freezing my ass off out here," said Buck.

"OK, OK, keep your pants on," Jesse said. "I'm just trying to imagine what she'd look like with her bush shaved." He looked at me again and added, "We'll take care of that when we get you to HQ. The leader likes 'em smooth. As for me, I'm kinda disappointed you weren't wearing a thong. Going commando is nice too, but there's nothing quite so boner producing as slipping a thong off a shaved twat."

"How childish!" I don't know why I said it. It was a visceral reaction. It was true, of course, but not a wise thing to say under the circumstances.

"I don't like your tone, ass mouth!" Jesse said. He slid his right hand down the back of his pants to his anal area, then pulled it out and shoved his index finger into my mouth. "Eat shit, bitch!"

Reflexively, I spat.

Jesse laughed. "We're not done with you yet, so don't bother to relax until you feel my stiff friend sliding into you. That'll be the ride of your life." He made a show of rubbing his crotch and then slapped my face several more times. "That's just to get your juices flowing." Then he reached down to scoop a handful of snow and slapped it between my legs. "And that's to get you lubricated," he added with a leer before following Buck into the house.

CHAPTER EIGHTEEN
ANGELS AND WITCHES

Alone now, I concentrated on the ***doomoo leeekaadzg*** technique that Key had taught me to raise my body temperature. As my limbs, torso, and head warmed, I began to think about escaping. No complete plan had formed in my mind, but I knew that temporarily leaving my body would be a necessary first step. But then I wondered if I could maintain body temperature while floating out-of-body.

"Yes, you can do both simultaneously," Sojourner said telepathically.

"Sojourner! Are you near? Can you save me?" I cried out, also telepathically.

"I will be there soon. Do not leave your body before I arrive," Sojourner instructed.

A wave of relaxation washed over me. Why hadn't I thought of contacting Sojourner or Pilgrim? A minute later, Sojourner appeared and began to untie me.

"Can you get me out of here -bodily?" I asked.

"Certainly," said Sojourner.

"I don't know why I didn't think to send you a message," I apologized. "How did you happen to be nearby?"

"I was at home," Sojourner explained while continuing to work on the ropes that bound me. "But your current location on the Coconino Plateau is only about 30 miles south of our enclave. You may not have consciously sent me a message, but at some level your brain did it for you. The call was faint but I heard it and tuned into your mind."

"Thank God they took me to a place so close to you," I said.

"I would have heard your distress call from many hundreds of miles away, Zara. Your Merven linguistic ability has altered your brain, amplifying your thought transmission," Sojourner said.

"So I have a kind of built-in providential protection," I said. "I'll need to remember that."

"Please do," Sojourner said.

All the bindings were now off, and I said, "OK, let's get out of here fast."

"Before we do that, it would be good, I think, to confront Buck and Jesse," Sojourner suggested.

This was something I had no interest in doing. "I thought Merven weren't supposed to interfere directly with humans but only influence them," I said. "Sticking around to confront my kidnappers looks like direct interference."

"So is untying your ropes," said Sojourner. "But I don't hear you lamenting that. Sometimes traditional practices need to be set aside."

"What do you have in mind?" I asked, leery and still frightened.

"If you care to, you could float into their house and perform whatever mischief comes to mind to spook them. I shall remain unseen outside guarding your body and, as the saying goes, telepathically mess with their minds," Sojourner said.

Now this idea did appeal to me. When out-of-body I was fearless, and I felt terror melting away simply from Sojourner's suggestion. A minute later, I was out of my body and floating toward the mobile home. Once inside, I heard Buck say, "Hey Jesse, are you really gonna rape her?"

"Maybe," Jesse said.

"Yeah but she'll tell the leader, and then *you'll* eat shit," Buck said. "And it's just my luck that he'll blame me for not stopping you." Buck seemed genuinely fearful.

I chose that moment to move into the space occupied by Jesse's body, settling into his abdomen, where I used all the suggestive power I could muster to cause him to lose bladder and intestinal control. As a surprised Jesse was soiling and wetting his pants, I flew into Buck's abdominal region and produced the same results.

While this was going on, Sojourner was planting a message in each of their brains that they were in big trouble, because I was a witch and my coven would soon seek revenge. Witches were flying in at this very moment.

I floated outside, returned to my body, and hid at the side of the house. Soon, two trembling and foul smelling men rushed outside and stared at the tree where I had been tied, seeing only the empty ropes on the ground.

"Get in the truck, Buck!" Jesse shouted. "We don't have time to change pants."

I jumped out from hiding and pointed a finger at them. "Since you know where I live, you probably know that the place is called Angel Nest. You know what that makes me?"

Their trembling increased dramatically. "I thought you was a witch, not a angel," said Buck.

"It makes me an *avenging* angel," I said. "Call me a witch if you like, but if you value your stinking lives, you will immediately return to your glorious leader and tell him what happened here. And you will tell him for me that if SCUM ever again attacks, threatens, or terrorizes any religious or social justice organization, he will learn first hand what real pain is. He will learn what it means to feel terror."

"You gonna kill him?" Buck stammered.

"Killing is too easy on him," I replied. "When I'm through with his putrid mind and sick body, he will beg for death but won't get it."

I gathered my clothes from the snowy ground, and Sojourner, clad now in Army fatigues, stepped into view and said to me, "Take my arm."

I did so, and in a flash, we disappeared. I regret not being able to see the expressions on the faces of my kidnappers, but Sojourner thought it imprudent to return and gawk at them. We rematerialized in the family room at Angel Nest.

"Zara!" exclaimed Mom and Dad simultaneously. They enfolded me with nervous embraces.

Pilgrim stood in front of me. "Have you been here while Sojourner was rescuing me?" I asked.

"Certainly," said Pilgrim. "Sojourner was giving me reports as the drama was unfolding, so I could reassure your family."

"We had no idea you'd been kidnapped," said Dad. "You hadn't been gone long enough for us to notice your absence. Then Pilgrim arrived and told us what had happened."

"And let us know that your rescue was in progress," added Mom.

"I was ready to call the FBI," said Dad, "but Pilgrim asked me to wait."

"You can still do that, Cloud," said Pilgrim. "But consider this first. SCUM wants publicity more than anything else. Kidnapping charges would give them that. The leader of SCUM doesn't care about his henchmen. They are expendable. If they were captured it would give SCUM international attention. Publicity that terrorizes is priceless. Denying them public exposure seems a suitable punishment."

"But this is a serious crime," said Mom. "Shouldn't we report it to the police?"

"Do you want to explain to them how Zara kept her body warm, who untied her, how she tormented her captors while out-of-body, and how she and Sojourner disappeared before their eyes?" Pilgrim asked.

"I could just say they were lunatics, which is true enough, and they'd done a lousy job of tying me up, so I got free by myself. I don't think anyone would ask me about keeping warm," I said.

"Do you really want to lie under oath?" Sojourner asked.

I hung my head. "No, of course not."

"And how would you explain how you got back to Angel Nest so quickly?" Pilgrim added.

"Pilgrim is right," I said. "And Sojourner and I have already given them enough feedback to cause SCUM to burrow even further underground."

"At the very least," said Dad, "we should organize a contingent of floaters to visit their lair and scare some more shit out of them."

"That might be fun, but let's wait and see what develops on its own," Mom said. "And there's the slight problem of not knowing exactly where they're holed up."

"It's somewhere in the Aquarius Mountains," said Dad. "With our intuitive tracking skills, we should be able to locate them easily enough."

"Let's let it go for now," said Mom. Her wisdom prevailed.

In the days that followed, I was determined to act as if my kidnapping had been little worse than the bullying I had experienced at school. I had been rescued before any real harm could be done, I told my family. After a week of encouraging me to talk about it, my family dropped the subject and I repressed memory of the event. My life returned to normal.

Nothing more was heard from SCUM for a year. No further attacks happened. Then in the spring of 2010, an article appeared in the Verde Valley Intelligencer that the leader of SCUM had been arrested based on information supplied by two members who had become FBI informants. They were identified as Buck Lurch and Jesse Kriep, and they had agreed to cooperate in exchange for having gun smuggling charges dropped.

A report the next day said that in a search of the SCUM compound, deputies had found five girls, ranging in age from 14 to 17, locked in a barred room in a barn. The words "Concubine Cage" had been painted on a sign above the door. In subsequent reports, the girls were identified as the subjects of missing person searches in Nebraska, Oklahoma, and South Dakota. Law enforcement in their jurisdictions presumed them to be runaways, but in fact each one had been kidnapped by sex traffickers. They were what we used to call milk carton kids.

As their story evolved in the media, it came out that SCUM members practiced biblical marriage, which meant that all the male members had access to concubines for their sexual pleasure. The girls were told that it was God's will they were in the custody of Sanctified Christians, and they had to obey God's commands.

It made me glad that SCUM was being taken down, but the thought of Buck and Jesse going free infuriated me. I started having nightmares about them kidnapping me again and Jesse actually following through on his thwarted threats. For weeks I was in a dark fog. My energy evaporated but my mind was on overdrive, causing me to flinch at ordinary sounds. I pushed myself to get through the days, but I couldn't concentrate on editing work or class preparation. All I wanted to do was sleep, but when I did, the nightmares returned.

Finally, Mom confronted me and said I needed to get counseling. I knew she was right, so I said, "Will you do a healing service for me?"

"If I thought it would do any good, I'd do it in a heartbeat," she said.

"But you already know my gift for healing psychological ills does not work on me or members of my immediate family. Sojourner told me it is one of those frustrating genetic anomalies. Your dad and I are here to support you in every way we can, but you need to talk to someone else."

"Yeah, I knew that," I said. "Unrealistically, I'm looking for a simple cure."

"We could gather a group to float inside your body," Mom suggested. "But you also know that's a temporary high. You need to take on the more difficult task of therapy."

She was right, and I knew it. "I'd like to keep this within the Angel Nest family," I said.

"How about Huxley?" said Mom.

I called my friend Huxley Askeladd, with whom I had grown up at Angel Nest but who now did counseling and therapy in Phoenix. It took Huxley no time at all to recognize that I was suffering from Post-Traumatic Stress.

One of the first things I said to her was that I felt like two different people.

"Elaborate on that," she said with an inflection of interest in her voice.

"The person you know from Angel Nest feels loved, healthy, secure, appreciated, accepted, and happy," I explained. "But these days, when I'm in the outside world, I feel wary, paranoid, vulnerable, and harshly critical of the stupidity and violence I see there."

"How long have you been experiencing this?" she asked.

"It has gotten slowly worse since my kidnapping," I said. "I know intellectually that it has everything to do with that, but I can't seem to shake it. I've long perceived the wider world as overrun with stupid people, but I had never before experienced it as dangerous."

"How much have you talked about the kidnapping with family and friends?" she asked.

"As little as I could get away with," I answered. "I want to keep it safely buried. My brain, I think, is powerful enough to box in that terror and keep it under control. At least I used to think that."

"Now you're onto something productive," Huxley said. "The more you try to keep it boxed in, the more it will rattle around and give you no peace. The only effective way to deal with it is to expose it to the air; shine light on it. It may take a while, but airing it out is the best way to dissipate the memories and ugly feelings."

For the next six months, I made weekly trips to Phoenix to work on rising out of my PTSD induced depression. Within a few weeks, the nightmares ceased, but in the course of therapy, I discovered that I had been repressing a great deal of painful experiences relating mostly to school.

"How do you feel about the taunts and bullying you endured prior to your college years?" Huxley asked in one session.

"I feel no compulsion to respect people who are willfully ignorant," I said. "It's wrong, of course, to harbor bias against people for things they have no control over, such as skin color or sexual orientation. That's how they were born. But people who enjoy first-rate educations and yet tenaciously cling to arrant nonsense are beneath contempt. It is reasonable, I think, to judge people by the content of their beliefs. People who choose to be stupid or irrational do not deserve deference. People whose worldview has not evolved since childhood need not be taken seriously. I have no problem with those who speculate about the irrational and the absurd, but those who claim such things are authoritative and factual are mentally defective."

"That's what you think," she said. "What do you *feel?*"

"I *feel* that I have been crapped on by teachers who knew better than the way they treated me. I feel that their actions were motivated by envy and spite. I feel that teachers, who were derelict in their duties, should have disciplined the bullies and morons among the students. I feel resentful about all of it. They were trying to make me feel like a freak, but I never did. And I hated them for trying."

"Better," she said. "Now, to what do you attribute what you describe as willful ignorance?"

"Inadequacy," I said contemptuously.

"That could be a psychological factor," she said. "Have you considered that a variety of psychological and environmental factors could have contributed to what you experienced as unjustifiable behavior toward you?"

"If I thought they were mentally unbalanced, I would need to show a little compassion," I confessed. "I think religious fundamentalism and excessive piety are signs of mental illness."

"Do you feel sympathy for such people?" she asked.

"I feel sympathy for people who have been brainwashed," I said. "But that does not mean I should be co-dependent with their delusions."

"OK," she said.

"I'm not narrow-minded," I continued. "People are free to believe anything they want, but that doesn't make any of it reasonable. No one has a right to impose their beliefs on others."

"What if they believe that they will go to hell if they don't make an effort to enforce their religious beliefs on the larger society?" Huxley asked.

"Then they are insane and should be treated as such," I replied. After a pause, I said, "That's how I *feel*. Intellectually, I know that people can be caught up in all sorts of religious delusion and dysfunction, and it is extremely difficult to rise out of it."

"The mind has powerful mechanisms to defend such beliefs," Huxley said.

"Yes," I said, "And I **think** that some of the problematic teachers and practically all of the rude students were suffering from brainwashing or some kind of mental dysfunction."

"Enough for you to feel a little feel sorry for them?" Huxley asked.

"Yes, but that doesn't make me *feel* better about the indignities I suffered," I said.

"Now we're getting somewhere," she said.

Looking back on my sessions with Huxley, I was able to set a goal of letting go of the painful experiences of my past. I highly recommend therapy for anyone who has been bullied, teased, made to feel like a freak, or undergone traumatic events.

Here's one last item of SCUM business: The government kept its word to Buck and Jesse by letting them off on the weapons charges, since they cooperated so fully. However, the kidnapped girls named them as the agents who bought them from their captors and also their repeated rapists. After being released from custody, they got as far as the parking lot, where a squad of officers loitered beside Jesse's truck.

"Do we rate an escort?" Jesse is reported to have said.

"Yes," said one of the officers. "Right back to the can."

They received long sentences, which caused me much relief.

CHAPTER NINETEEN
ALCHEMY AND FANTASY

When K. P. was five, I began taking him to the Saturday afternoon services of the Alchemical Church of Harry Potter Prophecy, which were held in the NCC chapel. The church had evolved from a college project initiated by Emma Round, who now led the humanist congregation. Members called themselves Holy Rowlings.

On his third birthday, I began reading to K. P. all seven *Harry Potter* books and he loved them. By the time he was six, he had read them by himself. We obtained the Jim Dale and Stephen Fry compact disc recordings of the series, and K. P. loved to listen to the American and British versions, gleefully pointing out changes in word usage between the two. He reminded me so much of my younger self when he did that.

In college, I had written a paper on the first *Harry Potter* volume and ultimately found the entire series delightful and spiritually rich. So I was intrigued but not surprised that a religion had developed around J. K. Rowling's Harry Potter theology. The Alchemical Church services were fun as well as profound, and K. P. and I savored the time we spent there.

As for basing a religion on a fictional character, I soon recognized that Harry Potter made a healthier choice of role model than many of those put forth by established churches purportedly based on the words of various so-called holy men. Churches organized around guilt and punishment are inherently unhealthy. Some religious traditions claiming to be centered on the love of Christ, for example, seem closer to worshiping Voldemort than Jesus.

Emma Round's sermons frequently explored the ways that the ennobling spiritual values in Rowling's novels stood apart from orthodox interpretations of Christianity, and she compared and contrasted the Harry Potter canon to the works of other writers of Christian fantasy, such as J. R. R. Tolkien and C. S. Lewis. Since I had read all of Tolkien's *Ring* related books in third grade, I paid attention to what Emma Round had to say about this. She brought out much that I had missed when I was younger.

The ACHPP made use of music from the Potter films. "Hedwig's Theme" served as a prelude to the services. K. P. and I have long enjoyed the music connected with the films. Whatever the shortcomings of the movie screenplays as compared with the books, the music exactly captures the mood and setting of Rowling's universe. I bought the soundtrack CDs and played them for background atmospherics while reading to K. P. Among our particular favorites from the first movie are John Williams' "Harry's Wondrous World," "Diagon Alley Theme," and "Leaving Hogwarts." From the third movie we like John Williams' "Double Trouble." From the fourth movie, Patrick Doyle's "Potter Waltz," "Harry in Winter," and "Hogwarts Hymn" are our favorites. For the record, I mention these pieces specifically, because my dear Merven friends, Sojourner and Pilgrim are aficionados of human music and also enjoy them.

K. P. and I were present on the day that Emma Watson, who played Hermione Granger in the *Harry Potter* movies, came to the service while on a visit to Sedona. Though I have never felt remotely inclined to participate in any celebrity fan club, I was quite pleased to meet and speak briefly with Ms. Watson. She is not a typical actress, if I may indulge in stereotyping for a moment, but bright, grounded, and seriously concerned with issues of social justice. I have a nose for narcissism and detected not a whiff of it in her. If ever I were tempted to be an actress rather than an academic, she would be an ideal role model. The fact that I am more than a dozen years older makes no difference to me. Age is neither a guarantor of wisdom nor a criterion for emulation.

I told Emma Watson about nude worship in the NCC congregation where the Harry Potter church is nested, and she seemed genuinely interested. Of course, she could have been acting to be polite, the way Queen Elizabeth must do when greeting all manner of oddballs from her far flung empire. My intuitive sense, however, is that Emma Watson was not acting and came close to accepting my invitation to a clothing optional service the next day. I've had a lot of experience introducing the subject of naturism to people and can tell when someone is shocked or dismissive. She was neither.

That night, I had a dream about engaging in a love affair with an actress. Who the actress was I had no idea. She was my age and clearly was not Emma Watson, yet that's whose face I saw. My mystery actress had a name similar to Emma that flowed in trochaic meter. The dream felt like a powerful premonition.

In 2013, I joined Facebook and had many adventures with total strangers with whom I became friends. My first Facebook connection was a friend of our family, Geneva Andrews. Geneva was a pastor in the Australian Natural Christian Church in Cairns who joined Facebook on her 90th birthday in 2010. My second friend, also from Cairns, Queensland, was the Queen's Paradise Bed and Breakfast, where my parents stayed on their honeymoon. Very quickly I began receiving friend requests from strangers around the world, most of which I accepted.

Facebook was an ideal way for an introvert like me to connect with people without having to spend time on relationship building in person, which has always been a draining activity for me.

Before long I learned that people lie a lot on Facebook. I was surprised to find many pseudonymous accounts, with people either acting out roles from novels, movies, and comic books for fun, or hiding behind fictitious names so they could cheat or prey on people. Some had legitimate cause to use fake names to protect themselves from trolls and cyber bullies. Also, people from third world countries would send friend requests to Americans and engage them in innocent conversations about the wealth of America compared with how poor they were. Then they asked for money. An amazing number of exhibitionist women posted seductive pictures of themselves on Facebook.

Since I put up front on my page that I am a naturist, I received many friend requests from fellow naturists, and I enjoyed sharing posts and messages with them. However, a fair number of requests came from horny textile men. Most of the latter turned out to be creeps, trying to engage me in conversations about not wearing clothes and asking me to send them naked pictures of myself.

One man, who identified himself as a naturist from New York and whose Facebook name was Jerry Springbad, wanted to engage in fantasy games by messaging. I thought his name was clever, although his profile picture was not real. It was a drawing of a bare-chested man with long hair and a full mustache that I recognized as the mid-19th century work of British artist Ford Madox Brown. The profile image suggested he was an educated man, but there was nothing on his page revealing what Jerry really looked like.

At first the messaging was innocent. He asked me what I imagined myself doing in another life and place. He mentioned something about a computer game called Second Life, where people can create an avatar of a second self, usually the person they would like to be if they could choose. I had heard of Second Life but had never gotten involved with it. Why would I need an imaginary second life when I had a wonderful secret life with my Merven friends.

At any rate, I played along with Jerry's non-sexual fantasy by inventing a previous life as a plane spotter in Hawaii during World War II. As a lover of solitude, I stationed myself on a remote beach on the North Shore of Kauai, where I kept vigil for Zero fighters, Zuiun reconnaissance planes, Hiryu bombers, and other enemy aircraft. But Jerry kept emphasizing the naked part and suggesting he would keep me company there. He said his middle name was NIFOC. That, too, was alright. Naturists will be naked, after all, including in front of the computer. Gradually, he introduced sexual innuendo into the conversation and asked questions about my real life, which I ignored. When he asked for my email address and phone number, I unfriended him.

More edifying friends came in response to my postings about being vegetarian, opposing animal cruelty, and challenging the practice of male and female genital mutilation, including circumcision. All the people associated with these causes proved to be idealistic and dedicated to improving society.

It was through Facebook that I learned about Femen. A member of Femen popped up in the "People You May Know" feature. I clicked on her profile and saw that she lived in Ukraine. As I thought it would be nice to have a friend in Ukraine, I sent her a Friend Request and also clicked "Like" on several Femen information pages so that updates would appear in my News Feed. She accepted my request about an hour later, and I was able to see posts on her Wall that were only available to friends. These included photos of groups of bare breasted women marching in the streets of various international cities.

Femen is a contraction of female energy. The protest movement started in Ukraine in 2008 and quickly spread around the world. It is dedicated to radical equality of women and men, beginning with the legal right for women to go topless in public as men are allowed to do. Femen philosophy is in tune with the free the nipple campaign and efforts to permit breastfeeding in public. Finding Femen was the most fortuitous thing to come from my flirtation with Facebook and ultimately resulted in making friends with women in Finland, France, Germany, Latvia, Lithuania, and Norway, plus a few more in Ukraine. My world was expanded in a salutary way through social networking.

However, I also recognized that Facebook can be addictive. Generally, I limited myself to no more than an hour a day, but I noticed that some people seemed to be logged in all the time. There were a few times when I found that I had spent four or five hours without a break doing Facebook searches and posts, and vowed to monitor this. And then, without warning, one day I got bored with it and stopped visiting the site.

During this time, my freelance work as an editor for independent authors increased. Unfortunately, too many of them had little of substance to say and even less skill with intelligible English sentences. I had no qualms about charging more for books that required extensive corrections.

The exception was Vestimenta Sine, a brilliant woman who wrote novels about naturism in academia. The willowy vegan with a wicked sense of humor created a fictional faculty of quirky professors of arcane subjects and an eclectic mix of earnest students who loved to run around naked while raising mischief and bantering intellectual notions. Rather than the usual town and gown tension in many accounts of university life, the tension in her novels was town and no-gown. She imparted an uninhibited Thorne Smith quality to her prose, suggestive but never crude and without Smith's culture of abundant alcohol.

It was a treat to edit her work. Though I found typos, such as words that should have been deleted and missing quote marks, Vestimenta never made grammatical or spelling errors. I searched in vain for a split infinitive or dangling participle. Her syntax was never clumsy or ambiguous.

Vestimenta had a Master of Social Work degree but had burned out from the enormous stress of that profession, suffering from a huge case of compassion fatigue as well as helpless disgust at the pervasive co-dependence among her clients. Hence her secluded lifestyle in which she carefully guarded her introvert needs. She lived alone, most of the time naked, on a ranch in the Weaver Mountains, east of State Route 89 between Yarnell and Peeples Valley.

We first connected on the Internet and worked from a distance but eventually decided to meet in the flesh. She, of course, knew from our correspondence that I practiced naturism, which made me an ideal choice to edit her books. So began a series of visits to her ranch, for professional consultation and personal enjoyment.

The first time I saw her in person, she was standing naked on her porch, adopting the pert posture of a teenager. I found this off-putting. The insouciant look of a fourteen year-old girl loses charm when adopted by a woman in her thirties. But it was merely a whimsical pose. As I got out of my car, she relaxed into a welcoming stance. Lines from John Milton's **Paradise Lost** came to mind as I looked at her: "In naked beauty more adorn'd, More lovely than Pandora."

"I just finished uploading my latest manuscript to my literary agent, and I'm feeling celebratory," she said. "I incorporated your suggestion about using naturist argot. Thanks for the tip."

"That's what you pay me for," I said. "It feels good to be useful."

She invited me to doff my duds there on the porch and settle into a rattan chair that was draped with a towel. We quickly descended into a discussion about the words manuscript and typescript.

"At root," I said, "a manuscript is something made by hand. The better term for a document produced on a computer would be typescript."

"Historically, that's true," she countered. "But in current usage, manuscript has come to mean the physical copy of any document, however produced. Typescript has a particular and limited meaning, while manuscript is generic."

She wanted to know about my life without raiment, and I responded with assorted tales of naturism. I suspected, accurately as it happened, that she was gathering fodder for another book.

In subsequent visits, we fell into a routine of sitting on her porch for hours, sipping her specialty organic fruit smoothies, munching on organic carrot sticks and raw walnuts, going over her latest drafts, and verbally dissecting all manner of interesting topics. Veganism was one of her favorite subjects.

"I'd like to help you transition from vegetarian to vegan," she said one day.

"I've thought about it but I'd miss yogurt too much," I replied.

"OK. I'll let it go for now," she said and switched subjects. "Did you ever wonder about the NPR program All Things Considered? Clearly it's a misnomer, because there are so many intriguing things the show won't or can't consider. It irks me that they bend over backward to be fair to people who don't deserve it."

"Still, I'm grateful for KJZZ and NPR," I said. "And it would sound silly to name the program All Things Not Too Controversial or Inconsistent with Puritanical Broadcast Standards Considered," I said.

"Agreed," she said. "Actually, NPR broadcasts some excellent and in-depth stuff, for which I'm grateful. But I feel entitled to criticize any organization I send charitable contributions to."

"I turn it off when they do those irritating pledge drives," I confessed.

"So do I," Vestimenta replied. "I send them money anyway, but only at times when they are not asking for it."

"You're a better man than I am Gunga Din," I said.

"And a better woman, too," she said with a knowing laugh.

"Well, what should we consider today that NPR wouldn't touch?" I said.

"How about my lunatic neighbors?" she suggested.

"I haven't noticed any neighbors on my drives here," I said.

"They're a few miles farther up the road," Vestimenta explained. "There's a coven of biblical prophets hidden away in an old house."

"A coven? Really?" I said.

"That's what I call them, because it would cause them apoplexy if they knew," she said. "They're Christian dumb-damentalists who call themselves the Biblical Order of Magi and Prophets. BOMP for short."

"'Who Put the Bomp?'" I could not resist saying.

Ignoring my musical pun (or perhaps not getting it), she said, "I ran into one of them shopping in Yarnell not long ago and got into a heated conversation about prophetic practices," she continued. "They claim to be related by blood to the Old Testament prophets and the New Testament Wise Men. I asked him if they ran around naked like the Old Testament prophets and you'd think he'd given himself a wedgie from the ghastly look on his unprepossessing face."

"I take it the answer was no," I said.

"I told him I ran around naked and wrote prophetic fiction and asked if I could join BOMP. I even invited him to the ranch to prophesy for me and I'd put his name and what he said in my next book. He accused me of being a witch," Vestimenta replied. "He said he'd had a vision about me riding a broom and eating dinner with Satan at a Wickenburg restaurant. He called it Wicked-burg and said everyone knows that Satan controls all the dude ranches in the area."

"How enchanting," I said. "Was the food good?"

"Heavenly," she said.

Naturally, on many occasions we talked about writing. She freely gossiped about the bawdy and profound things her fictional characters told her.

"They talk to me all the time," she said. "And I dream about them too. Many times I've written a scene only to have a character tell me she wouldn't do what I'd written or he was inclined to do something more audacious. Sometimes they want me to describe them doing things that go beyond the boundaries of propriety I've set for them."

"Do you listen to them?" I asked.

"Always," she replied. "But I try to tone down their behavior or make it seem more elegant than it really is. You can do that if you know how to handle words."

"I've noticed that your sex scenes are never vulgar," I said.

"No thanks to my characters, some of whom are unrestrained hedonists," Vestimenta proclaimed. "It's all an author can do to keep them out of unseemly orgies."

"As opposed to seemly orgies?" I responded.

"Of course," she said. "All my orgies are seemly."

On a warm afternoon as we were relaxing in the buff on her back porch, a storm that had been moving slowly north from the Gulf of California let loose a gentle rain upon the desert landscape stretching before us. I breathed in the scent released by drops of water falling onto the dry earth and was aroused.

"I love petrichor," I said.

"Oh, you know that word too?" Vestimenta said. "Not many people do. I've been tempted to use it in one of my novels, but haven't found the right place for it."

"There's something about the smell of rain on the desert that affects me like an aphrodisiac," I said. "Maybe you could have a pair of your naked professors get randy in a rainstorm. Surely one of them would be sufficiently educated to know the term."

"That's a great idea!" she said with a laugh. "They would probably want me to let them mud-wrestle in a large puddle, but I could make them carry on a literarily elegant conversation first. The feel of warm and gentle raindrops on one's skin combined with the scent of opening earth can produce powerfully erotic feelings."

I could see her nipples growing erect.

"Have I ever told you that I am bisexual?" I said.

"Perhaps," she replied. "But if you haven't explicitly said so, I picked up the idea somewhere along the way. That's one of the things I like about you."

"Do you have any interest in behaving like some of your characters would if you let them?" I asked. "Erase a conventional boundary or two?"

"A great deal of interest," she said as she rose from her chair and straddled my lap, leaned forward, and kissed me. My fingers found her erect nipples and squeezed. A few minutes later, we were joyfully wrestling in the mud.

For the most part, this was a pleasant and comfortable period in my life. Vestimenta invited me to her ranch from time to time for pleasure as well as occasional business. But neither of us made emotional claims. We treasured each other without possessiveness. She needed solitude much more than I did but was elated by my visits at convenient intervals.

I loved being part of the Angel Nest community, and everyone there happily accepted my eccentricities and acerbic tongue as authentic expressions of my personality. Still, I continued to apply for teaching positions at suitable colleges and universities, with only disappointment to show for it. And then came an unexpected invitation to teach at a place to which I had not sent my resume.

Wakhan and Camelot invited me to lunch at an upscale restaurant in Sedona to discuss the job offer. It wasn't that there were potential pitfalls that warranted consideration, but Wakhan had an interest in the particular institution.

Our table was against the wall on the side of the room away from the entrance. As I was putting a bite of salad into my mouth, I saw Thirel Messer enter the place with a gaudily dressed young woman. They were escorted to a table on the opposite side, and he did not look in my direction. Our salad plates had been cleared away, and we were waiting for the entrees when I said, "Excuse me while I go to the restroom."

I locked myself in a stall in the women's room and floated out of my body. Arriving bodiless at Messer's table and hovering behind him, I perceived that he was doing his best to seduce the young woman.

"I heard you were first runner-up in the Miss Yavapai County contest," he said.

"Wow, like I'm impressed you keep up with the social news," she responded.

"Senator Thirel Messer keeps up with everything going on in the area. It's a professional requirement," he said, referring to himself in the third person. "But I don't think you deserved to come in second. I think you were robbed. You're much prettier and more talented than the one who won."

"Like thank you, Thirel," she said.

I could take no more of this. Acting on a spontaneous whim, I floated into his abdominal area and performed a Buck and Jesse treatment on him. Immediately, he lost bladder and intestinal control, and the startled look on his face was priceless. The stench spread among the nearby tables, and he carried it with him as he rose and ran for the men's room. Being out-of-body, I preceded him as I zoomed into my stall and entered my body. I was walking down the hall as he approached in a panic, seeking the men's room just beyond the women's. He had to go past me to get there.

Grimacing, I said, "Phew! What happened to you, Senator from SCUM?"

He recognized me and glowered but said nothing, pushing past me and wrenching open the men's room door.

Back at our table, Wakhan gave me a knowing look and said, "We just saw Messer rush by in great distress. What's going on, Zara?"

"He must have encountered an avenging angel," I replied.

Messer had not come back to the dining room by the time we left. I waited until we were in the car en route to Angel Nest before telling Wakhan and Camelot the whole story. Camelot, who was driving, laughed so hard he had to pull into a parking lot until he calmed down.

Wakhan said, "It's a good thing you have a job offer out of town. He might blame you for poisoning his water or something."

"I'm not worried," I said.

III

A STILL HIGHER DESTINY

Man may be excused for feeling some pride at having risen…to the very summit of the organic scale; and the fact of his having thus risen, instead of having been aboriginally placed there, may give him hope for a still higher destiny.

Charles Darwin

Much of the evil in the world is due to the fact that man in general is in general hopelessly unconscious.

Carl Jung

There is almost a sensual longing for communion with others who have a large vision. The immense fulfillment of the friendship between those engaged in furthering the evolution of consciousness has a quality impossible to describe.

Pierre Teilhard de Chardin

CHAPTER TWENTY
HARBINGER OF PARADISE

Pacific Crossroads Theological Seminary, in 2014, invited me to join the faculty there to teach Semitic languages and biblical studies. A faculty search committee had gone through a lengthy and frustrating process that yielded no satisfactory applicants, and so the dean decided direct recruiting action was needed. She remembered me as a student there and had followed my progress at Stanford.

I went through alternating spells of laughter and gratitude all afternoon and evening before calling the dean to accept the offer. What made this so hilarious was that it had never occurred to me to apply to my alma mater, but it was a perfect fit for my peculiar interests. My only hesitation was uprooting K. P. from his beloved Angel Nest family, as he was approaching seven at the time. However, he thought relocating to Maui would be a great adventure.

K. P. and I moved to the island, where he quickly found a new pack of adoring substitute parents, and I enjoyed a supporting community of progressive scholars. K. P. soon came to love Lahaina, a feeling that grew stronger through the years he spent growing up there.

My mother's favorite theology professor, Ogden Cobhart, had retired the previous year at age 85, and he graciously opened his home to us until we could find our own place. In short order, he discovered that he was lonelier than he had allowed himself to admit. Very much an introvert, he had satisfied his few social needs by interacting with students and fellow professors at the school. But now that he had no classes to teach or faculty meetings to attend, he experienced an unanticipated desire for people in his life. He very much liked having us stay with him and promptly asked us to make it a long-term arrangement. This we gladly did. He also enjoyed babysitting for K. P. when I had to be away for any reason or wanted to socialize with sexual intent, and he cared for our cats when K. P. and I were both away.

One of the first things I did upon settling in Lahaina was to visit the animal shelter in search of a house cat. More accurately, I was in hopes that a cat there would choose to go home with me. As it happened, two cats vied for my attention, so I adopted them both.

Thus care of my two longhair male cats often fell to Ogden, who pretended to protest this as an undue burden, but secretly he loved tending to them. He confessed to me once that when K. P. and I were away, he fed them avocados and poured small amounts of beer in their water dishes, receiving purring affirmation from Quetzalcoatl and Yggdrassill for doing so.

K. P. inevitably shortened the cats' names to Quetz and Ygg, which I accepted reluctantly and which bemused Ogden. Most of the time, I continued to call them by their full names.

It proved to be a bonus for Ogden that K. P. and I are naturists, since he did not have to bother with clothing around the house. Our presence did not disturb his morning routine of sitting nude on the lanai to write theology, which practice he continued to the day he died. *Eternal Becoming*, his encyclopedic study of process theology, was published to great acclaim six months before his passing in 2018. I assisted with the final editing of the tome, absorbing a great deal of useful theology along the way.

Ogden, K. P. and I had four wonderful years together in that house. The old academic was graciously elastic with regard to changes in household routine. I'd been on the scene about a month when I mentioned to Ogden that most of my life had been spent in residences with names: Strange Haven and Angel Nest. He had thoroughly enjoyed his many visits to Angel Nest and immediately suggested that I name his place, too. So I thought about it for a few days and finally came up with an old name translated into the local language.

"Let's call it *Anela Punana*," I said. "Angel Nest in Hawaiian."

"Excellent!" he exclaimed. "But why don't you add *lua* to distinguish it from the old nest."

"Perfect," I said. "Angel Nest Two." And so it was named, although we rarely used *lua* when we said the name, believing that the Hawaiian vocabulary was sufficient distinction.

Thankfully, Ogden had arranged for me to assume the lease on his home upon his death, and I still live here in ***Anela Punana***.

Often during school winter and summer breaks, K. P. and I would go to Angel Nest or Uluru to enjoy the company of family and friends. We also flew across to Oahu to visit Grandma Penny and Grandpa Randall. On one such visit, Randall's son from his first marriage was visiting. Edsel worked in the computer software industry and was a multimillionaire, holding dozens of copyrights and patents. While the others were out on the beach, Edsel and I engaged in idle conversation that took an uncomfortable turn.

"With your IQ, you could be doing all sorts of things to benefit society," he said.

"What do you mean?" I asked.

"I've often wondered why you didn't go into science or technology," he replied. "With your creative genius, you might have invented something incredibly useful or made some great scientific discovery. I'm working on an app to cure cancer."

This stung, because I had long recognized that my graduate work was in an arcane field, and my work was so much fun that it often seemed self-indulgent. Without doubt, I had followed my bliss. I didn't want to admit that he had touched upon a sensitive issue but didn't want to be defensive either. But then he kept talking, which was a mistake.

"Instead, you're wasting your genius on the dead languages of a dead religion when you could be saving humankind. You've got the brains for it."

"What if I don't ***want*** to save humankind?" I spat back.

This startled him, because Edsel thought he had been complimenting me for my high intellect. He never married. One wonders why.

"Well," he said with a reproving tone, "I thought anyone with the passion for social justice that you have would be hell bent on saving humankind."

My conversation with Chief Librarian Key about humans heading for an evolutionary cul-de-sac came back to mind, but I was not going to bring that into the conversation.

"I certainly don't want to hurt people," I said. "But I happen to believe that the work I'm doing does contribute to a better world. I'm not sure the same could be said about the mind-numbing, time wasting computer apps you've created." I would never have said this if he had not provoked me, but it slipped out, the unfortunate result being two hurt people.

"You're hopeless. I was just trying to help you," he said and stomped from the room.

At dinner, Edsel played with his phone the entire time but seemed to have put our unpleasant conversation out of his mind, for he adopted his usual benign indifference to my presence. Grandma Penny and Grandpa Randall never suspected anything disagreeable had happened.

I bought a used 2008 Toyota Prius for general transportation around the island, but I also enjoyed the luxury of being able to walk to work and for most of my grocery shopping. The car sat in the garage for weeks at a time, but I was grateful for its convenience when I needed it.

Many academic institutions in those days had a "publish or perish" ethos. Faculty members were pressured to publish articles and books in order to gain tenure and promotions. This detracted from the time professors had to share with students, but administrations did not care much about students apart from their tuition. This was not the case with PCTS. My eventual tenure was never in doubt. Nevertheless, I did produce a number of articles that appeared in print in various academic journals.

An article called "Holy Metaphor!" was the first piece I published as a seminary professor. It dealt with the centrality of metaphor in creating and subsequently interpreting religious texts. Another was "Ancient Metaphors Resurrected," which explored the ways metaphorical images and themes in scripture had been damaged by later literal interpretations. Somewhere along the line, I learned that students had begun calling me Metaphor Morgan among themselves. I loved the epithet! Aristotle taught that the greatest thing one could be is a master of metaphor. Recently, I did a survey of all my academic publications over my entire career and discovered that the word metaphor appeared at least once in every one of them.

My first scholarly book was a compilation of my writings about metaphorical language, and I teased my editor about wanting my name to appear as Zara Metaphor Morgan, PhD. But of course, I would never miss an opportunity to display my real middle name, because it represents my maternal side, of which I am sinfully proud. Over my lengthy academic career, I published five books and hundreds of articles, none of which I will belabor here. They are all represented in the Merven Library at Uluru, for any Merven scholars who may wish to pursue these arcane subjects. Let me add that two books I participated in writing, using a pseudonym, are also shelved in that library. For human scholars, these works may be found in the sacred library at the Sedona Natural Christian Church. Clearly, my books are not sacred, but the library contains copies of all the published works of Angel Nesters.

Since I was a member of the Natural Christian Church (and still am), the dean at PCTS asked me to teach History and Polity of the NCC occasionally, when we had students who needed the course to meet ordination requirements. I was happy to oblige. The most fun part of teaching NCC history is that my paternal grandfather and both my parents played significant roles in the evolution of the denomination as a progressive church.

My early years as a seminary professor were contented ones. Most of my socializing was among faculty members and their spouses. K. P. also found a supportive community among faculty children, one of whom invited him to join a Harry Potter Appreciation Society, which greatly pleased my son. K. P. and I had whimsical fun exploring the many New Age activities on Maui, but no intimate relationship opportunities developed for me as a result.

Apart from the seminary environs, the intellectual ethos on the island was limited. No one on the faculty was suitable for dating, which was fortunate, because I did not want to complicate my role as a colleague by getting emotionally entangled with any of them. A few unmarried intellectual men had retreated to Maui in those years to reflect, meditate, and write, and I had flings with the entire few.

My general goal was to get involved sexually only with men and women with creative and questioning minds. As a sapiosexual, I find brains erotic and can be turned on by witty repartee and profound reflection. I was sure there must have been such women on the island beyond the seminary community, but in the first few years living there I didn't meet any. So for half a decade residing in Lahaina, my behavior was exclusively heterosexual. Since I had said nothing to colleagues about my sexual orientation, and was seen in public social settings only with men, they assumed I was straight.

In my first year at PCTS, I organized a retreat for all my biblical studies students. I called it Fireside Fantasy, and it took place on Kaanapali Beach on the eve of the last day of class before Christmas break. The retreat became so popular that I continued leading it for the rest of my professorial career.

The students brought food and beverages, and I laid out wood for a bonfire. After the sun had set, we lit the fire and the students took turns inventing their own oral myths about creation, the first humans, or any other biblical theme they wanted to speculate about. Over the years, students gained insight into the strength of ancient oral traditions and spun out memorable and bizarre alternative accounts of parallel biblical texts.

At the end of the spring term, I had the students work by consensus to decide which Fireside Fantasy should be included in the canon of Kaanapali scripture and then to redact the chosen one to satisfy the group. Inevitably, the students vividly remembered a few fantasies that had struck them as particularly good. But the process of coming to agreement on which one to add to the canon that year proved difficult. I loved to watch them struggle to agree. And then they had to struggle again when it came to editing and perfecting the text. The one who had created the chosen fantasy was not allowed to speak during the redacting process, and this proved frustrating to all of them, especially when the group added or subtracted material that took their myths in directions they did not approve of. Any one of them could have done these tasks easily as an individual, but working as a group was exceedingly difficult and instructive.

Without exception, students who had been through the retreat and redacting exercises all aced my subsequent class on the historical process of canonizing the Hebrew and Christian scriptures.

Ployglot was 138 years old at the time we first met, and therefore it did not consciously occur to me that I would find the new librarian sexually attractive, Nevertheless, a general sense of excitement flowed though my body as I set out for Uluru that day in 2018. My relationship with Key had been so natural and easy, as if Key were my grandparent, that I was afraid this new one would be awkward and difficult.

I need not have worried about difficulty, but awkwardness certainly intruded on the scene of our first meeting. From the instant I saw Polyglot, I experienced sexual attraction, which time demonstrated to be mutual. At that first moment I wondered how I could possibly have romantic much less erotic feelings about someone nearly a century older than I. But I did. It needs to be acknowledged, however, that the effects of aging occur more slowly among Merven than among humans. A typical 150 year-old Merven can run rings around the average fifty year-old human. For all that, I found Ployglot an exceedingly attractive being, with a compelling face and exquisite body.

My love affair with Polyglot was intensely erotic and as equally intellectual. The useful German term *Jungfräulich Erlebnis* well described the first time I had sex with a being of another species. It felt like a virginal experience, although I did not act like a virgin, but this was yet another end to my various states of virginity.

There was no pain or sense of loss. I had no sense of taboo about what we were doing. But it felt as if I had passed a threshold from which there was no return to innocence. It was an experience far more intense than any of my bisexual adventures. Passionate conversations evaluating the cultures and civilizations of all sentient beings on earth kept us up many nights. As dawn broke on some such discussions, we fell into one another's arms and made love as passionately as we had bandied paradigms.

Without intention but with much happiness I became pregnant again in the summer of 2018, via intercourse with Polyglot. Hoary members of the Uluru community expressed unease about my carrying a mixed species child, owing to the plethora of ancient myths and more recent anecdotes about the frequency of such offspring being stillborn or hideously malformed. One resident of the Australian enclave declared that the evolutionary implications of such a birth were akin to the misbegotten results of a Neanderthal mating with a Cro Magnon. Nothing good could come from it.

Key's affirmation about the good prospects for my conceiving a child with a Merven partner, however, resounded in my memory, and therefore I was not at all worried. In my first pregnancy I did not know the identity of the father, and yet I sailed through the gestation period with no angst. This time I not only knew whose sperm had impregnated me but could rely on Polyglot for emotional support, which was readily given. I perceived a mystical protective aura surrounding my womb, which I suppose is an indicator of the paranormal genetic inheritance I gained from both my parents. One of Key's associates rather petulantly described me as naively cheerful, but I felt confident throughout the marginally longer than normal (for humans) 40-week term of the pregnancy.

My labor was attended by three Merven midspouses. They insisted on this because it was a mixed species delivery. But everything went as smoothly as possible in such circumstances, with no complications. I delivered in a squatting position as I had done with K. P. The child weighed in at 3.5 kilograms and measured 55.9 centimeters in length.

Once again on my birthday, my forty-first, I gave birth to a perfectly healthy intersexual child, this time in the Australian early spring. We named our offspring Harbinger and raised him at Uluru, jointly at times but for long periods by Ployglot as a single parent, as I was still teaching at PCTS. To my great regret, I was not able to breast feed Harbinger (as I had K. P.) because of my teaching commitments in Hawaii. We utilized a Merven wet-nurse, which was probably more beneficial to Harbinger than my human breast milk. That, at least is my rationalization for abandoning my maternal duty.

I had been vague about my pregnancy at school. The seminary staff knew that I had become pregnant as a result of a relationship in Australia. They assumed that my partner was human. Better said, they had no context for considering my partner to be anything but human. When I returned to campus without a child, I told people that Harbinger was being raised by family in the Northern Territory and that I planned to visit the baby as frequently as I could.

K. P. nearly always came with me on visits to Uluru and thoroughly enjoyed having a younger sibling, and more significantly, gloried in being an older sibling.

Harbinger has the face and oval head of a human but the fine white hair and tall body of a Merven. Apart from cranium shape and physiognomy, Harbinger possesses all the traits and abilities characteristic of the Merven species, some of which coincidentally I also possess. From an early age, Harbinger was seen as exotic by Merven contemporaries and therefore has not suffered isolation but rather has enjoyed perhaps more social and romantic attention than most others in the Uluru community.

Over the years, Polyglot was kind enough to bring Harbinger on periodic visits to *Anela Punana* and on some occasions to Angel Nest reunions. The visits to Lahaina had to be discreet, because the seminary community knew nothing of Merven, but Harbinger enjoyed the run of the place in Sedona.

At one visit to Angel Nest, Harbinger, age seven at the time, asked to be anointed and immersed, saying, "I want to demonstrate solidarity with the human side of my heritage." Mom and Dad officiated, and my face splashed with tears of joy.

Notwithstanding the ardent nature of our affair, Polyglot told me before the first time we had sex that our relationship never would be exclusive. I accepted this quite calmly although, for the first time in my life, I was heels-over-head in love with Polyglot. Parenthetically, heels-over-head is the original wording of the expression, dating from the 14th century, but somehow and nonsensically it got turned on its metaphorical head. The commonly used form head-over-heels makes no sense as an expression of a state that causes elation because this is the normal orientation of one's head and heels. Unless, that is, one is in bed and they are of a level, which of course leads to speculations about sexual positions with heads being over heels. Yet even in this context, I think, the original expression, with heels up, is better suited to such endeavors.

At any rate, the reason for non-exclusivity, Polyglot explained, was that despite my profound attractiveness, I lacked male genitalia. Clearly, this continuing deficiency was not of my own creation, and we sought to overcome it by becoming adept at using sex toys to simulate maleness. Nevertheless, for Polyglot this did not produce the same qualitative satisfaction as relations with a real Merven partner.

From this experience, I gained a level of understanding of how some of my previous lovers had felt when they had become enamored of me and claimed to love me, but I had no interest in being bound to them. I did not engage in histrionics or mope around crying woe is me, but I did feel a new form of emotional pain.

As I reread this last sentence just now, I was tempted momentarily to rewrite it grammatically to say woe am I. There was a time when I would have done so, but I'm past that. And woe am I isn't correct either, for I am not a woe but rather feel woeful. Idioms will be idioms, and grammar nerds such as I should let them be.

Looking back, I am grateful for Polyglot's confession, since in the ensuing years we have both taken wonderful lovers. As far as I know, Polyglot has not connected sexually with any other humans, and I can affirm that I have had no other sexual relations with any Merven.

CHAPTER TWENTY-ONE
ELKE

Although I did not then know her name, my eyes locked onto Elke's. Her irises were galactic blue, radiating a cosmic joke and daring me to get it. Her mouth was set wide in knowing response to the joke told by her eyes. The long hair framing her face was lighter than mine but still a few shades shy of anything that would be called blonde. A breeze swirled strands of fine hair across her cheek and she pushed it back with delicate fingers without losing eye contact with me. I judged her to be about an inch shorter than I, and had she been wearing a dress, it would have been a size smaller than what I would wear. She wasn't wearing a dress, though, but very short cut-off jeans and a loose tee shirt bearing the face of Vera Brittain. Her posture was confident and casually erect.

My eyes dilated and my mouth spread into a foolish grin.

At the farmers' market in Lahaina on a perfect day in 2019, I noticed her holding a jar of *lilikoi* butter while I, a few feet away on the other side of the display bin, was also holding a jar of the island-made passion fruit spread. I won't call it love at first sight, but it was certainly strong chemistry at first sight.

"The *lilikoi* butter here is the best in the world," I said to her, for lack of anything profound that could escape my smitten mind.

"Yes, it lives up to its English name," she said. Her voice carried a slight Scandinavian accent.

A feeling of passion radiated between us, and my intellect went on holiday. "I also love their onions and chocolate banana bread," I managed to get out almost in a whisper.

"And their homemade chocolate chip cookies, lemons, limes, and avocados," Elke whispered back.

Food can be exceedingly erotic. Some say it is a substitute for sex, but I experience it as foreplay. I had the receipt to prove that I paid for my purchases but don't remember actually doing so. My next recollection is walking with Elke Goodsen to my place in order to continue our conversation. My memory may be playing tricks on me, for I don't specifically remember this happening, but in the myth-making part of my mind, we held hands as we walked. If not, I certainly thought about taking her hand.

"Either you like Vera Brittain or someone gave you that shirt as a gift," I said along the way.

"The former," she said. "Have you read her?"

"I've read **Testament of Youth** three times so far," I answered.

"Me too," she said.

An image of the two of us reading it aloud to one another for a fourth time swept through my consciousness but I kept it to myself.

When Elke sat down on my couch, Yggdrassill and Quetzalcoatl jumped into her lap, each one seeking belly rubs. She set them on either side of her thighs and did as each one directed her. "They probably smell Zoey," she said. "Actually she's Zodiac, but I've fallen into the bad habit of calling her Zoey. She's a very robust black cat."

"I'm glad that you're a cat person," I said, gently shooing both of mine from the couch so that I could sit with Elke.

I perched at a right angle to her and tucked in my legs so that I could see her as we talked, and she moved into a similar position facing me. The legs of my khaki shorts had bunched up, so I wiggled to adjust them before saying, "I'm the in-house heretic and professor of all things Semitic at PCTS."

"I'm a writer of erotic novels," she replied, matching my career with hers. "I decided to lease a cottage in Lahaina because I thought it would provide inspiration, and just because I like it here."

"I've read novels that had erotic passages, but I don't recall reading anything specifically tagged with the erotic novel genre. Are your books available in any local stores?" I asked.

"There are several places on the island, but most of my sales are through the Internet. I use the pseudonym Joy Swallow," she explained. "But you don't need to rush out and buy them. I'll gladly lend you a few of my copies so you can decide whether you like them. The genre is generally fun but not deep. Some erotica out there is dark and sadomasochistic, but not mine."

A pleasant tingle rushed through me, making me aware of my physicality. Conscious that I had borne two children to term, I nevertheless felt confident about my body, which had returned to my pre-pregnancy shape shortly after each delivery. Only small indications showed that I had been pregnant, if one looked closely. I admitted that I would soon be 42, and Elke said she had pegged me for a decade younger. She was born the same year as I, and when we were at the market I had judged her to be early 30s as well. That coincidence provided us mutual emotional boosts.

K. P. was out surfing with school friends and would be gone all day, so with nothing more than a mutual confession of bisexuality and sly nods, we ambled into my bedroom and made love. This was the first and last time in my life that I had sex with someone on a first meeting, but in this case, it felt as if I had known her for years. The feeling had a rational basis, but there was a great deal about Elke that I did not know.

Noting my all-over tan as we lounged in bed afterward, Elke asked about it, and I told her the story of my naturist life. I then said, "You didn't wear a bra today. Is that normative for you?"

"Oh, I hate those damn things," she replied. "Most of the time I go without. My characters wear lacy or see-through bras, but I prefer comfort."

"Me too," I echoed. "In fact, I have never worn one in my entire life."

"You should try one on sometime just to see what other women have to bear for the sake of fashion or propriety," Elke said. "Mine are a little big for you, so it wouldn't give you a true sense, but you're welcome to try one on."

"Thanks anyway, but I'll pass," I replied. "I wouldn't want to jeopardize my thirty-year braless streak."

Then without a trace of embarrassment, she told me about her career as an actress in porn films. A vivid and pleasantly erotic dream I'd had when I was a college undergraduate flooded into my mind. The dream had involved a porn star in tropical Denmark, and at the time I had interpreted it as representing my upside down world. But now it made a different kind of sense, because Elke was a Danish porn actress living in Maui. I told her about my dream, and she said that in the farmers' market she had picked up a mental image from me about our having met in a dream.

"How did you come to work in the porn industry?" I asked.

"I was born in Copenhagen, where the industry has been legal since before my birth," she said. "My mother was a stripper and occasional porn film actress. My father was a reclusive electronics wizard who never married my mother but who visited our apartment many times over the years. He was obsessed with my mother's sexuality. Since he was wealthy, he provided financial support, but erratically. It was not enough for us to live on without other income. But he gave me an extraordinary gift. My IQ has been measured in the genius range. That certainly did not come from my mother's genes."

"I inherited my high intelligence from both my parents," I said. "Sorry to interrupt the flow of your story. What happened next?"

"I don't mean to disparage my mother about not having genes for intelligence," she added. "My mother contributed valuable gifts to my genetic makeup, certain extrasensory skills, for example, and an adventuresome spirit. But she is no intellectual."

"When I was eleven, my mother said I should address her by her first name and not call her *mor.* So from then on she was Esther to me, not mom. Not long after that, she announced that it was time for my sex education lessons," Elke continued. "Rather than the expected facts of life talk, Esther allowed me to watch while she had sex with my father and, after a while, with other men."

My mouth hung open but I did not speak.

"Esther and I also masturbated together and talked about the things that led us to orgasms and about safe sex techniques. By the time I was 13, I was masturbating while watching Esther having sex with men and commenting aloud on what she was doing. Esther's partners seemed to love it when I did that. At age 14, I lost my virginity in an arrangement with a teenage boy whom I had previously watched Esther have sex with. After that, Esther and I did threesomes and foursomes together, including several times with my father.

"I never had direct sexual contact with Esther, although I would have if she had been open to it. When I was 15, I had a sexual affair with a forty-something lesbian who lived in our apartment building. She invited me to move in with her, but I wasn't ready for that kind of relationship."

I wanted to ask if Elke had been paid for the group sex sessions but hesitated, which was wise, because she answered without my needing to do so.

"Esther never asked for money from any of her sex partners, but many of them offered financial gifts, which she always took. Some of them gave her jewelry, which she usually sold. I was not paid directly for my participation, but I did receive an allowance from Esther that came whether or not I had entertained any of her men," Elke said.

"At that point," I noted, "you were still too young to work in the porn industry. At least not in the legal industry. Were you in school?"

"Yes," she said. "And that's an important element in the story. A very wealthy married businessman, who wanted Esther available for sex at a moment's notice without the hindrance of a minor daughter in the apartment, offered to pay for me to go to boarding school. I was thrilled with the proposal and was thus sent to the United States to Orme School in Mayer, Arizona, where I spent two wonderful years. About a third of Orme's boarding students are international. At any rate, this businessman had no idea that Esther and I had functioned as a team, or he would have kept me home. But Esther wanted me to get an education and so never revealed this to him."

"Silence is golden," I said.

"Indeed," she said. "Then, after graduating from Orme School, I returned to Copenhagen and got a job doing computer data entry for a bank. It was tedious and mind numbing, hour after hour at the keyboard typing in numbers. At night, I had dreams of being on a treadmill and attacked by armies of numerals, all of them trying to knock me down. One day Esther told me she had been cast as the mother in a *faux* incest movie and invited me to the set to watch the filming. I was so bored at my bank job that I thought it might be fun. So I showed up.

"The director liked my looks and asked if I'd be interested in a minor role in the piece. He offered me a thousand **kroner** for ten minutes' work. I thought, why the hell not? I was cast as the sister who walks in on her brother having sex with mom and who little by little strips and masturbates while watching them do all sorts of sex acts. I had never before been in front of a movie camera, but the director raved about my naturalness in the scene. At the end of the shoot, he offered me a contract to act in sex films. Working at the bank was safe and secure but deadening. So I signed a contract for three films, adopting the stage name Tina Joy.

"Over a three-year period, I made a dozen films in Denmark and Sweden. I missed out on some roles because I refused to shave my pubic hair. I trimmed but would not shave, because pubic hair evolved for a purpose, to ease friction during intercourse, which those movies were full of. I also proclaimed that shaving pubic hair was a sign of infantile ideation, which angered directors, as I usually did this on the set in front of other actresses who had shaved. I never blamed any of the women, however. I made clear that my rebukes were aimed at men who never grew up. Sometimes I called them wanna-be pedophiles. One director banished me from the set any time I was not in a scene.

"I only did things in films that I liked to do for my own pleasure, and this showed through on the screen. Tina Joy films were noted for fun sex. That's what made me a star. I would not participate in anything that involved what I believed demeaned women, including violence, slapping, torture, bondage, duress, sadism, and masochism. I refused roles in which the script had men saying derogatory things to or about women. I did one piss film, because the pissing was reciprocal. Both sexes peed and were peed upon. But I wouldn't let anyone pee on my face, only below the neck."

"How did you get away with that? I thought porn flick producers were domineering, ruthless, and demanding," I said.

"That's the stereotype, but this was **Denmark**!" she said. "Scandinavians are notoriously agreeable. And it didn't hurt that doing it my way gave them a very profitable franchise."

"Did you share in the profits?" I asked.

"To a degree. I got much more money in my second and third contracts. And I lived with Esther during this time, so I stashed away the money from acting. The man who had financed my boarding school education was now out of the picture, and my biological father was erratic with money support, but I had few expenses and thus saved nearly everything I made in those years. My plan was to further my education."

"So, you went to college..." I said.

"I returned to the United States and enrolled at Scripps College in Claremont, California. It's now part of the Claremont Colleges Consortium. At Scripps I earned a degree in English. While in college, I sold some erotic short stories, and after graduation, with encouragement from an editor who got me an agent, I began writing novels. There is a huge market in this country for erotica written by women, so I have been able to make a comfortable living with it. The downside is that the plots are formulaic, so it can get boring writing the same characters over and over but with different names, doing the same sexual experiments in various time periods and geographical settings.

"I took a master's degree in American literature at UCLA, and gained my green card, but I was getting fed up with the daily hassles of living in Southern California. Last year I moved to Lahaina where I could enjoy the sun, sand, and tropical breezes, even when my plots were boring."

"A fascinating story," I said. "Having gone to grad school in California, I resonate with the part about daily hassles."

"Are you put off by any of it?" Elke asked straightforwardly.

CHAPTER TWENTY-TWO
POETIC LICENSE

"**Honestly**, there is something in your story that bothers me," I said. "Not your acting in x-rated films. I'm queasy about the incest. Something inside me says that it's creepy at best and a major boundary violation in general. It feels ethically and morally wrong to me."

Elke produced a relieved laugh, not at what I had said about incest but that her acting career was not an impediment to a potential relationship.

"I see you as a victim of incest," I continued.

"I don't evaluate that experience in terms of moral right or wrong," Elke responded. "I recognize that it goes against prevailing social norms and certainly there can be an issue of violating personal autonomy, but I don't find puritanical morality a useful guide for evaluating it. Quite definitely, I don't see myself as a victim."

"I'm hardly puritanical," I responded. "I am impressed by the way you have overcome the...the...I'm searching for a word other than dysfunction but can't find one. Your story seems to be one of overcoming childhood circumstances."

"Dysfunction is not an inappropriate term," Elke said. "And I agree that incest is completely wrong when coercion is involved, psychological or physical, or when it involves prepubescent children. I would even say it is evil in those circumstances. In my case, I was not coerced but invited into the incestuous behavior. In physical sexual development, I was an adult. I won't claim emotional maturity, but this was something I was curious about and found exciting, and I freely joined in with it."

I thought but did not say that this was a psychological defense mechanism to keep inner rage under control. Instead, I said, "But given your early upbringing, you weren't in a position to set reasonable boundaries or make ethical judgments."

"Although I lacked the technical vocabulary at the time," she replied, "I recognized that my mother had no personal boundaries. She may have had them once upon a time, but someone demolished them before I was born. Even before my sex education lessons, I was determined to set my own boundaries and maintain personal dignity. I've been on a quest for personal autonomy since I was a teen. Doing porn films was an act of adventure, taking a path to establish an authentic identity apart from the norms of conventional society. My decision to quit the porn business was also a step on that journey, but even when I was making the films, I set boundaries about what I would and would not do."

"It's refreshing to be in a relationship where I'm the prude," I said.

"So, we are already in a relationship, yes?" she said.

"Unless you object to the term," I said. "Without doubt, I want to see you again."

From our first meeting, we began to spend a lot of time with each other at her place and mine. While walking to her cottage after a visit to the farmers' market for fresh fruit to make a luncheon salad, Elke told me that she has the ability to absorb thoughts and mental images from sex partners.

"This is a trait I inherited from my mother," she said. "This is how Esther was able to captivate wealthy men using her sexuality. She used her physical beauty to get their attention, but then she was very skilled at acting in ways that connected with their inner lives. That kept them coming back for more. Of course when they did come back, she let them walk all over her."

"That absorbing thoughts trait runs in my family too," I said.

"Really? Then I must be very careful around you," Elke said.

"Don't worry about it. Just be yourself. I'll know if you're faking," I replied.

An impish grin covered her face. "While making films, I liked to spook other actors by asking them about a memory or image I had picked up during the performance."

"Do you remember any particular thoughts you absorbed?" I asked. "Do any of them stand out in your mind?"

"Most of them were not worth remembering," she replied. "There was an exceedingly egotistical stud who regularly thought about how great an actor he was while he was screwing me for the camera. I could have been an anatomically correct manikin for all he cared. Another one imagined I was his sister. A lot of the girl on girl action was faked, of course. Well, so was the screwing. But I remember one *faux* lesbian making a list of the chores waiting for her at home while pretending to enjoy licking me all over. Apparently she was behind with the laundry."

"What about when you had sex with your father?" I asked. "What was he thinking?"

"I had trouble reading him. He tended to simply enjoy the physical experience," she said. "His mind was inside his penis. I suspect he blocked out the significance of what he was doing."

"Or whom he was doing?" I quipped.

"Yes, but only while he was doing it," she said. "Afterward he was kind and affectionate and spoke endearingly to me. It almost felt like he was apologetic."

Given her extrasensory gift, I had no trouble teaching Elke to float. She was a natural at leaving her body.

One of the fun things we did together early in our relationship was watch videos of her Tina Joy films. They had been made originally as VHS tapes, but she had her personal collection transferred to DVD.

My favorite among these films had the Danish title *Traek Deres Busker Ned* in which Elke played a nurse who took very good care of her patients, male and female. The English release, Elke told me, bore the title *Pants Off!*

Another fun thing we did in those days was to google various websites to find photoshopped stills from her movies, where her face had been replaced by pictures of other women, including news reporters and anchors, politicians (members of Congress and governors), famous actresses, and commercial spokeswomen. Elke told me this was a form of social satire ubiquitous on the Internet, and male politicians and celebrities were also lampooned this way. Once she had pointed it out to me, I encountered it repeatedly on news and opinion sites. Some of it was witty but most was crudely offensive.

"Look for the NSFW disclaimer when you're surfing political news pages, especially right wing ones," she told me. "That's where you'll find photoshopped satire."

For the benefit of Merven readers who have never used the Internet, NSFW stands for Not Suitable for Work. Historically, there was a time when human employees were expected and in some cases rigidly required to separate rather than integrate their personal and employment hours. Productivity suffered, of course, but that was the prevailing philosophy in those days.

One of the witty photos showed Elke having oral sex with a well-endowed male, but her face and her co-star's face had been replaced with those of a couple from a "four-hour erection" commercial, demonstrating how amazingly well the pills worked. Lest anyone miss the joke, the name of the erectile dysfunction pill and a satirical disclaimer were superimposed on the scene.

Once when I was carrying on about the intricacies of interpreting biblical texts, Elke commented that the Bible had proven to be a good source of material for her films and erotic fiction.

"So your porn used biblical themes?" I said. "Tell me more."

"Given your doctoral thesis, you already know there's a lot of erotica in the Bible," she said.

"Well I know," I replied. "A lot of sex anyway. Some of it is not very erotic. Which did you use for your films?"

"The Song of Solomon is all erotica," she said. "And then there's all those men going into their concubines. Sarai urged her husband Abram to have sex with his concubine Hagar. In the movie version, instead of being infertile, we made Sarai frigid but getting her jollies from watching Abram do Hagar. I played Hagar. That's a porn version of biblical interpretation.

"Susanna is about two men watching a naked woman bathing and blackmailing her into having sex with them. I played Susanna, resisting at first but then coming to love doing both of them at the same time."

"In the biblical text, she successfully resisted them," I said.

"I know. We took poetic license," Elke said. "The king in the book of Esther wanted his wife the queen to parade naked in front of his friends at a drunken revel, wearing only her crown. In the Bible, she refused. In the film, she not only did it but also did the king's friends, which bummed him out and made him impotent. I see it as his just desserts for wanting to show off his wife's beauty. In that sense it's a morality play.

"Sodom and Gomorrah and its aftermath provided a lot of salacious material. I did a film about Lot's daughters having incest with him. In the Genesis 19 account, the daughters seduce him one at a time. In our film, we turned it into a threesome, which I think is in keeping with the spirit of the biblical story.

"I wrote a short story about Jesus turning water into wine. That text is borderline erotic. In my story, the wine is made in 30-gallon containers for bathing. The idea of the bride and groom bathing in wine and all the places they could suck wine from each other's bodies makes an appealing and joyful image."

"Not to be overly critical, but your screenwriters took significant creative liberties with the passages," I said.

"As they do with every book that is turned into a movie, including the sappy and pious religious sagas and biblical epics," she said.

"I can't argue with that," I replied. "By the way, you seem knowledgeable of the Bible. One of the things we haven't talked about is religion. Am I apt to start an argument if I probe that area?"

"I think it's time to do that," she replied. "My biblical knowledge was initially absorbed from the screenwriters of my films. This interested me, so I read portions of the Bible for myself, although most of it made little sense. In college and grad school, I learned more and gained a level of sophistication about it."

"What a delicious irony that you were exposed to the Bible by pornographers," I said. "What about church?"

"I have never been inside a church in my life, much less a religious service," she explained. "Not even for a wedding. Piety and churchy morality give me the creeps."

"Me too," I said. "Although I grew up in a church where both my parents are clergy. They are neither pious nor moralistic."

"I'm not opposed to the idea of God," Elke continued. "I think of myself as an agnostic and definitely not dogmatic about the existence or non-existence of God."

"I know many atheists, and I respect their rationality," I said. "For the most part, I enjoy their critiques of the Bible and doctrinal religion.

This world would be a much worse place without atheists and other skeptics. But I'm drawn to the mythic and mystic realms of existence. I need to explore realities that lie beyond what can be merely measured and catalogued. There is a sentient intelligence in the world that is bigger than any individual. That to me is God."

"I can't argue with that," Elke said.

I found a copy of **The Timberscape of Memory** on a bookshelf in Elke's cottage and told her that Chaucer Dickinson was my favorite professor in college. Elke really liked **TOM** and had read it several times. I added that Chaucer and I had each advised the other to write additional books and confessed that I had written a thousand-line poem for credit in an independent study with Chaucer and Bookman Donne. Immediately, Elke asked to read **The Third Song of Creation**. The next day, I dug out my copy of it and gave it to her.

The day after that, she came over and said, "I'll refrain from teasing you about the significant creative liberties you took with the biblical creation accounts. This is wonderful. You should try to get it published."

My response was, "Touché! My intent, of course, was to go beyond scripture. It's a youthful work. I've outgrown some of its assumptions."

"But it's a great piece of work," she said. "Would you mind if I showed it to my agent?"

"Let me think about it," I said. I've been thinking about it ever since.

This conversation about my writing skill led to the suggestion from Elke that she and I co-write something with mythical dimensions.

"How about lesbian and bisexual fairy tales?" I said jokingly.

But she thought it was a splendid idea. In no time at all, we had come up with a number of ideas: Alice does the Queen of Hearts, Cinderella does her fairy godmother, Hansel and Gretel do a three-way with the witch, Goldilocks does all the bears. We laughed and laughed as we developed more bizarre story lines.

Not long after that, Elke borrowed my copy of Ogden's massive work on process theology and became absorbed in it. Every day she would ply me with theological questions, notions, or insights she had gained from **Eternal Becoming**.

"You're turning into a first rate divinity student," I said.

"Heaven forbid!" she replied. "Next thing you'll have me transforming into a new Augustine."

"Not a chance," I said. "You could never take on the pathological guilt he wallowed in over his youthful sexual antics. And process theology is far removed from orthodox ideology."

"Well, I do find it fascinating," Elke said.

"You are welcome to sit in on any of my classes if you like," I offered.

She liked that idea very much, and in fact registered with the seminary to audit a variety of classes.

Elke also began accompanying me to faculty social events and school receptions. A few of my colleagues seemed surprised at my relationship with a woman, but no one had any objections. A church and society professor, who was in a same-sex marriage, stopped me in the hall one day and asked why I had only recently come out after teaching at PCTS for so many years.

"I've been out since I was twenty," I said. "It never occurred to me, however, that it was necessary to inform my colleagues of my sexual interests."

"I'm sorry," she said. "I didn't mean it that way. It just seemed that you always socialized with men until recently, so I assumed...."

"It's alright," I said. "I'm bisexual, and from my perspective, men are as suitable as women. But until I met Elke, I hadn't found any unattached women on the island I wanted to engage with."

"Again, I apologize if my question was offensive," she said. "Of all people, I should avoid making assumptions about other people's sexuality."

One day, in 2020, Elke and I decided to pack a picnic and drive to Kaupo on the southeastern shore of Maui. Taking K. P. along, we picked up Route 31, the Pi'ilani Highway, and drove south to swing along the southern shore and up to desolate Kaupo, where we found a grassy field away from the carloads of tourists creeping by in identical economy rentals. We spread a blanket and sat to listen to the wind, watch the sea, and wonder at Haleakala.

K. P. was 13 at the time and enjoyed the doting attention of two women. Elke said she regretted never having children and enjoyed sharing in the life of K. P. In a moment of family intimacy, K. P. and I together told Elke about the Merven and my love affair with Polyglot and having a half-Merven child named Harbinger. She was stunned and bemused at the same time but recognized intuitively that we were telling her the truth. I dramatically intoned sentences from the Merven language for her edification, and K. P. spoke a few of the phrases that he had picked up. I thought that one day he would be a better Merven linguist than I.

Elke entertained us by reciting bits of absurd dialog from her films, edited slightly for K. P. Out of context, many of the lines she spoke were hilarious, and we all laughed so hard our sides ached.

Several times over the next few weeks, Elke made humorous comments about being jealous of me for having two beautiful children. On other occasions, she spoke about regretting never having a child. "Esther didn't want me when she got pregnant, and wasn't the world's best mother in the first few years of my life, but she told me before I left for Orme School that she was glad that I was her daughter. She said I had turned into a real joy."

Elke and I made a winter trip to Denmark in December 2021. Since it was school break, K. P. came along. We met Esther, who looked young for a woman in her sixties. She was retired and now living a contented celibate life. One morning, she offered to spend the day with K. P. making cookies, so that Elke could show me the place where both mother and daughter had worked as actresses. The studio was still churning out sexually explicit movies.

Because of her reputation as a former porn star, Elke was able to arrange a tour of the facility, and we observed a new film being made. Afterward, Elke said, "They were sexier in the old days. The actresses these days look like flesh-covered hairless robots making insipid sounds."

"My thoughts exactly," I said. "I didn't come close to being turned on by any of it. But all you have to do is teasingly brush my cheek with your hand and I'm on fire."

She put her hands on my hips and said, "Oh Zara, I do love you so."

That night, we binged on hot chocolate and cookies in Esther's apartment.

During a snowstorm, I demonstrated my ability to be outside naked while remaining warm. Unsurprisingly, she wanted to learn the technique, and I taught her. As with floating, she learned rapidly.

When we returned to Maui, she asked if I would teach her to speak Merven. I agreed to give her a few words and phrases to try out. She mastered them with relative ease. I then contacted Pilgrim for wisdom about further lessons. Pilgrim said that Elke would need additional instruction from a real Merven, and to my surprise, volunteered for the task, adding that it was time to begin formal instruction for K. P. as well. Thus, over time, Elke and K. P. added two more humans to the list of Merven linguists.

During this period I encouraged Elke to write a novel based on her childhood. "It's such a compelling story," I said, "with so many psychological and ethical layers."

"I've been thinking about that," she replied. "But there's another story I need to write first, something with more energy behind it."

And so, Elke began work on a general fiction novel about the sexual obsessions of a Scandinavian man. The protagonist was a composite of her biological father, the man who paid for her private schooling, and several other men who had been involved with Esther. Through the writing, Elke worked out deeply held feelings. Published with the title **The Longing**, the novel received critical acclaim and sold well. Elke used her real name as author, and gained a modicum of fame as a result of its success.

She never did write a novel based on her own life, but stemming from her continued studies at the seminary, she published three more non-fiction works on feminism, the nexus of politics and sex, and anti-intellectualism in the United States.

CHAPTER TWENTY-THREE
BRAIN MANAGEMENT

It came as no surprise to learn that K. P. has a genius IQ and also that he is bisexual. Like mother (and very likely father) like son. He tolerated elementary school in Lahaina, his education supplemented with private instruction from Elke, various of my seminary colleagues, and me. When it came time for secondary education, however, we decided private school was necessary and enrolled him at Punahou on Oahu. Ostensibly, he stayed on the North Shore with his great grandmother Penny. She was now a widow and appreciated his company. Since the commute from her house was difficult, however, he often spent the night with friends in Honolulu. On some ordinary weekends and for all extended school holidays, he came home to Lahaina.

When K. P. was fifteen, he discovered that he could control certain of his brain activity. The amygdalae, those areas in humans poetically referred to as our rat brain are responsible for the fight or flight response and all sorts of primitive, emotional, and violent behavior. K. P. taught himself how to modulate his rat brain through meditation. When he encountered youthful aggression or bullying, he did not instinctually prepare for conflict and instantly react with adrenaline induced fervor but rather used his mind to control the emotions of his antagonists. Usually, he simply calmed their minds, but on occasion he chose to make them feel afraid and thus flee.

We live in an age when parents learn from their children. K. P. taught me to manage my rat brain and also how to manipulate certain of my genes by turning them on and off. This also is achieved through meditative consciousness. The result is that I have intentionally modified my genetic structure to slow down the aging process. It's not likely that I will live as long as a typical Merven, but I'll be disappointed if I don't reach 150 years. It's not a once and done process, however. Continual monitoring is required, along with mental maintenance to keep organs and tissue healthy. I asked him to teach Elke as well, and he did so gladly.

He also taught me something far more mundane but great fun. K. P. is an excellent surfer, and he gave lessons to Elke and me on the proper use of a surfboard. I've often floated in, on, and above water, but surfing provides an entirely different feeling, at once bracing and sensuous.

K. P. also became a minor celebrity when he posted a video on YouTube, in which he enthusiastically explained how easy it is to become rich by surfing. Surfing is the hidden gateway to wealth, he proclaimed. Investing in a board is the first step to building a fortune. The whole thing was a spoof, but it went viral because most viewers didn't get the joke. K. P. received offers from get-rich-quick seminar promoters offering him sizeable amounts of money to do workshops at their events. They had gotten the joke but didn't think that was a disqualifying factor. He turned them all down, noting that he thought they were a pack of crooks.

An invitation to deliver a lecture at another seminary came as an indicator that my academic career was on solid ground. Universal Kerygma Anthropo-Theological Seminary in Pasadena, California offered me a significant honorarium for making a presentation on recent developments in Semitic linguistic analysis. The timing fit my schedule, so I readily accepted. UKA-TS holds denominational affiliation with the Universal Salvation Church and is on the approved list for pastoral candidates in my denomination.

Elke went along with me, visiting her alma mater, Scripps College, while I was lecturing at the seminary. Afterward, we spent a stress free weekend at the Glen Eden Nudist Resort in Corona, before flying back to Maui.

Elke and I published a collection of our jointly written lesbian and bisexual fairy tales with Elke's publisher, but added a new pseudonym for me, because I didn't want these light-hearted pieces to be reviewed along side my scholarly works. We called the collection **Cinderella Comes Out**, by Joy Swallow and Polly Antic. This proved to be so successful that we quickly came out with another volume called **Bi Vibes in Valhalla**. Most of the reason for the success of these stories was that Joy Swallow already had an audience ready to buy anything with her name on it.

On a whim, we decided to pack **Bi Vibes** with retronyms. Elke bet me that our editor at Strange Angel Press, Lawn Griffiths, would not notice the large number of retronyms. The loser of the bet would have to perform oral sex on the winner. Of course I took the bet, seeing as paying off the bet was a win for both of us. Elke saw it the same way, which is why she proposed it. As it happened, Lawn did notice our linguistic inclusions and commented on them using more retronyms of his own.

Without checking in the book, my recollection is that the retronyms Elke and I used were: manual typewriter, manual transmission, black and white television, British English, cloth diaper, dairy milk, hot war, horse cavalry, inground pool, Old Testament, opposite sex marriage, organic farming, raw milk, sit-down restaurant, Old World, natural turf, acoustic guitar, and organic food. We found ways to make them sound erotic or to convey sexual connotations. Lawn's reply included: 2-D (referring to the flatness of his letter, it not being written in 3-D), monaural sound, hard copy, and snail mail.

With Merven consent, K. P. and I took Elke along on a visit to Harbinger and Ployglot at Uluru in 2023. This provided an excellent setting for Elke to practice speaking Merven. On this auspicious visit, Polyglot offered to teach K. P. and me how to disappear and reappear as the Merven do. I had already done this once, by taking Sojourner's arm during the rescue from SCUM. But I was only a passive passenger at the time. The Merven word for the action is **dzjing** [rising sigh], which is much easier to say than transport oneself instantly from one physical location to another.

Polyglot diplomatically told Elke that if she desired it, she might be taught various Merven skills after she had spent more time in their presence. "Zara has been among us since she was a child, and it is only now that we are offering her this skill. And though young, Key Person has also known us since childhood."

"Don't worry about me," Elke said. "I fully understand. I am not ready."

My intuition told me, however, that though she did indeed intellectually understand, she nevertheless envied K. P. and me.

We were told to select a line to chant as a trigger for the necessary mental state until we were able to do it without chanting. I chose a line from **The Third Song of Creation** [XXXIV]: "So slight was Corposant, so lightly boned that breezes often challenged him to fly." The purpose of this instruction was to make it easier for us to visit the Merven enclaves in Havasu Canyon and Uluru. These were the only ones where I had Merven friends and had visited, but the technique could be used to transport to any enclave in the world, as long as I knew where they were.

K. P. and I mastered the art of *dzjing* [rising sigh] more quickly than I had anticipated. Polyglot's final instruction was that we should first call telepathically before doing it. This was common courtesy among all Merven. Failure to do so was considered rude.

The first time I used the *dzjing* [rising sigh] technique, I did it alone, having first politely inquired telepathically. I had some books for Harbinger, along with some recordings of Beatles music, which he had asked for. Delivering them this way was much easier than shipping them in a package via commercial carrier.

While there, I asked Polyglot for more information about a dimension of altering one's DNA that I had been musing over. "K. P. couldn't answer this, but maybe you know. Can DNA for sex orientation be changed?"

"Do you want to change your bisexuality?" Polyglot asked in a surprised voice.

"Not at all," I replied. "Why would I want to do something that would limit the possibilities in my life? I'm just curious. All this pray away the gay blather coming from the religious right set me to wondering. We already know that DNA can be altered. Apart from their junk science about reparative therapy, is it possible to change sexual orientation?"

"Indeed you are curious," Polyglot said. "And the question is legitimate. The answer is yes, but only to broaden orientation. It is not possible to delete genes for sexual orientation, but for those desiring wider arrays of experience straight can be added to gay and vice versa, thus creating a bisexual orientation."

"I know some people whose orientation I'd like to broaden," I said sarcastically.

"I suspect, however, that they would not be willing participants in the project," Polyglot noted.

"No, but it would do them all a world of good," I replied.

"Yes, but some of them are already broadly sexed but are in denial about it," Polyglot noted.

"Is there a gene to overcome denial?" I asked.

"If only," Polyglot said.

Though now well into our forties, Elke and I both still looked about thirty, thanks to the genetic instruction of K. P. and the influence of the Merven, as well as healthy lifestyles. The aging process had been successfully slowed in our bodies.

As a gift for K. P.'s sixteenth birthday, and with my prior assent, Elke initiated him sexually. She made clear to him that this would only happen once, and she would never have sex with him again. Afterward, K. P. said ending his virginity was the best birthday present he could have imagined.

Two months later, during a visit to her cottage, Elke told me she was pregnant. My first thought was that it was risky to have a first pregnancy at such a late time in life. Closely following on that came the assumption that K. P. had been the sperm source. This made me angry but I chose not to show it at that moment.

"Are you worried about being pregnant at 46?" I asked

"Really, I'm not," she said. "I have the body of a much younger woman."

"Nevertheless, the pregnancy must be considered high risk," I said.

"I'm prepared to take the chance," Elke said with determination in her voice. "This is my only chance to bear a child, and I'm going to take it."

"I have to ask this," I said, now allowing a hint of my anger to show. "Is K. P. the contributing male?" I did not want to use the word father, because I found it painful to imagine my teenage son in that role.

Elke gave me a reproachful look and said, "Yes. There could be no other source."

"I assume you would not consider an abortion," I said.

"Not unless medical tests revealed a profound defect," she said.

"Then K. P. must never know. Never! Do you promise?"

"I could not agree to never, because circumstances may make it advisable that he know when he is much older," she said. "But I agree that it's wise for the present that he be blissfully unaware. I will tell him and everyone else that I used a sperm donor. How about the same one you used?"

"No, not him," I said. "Say it was a local one, which is, in a way, true."

"Can you be happy for me?" she said cajolingly.

"I don't know," I said. "Not at this moment. I need time to consider the situation of my lover bearing my grandchild."

"You know that I'm not in love with K. P. I love him like a son but have no desire to have a romantic relationship with him," she explained.

"That makes conceiving a child with him incest," I said. "We've already had an unhappy discussion about that subject."

"Yes, we have, and you and I must agree to disagree about it," she said. "The problems associated with inbreeding are absent in this situation, and you and I are not married, so there is no legal basis for incest."

"It's de facto incest," I said. "That's bad enough."

"Now don't get all moralistic about this, Zara," she said. "I've read **The Third Song of Creation**. Incest is a powerful theme in it, so despite your protestations of disgust, the subject must hold a certain fascination for you. And you treat it sympathetically in your poem. You have no rational case for objection."

"Don't go throwing in my face something I wrote in college," I responded.

"You mean back in the days when you were open-minded?" she said sarcastically.

"For your information, Miss English major, I was writing classical mythical themes. It was literary incest, and there was nothing Oedipal about it," I said with a raised voice. "If anything, the incest in my poem was a slam against biblical literalists who insist that Adam and Eve were the first and only humans until they had children. Therefore, their children must have been incestuous in order to populate the earth!"

"Don't matronize me," Elke said. "You have no need to be defensive. I'm merely pointing out a logical inconsistency in your position. It happens to everyone."

That hurt, so I fired back. "There's the technical matter of statutory rape."

"To which you are a contributing party," she said calmly. "It's funny that you didn't think of that or of incest when you said it was a great idea to give K. P. the opportunity to end his virginity without the usual teenage fumbling. Are you going to report me to the police?"

"No, of course not, but I need some time alone to reflect on this," I said. I was angry at Elke and more so at myself. "I don't think we should see each other for a while."

"I'll leave it to you to tell me when you're ready to meet again," Elke said and quietly added, "and also to tell K. P. about my being pregnant. You can tell him I'm having morning sickness or discomfort or something to explain why I'm not there in your home."

"I'll do that," I said and left to walk back to my place at a furious pace.

Before moving to Maui, I burned a batch of compact discs with my favorite songs from my dad's record collection. Now I felt the need to listen to some of them. Music had always provided solace for me when I needed it, and I had major brooding to do. The first CD I selected was all Beatles music. I turned to the Beatles for help, starting with "Help!" Playing and replaying the songs, I worked my way through "I Should Have Known Better," "Things We Said Today," and "In My Life." Each one assisted me to move through the emotional trauma I was feeling.

Although I am generally inclined to handle things by myself, I recognized that this was a situation, as the Beatles so aptly sang, where I needed help. After sulking for a week, I communicated mentally with Ployglot, seeking counsel. Sojourner or Pilgrim might have been better choices given the circumstances, but I wanted advice from a lover and not a parent figure.

"I have something vitally important to talk with you about. Is it convenient for me to transport myself there in the next few minutes?"

"First give me a synopsis telepathically, and I will assess whether you need to be here in person," Polyglot said.

I described the situation.

"This creates complex issues for humans," Ployglot said. "I can see how difficult this would be for you, given the emotional dynamics of human society."

"How would a Merven respond to a similar situation?" I asked.

"Substantially the same with regard to the interpersonal issues," Polyglot replied. "But there would be no overlay of jealousy."

"I'm not jealous!" I proclaimed, feeling on the defensive. "I'm concerned about my teenage son being father to my lover's child."

"You overlook that Elke has long been envious of you for having two gifted children while she has none. This is an opportunity for her to be your equal as a mother," Polyglot said.

"She doesn't need a child to enjoy equality and mutuality in her relationship with me," I said. "I have never thought less of her for not being a mother."

"It is not a matter of what she needs but what she deeply wants," Ployglot said.

"So, you think she's right and I'm wrong," I said.

"Feel free to get a second opinion from Pilgrim or Sojourner," Polyglot said with a kindly inflection. "Or from Huxley."

"That's not answering the question," I said.

"From a Merven perspective, this is not a matter of right or wrong," Ployglot responded. "Yet there is an overriding issue at stake here."

"What could that be?" I said with a hint of sarcasm.

"From the perspective of evolutionary developments, considering the genetic mutations that K. P. enjoys, Elke bearing a child with the contribution of his genes is a fortuitous event. Apart from the human relationships involved, a child born to K. P. and Elke is very likely to be another step forward in human evolution."

With those words, a great burden lifted from my mind. But I was still mad at Elke and not ready to forgive and forget. I continued to brood, indulging in alternating spells of depression and righteous indignation. Two days later, I contacted Polyglot again and asked if I could **dzjing** [rising sigh] for a personal visit.

"What do you have in mind?" Polyglot asked.

"It's not so much in mind as in body," I said. "I'm feeling the need for physical intimacy."

"I think not," Polyglot said.

"Why not?" I responded. "We love each other."

"Revenge is not a healthy reason to have sex," Polyglot said.

The words felt like a slap across my face. Polyglot was right, of course. My motive for wanting sex was to spite Elke, and I felt ashamed.

"Ouch, Polyglot! I guess I needed that reminder," I stammered.

"I do love you," Polyglot added.

"I know," I said.

For two more weeks, I continued to brood. Near the end of that time, I woke in the middle of the night with a flash of awareness about a mystical experience that happened when I was two. I had touched an antique doorknob in Mary's studio and saw a vision of a brother and sister who were being forced to separate. Clearly these two represented my bisexual nature that society did not approve of. Recognition that even then at some preconscious level I was struggling to assert my true identity and grieving the prospect of caving in to societal norms was not the surprising part of this new insight. I was neck deep in challenging society at the time I wrote the *Third Song* when I was in college. What struck me so powerfully now was the realization that I had expressed this inner struggle through the incest of the characters Moon and Meteor. Elke was right that I was in denial about my fascination with incest. That it was incest between me and myself was no excuse. I had been nursing a grievance on false pretenses.

Reconciliation with Elke was now imperative. When she answered the door of her cottage and saw me standing there holding a jar of *lilikoi* butter, she carefully took the jar from my hands and set it on the doormat, burst into tears, and fell into my arms.

"I missed you so much," she said while hiccoughing.

"I missed you too," I said.

Though neither of us has made any promises or uttered a word about it, we have remained monogamous and faithful to one another ever since.

Her pregnancy advanced in normal fashion. There were no signs of pathology in the fetus, and no complications with the mother. On July 7,

2024, at the West Maui Hospital, Elke delivered a healthy girl, (7 pounds 7 ounces, 21 inches) whom we jointly named Athena Makana Goodsen, and whom we would raise together as our daughter. Enjoying the same non-coincidence as with my children, Athena was born on her mother's birthday.

The attending obstetrician and doula both expressed surprise at how smoothly labor and delivery had proceeded. Elke and I knew that genetic manipulation greatly contributed to the easy birth but could not tell them that. Elke told both women that her vegetarian diet and regular exercise were factors, which she believed to be true.

Despite his impressive intuitive power, K. P. never suspected that Elke's baby was his biological daughter and my granddaughter. Perhaps he did not want to know this, because as she grew, Athena showed obvious facial similarities with my family and the extrasensory gifts associated with our clan.

K. P. graduated from Punahou in 2025, re-establishing a family accomplishment when he was named valedictorian. My mom enjoyed that honor, but it skipped my generation. The Honolulu Star-Advertiser published a nice article about K. P. including that he came from a family of naturists. He then followed the family tradition of enrolling at Anasazi College in Sedona and was delighted at the opportunity to live once again at Angel Nest.

Elke, Athena, and I also visited Angel Nest, where many people fussed over the baby. As previously worked out, Elke and I left Athena in the care of family there, while we embarked on a cruise to New Zealand with stops at Tahiti and Pitcairn Island on the way and Fiji and Cook Island on the way home.

Time at sea among the hordes of tourists on the cruise ship felt like energy-sapping introvert abuse to us, but we recharged by regularly floating out of our bodies and exploring the ocean depths and riding the wind with flocks of birds. As neither of us use alcohol and both of us are vegetarians, the food and drink on board seemed disgustingly excessive. The worst part was watching our fellow passengers ingest and imbibe vast quantities of harmful things. It brought to mind Key's comment years earlier about Homo sapiens drugging themselves with food, eating themselves into an evolutionary dead end. Here was evidence of that.

Frequently we made love in our cabin, inventing a new way to do it.

While Elke lay on the bed, I left my body and nestled inside hers, focusing my energy on bringing her to orgasm. Then she did the same for me. The climactic sensation is tremendous, different from a normal orgasm and more prolonged. She likened it to having sex with a ghost and then clarified to say with an angel.

"Or maybe a witch?" I said.

"Witch or angel, either would be good. It feels like magic sex, in any case," she replied.

Whenever we got to a port, Elke and I set off on our own, avoiding the tourist shops, and explored areas where we felt mystical energy. We did this in and out of our bodies. Every place pulsed with transcendence, but not in the places tourists tended to congregate.

Then we retrieved Athena and flew back to Maui. Although she was happy to see us, Athena clearly had been spoiled while we were away. I think she would have been content to stay at Angel Nest.

Once we were again settled in at ***Anela Punana***, Polyglot came to visit to teach Elke the ***dzjing*** [rising sigh] technique so we could more easily travel to Uluru and Angel Nest as a family.

CHAPTER TWENTY-FOUR
METAPHOR AND FAMILY

Recounting tales of sexual adventures can become tedious after a time, so I will not risk dulling the reader's mind or depleting the reader's energy with further repetitive details of these matters, except to say that I'm still having them on a regular basis.

Now in 2044, Elke and I are still together, although neither of us has felt any need for a formal marriage ceremony. She is fond of telling me I am *sui generis* and I say the same to her. If either of us does something unusual or outside the norm in a public setting or causes a salesclerk, for example, to do a metaphorical head-scratching, the other will quietly say, "S. G." It's our private endearment. Together we are auctors of a new form of humanity, each contributing adaptations aimed at aiding and encouraging evolution. We would make good subjects for an evolutionary psychology project seeking to identify mental and conceptual adaptations in addition to the changes in our physical organs.

Dull repetition can also arise when writing about teaching, even in graduate school. I take pride in my accomplishments as a professor, but that position does not define my identity. Rather than become an antiquated fixture in the classroom, I opted to retire at the end of the last academic year. Most of my colleagues choose to continue teaching into their seventies or even beyond. Not me.

Each class was interesting in the gestalt of the moment, but a certain degree of repetition inevitably invades the narration in the enterprise of education. Despite odd tidbits of revised data and the momentary excitement of novel paradigms, lectures turn into oral blurs. The faces of students blend into anonymous icons in my mind because over the years so many of them with different names and faces were nevertheless so much alike in personality and intellect.

Multiple voices asked the same stale questions and repeated the same old objections to new perspectives and emerging concepts. Looking back, I am amazed at how patient I became with timid minds who worked so hard at compartmentalizing their thoughts, lest they integrate their actual experiences with science and spirituality. As budding theologians, they sought to force metaphors into doctrines, rather than deftly use metaphors as doorways for comprehending reality.

Only a score of my students retain their individual identities in the cells of my brain. A rare few were brave enough to mix clay and fantasy with vigor and joy, but those memorable few have made the enterprise spectacularly worthwhile.

Since my teaching career was in graduate school, I never had occasion to deal with young students who behaved like I had in stultifying primary and secondary educational environments. But I did encounter students who had gone through public school experiences similar to mine. Whenever I could gather together two or three of them, I arranged extra credit tea parties so they could exchange memories and expose old frustrations to the light of appreciative and comprehending conversation. Not only was it comforting to reinforce the notion that they (and I) were not alone, but it was outright rollicking fun to tell outrageous stories without censorship or exhortations to grow up. All in all, these were therapeutic socials, which benefited me as much as my students.

I have not retired to sip fresh fruit smoothies on the lanai, however. Elke and I do that, but we have active agendas for the years ahead.

What most excites me today is the Metaphorical Scripture Seminar, an organization that I conceived, developed, and now serve in unhierarchical fashion as Convener. Our first in the flesh convention occurred last February here in Lahaina, although many of us had been meeting electronically for years. Pacific Crossroads graciously made available an auditorium and housing for participants, and it was not difficult to convince scholars and religious leaders from northern and southern climes to gather in temperately balmy Maui that time of year.

The Metaphorical Scripture Seminar attracts eminent participants representing all the major religions around the world. Our primary goal is to encourage people to embrace the scriptures of their particular traditions as metaphorically true rather than literally so. We believe that if Buddhists, Christians, Hindus, Jews, and Muslims would focus their religious energies on the figurative truths in their traditions rather than defending them as exclusive and infallible, comprehensive world peace could be more than a naïve dream.

A secondary goal is to provide moral and intellectual support to progressive reformers in various religious organizations. The common view of MSS participants is that Christianity and Islam stand in greatest need of doctrinal reform, Hinduism and Judaism only slightly less so, while Buddhists could benefit but are least needful among the big five.

Leaders from many other world religions take part in our proceedings, of course, but these five traditions currently contribute the most to international instability and thus deserve the greatest scrutiny because of their cultural impact.

Now, none of these religions is monolithic, and despite the continuity of hyper-orthodox elements, each has healthy progressive movements active within it. Yet speaking for my tradition, too many pastors and priests who clearly know better are nevertheless afraid to tell their lay people that for all its spiritual riches the Bible is self-contradictory and cannot reasonably be taken literally.

Thus the word *encourage* in our primary goal is most apt. We seek to hearten and instill with courage those who must carry the news of metaphorical scripture to their members. Literalist clergy tend to have rigid spines to stand up for their arrant nonsense. Why then shouldn't progressives show their backbones as well?

I expect harvesting the fruits of the Metaphorical Scripture Seminar to account for a major portion of my remaining lifetime. Yet without doubt I shall continue to pursue other interests, such as studying evolutionary trends in various languages and searching out the identity of the biological father of my son K. P.

The word heretic is a noteworthy example of how words shift meaning. A heretic was once someone who proclaimed false doctrine, the word carrying entirely negative and antisocial connotations. In the 20th century it took on the additional more positive sense of a person who challenges conventional orthodoxy, though retaining its technical meaning with regard to religious traditions.

In this century, the primary meaning of heretic has come to be one who thinks independently and is not mindlessly bound to moribund dogma or pathological superstitions. Hence heresy has evolved etymologically from a wicked act into a virtuous intellectual enterprise. How wonderfully ironic!

Another interesting linguistic shift has occurred with the word God-fearing. Originally it referred favorably to the quality of respecting God but changed to mean fearful of God with regard to human moral behavior. Now God-fearing is taken to describe cowardly cringing at the supposed malevolence of God.

From an early age and without changing my approach to matters of religion or science, I have used the word heretic self-descriptively, bearing the epithet proudly. For the formative years of my life, this placed me in a class of socially suspect people, and so did being a naturist, but I gloried in the essential iconoclasm of both endeavors. Now it seems on both accounts I have become -wonder of wonders- a role model.

Suffice it to say that thus far my family life, my love life, and my professional life have been immensely satisfying, with far fewer episodes of grief than I could have expected given the contrary nature of my personality.

To the long painful ordeal of my primary and secondary education, I now have a less caustic understanding, thanks to a chance encounter nearly a decade ago. By coincidence, I was visiting Angel Nest during the same week as the 40th year reunion of my high school class. I did not attend, but while doing an errand in town, I happened to meet a classmate who had been among the coterie of my tormenters.

She recognized me first and called my name. When she told me her name, I mentally noted that she had put on a lot of weight but seemed comfortable with it.

"You should pop in at the reunion," she said. "You've gone further than anyone else in the class, what with a PhD, and writing books, and being a professor, and all."

"I have no interest in seeing people who called me a freak," I said.

"I always admired you, Zara," she responded. "And so did lots of other girls."

"I never had that impression," I replied.

"You always seemed to have it together. The rest of us were insecure, trapped into playing roles assigned to us by the dominant girls. We were all confused, scared, and embarrassed of our flaws. Eventually, though, most of us grew out of it."

This brought me a sense of peace and understanding that felt like a gift of grace.

I have produced this brief memoir three years earlier than Key's benchmark of age seventy. If my life continues to evolve as I hope and plan, less than half my span of years has passed, but in any case, barring an unforeseen catastrophe, I anticipate having more to chronicle in as little as three or four decades from now.

My parents are still living, though long retired. My dad became a chipper centenarian last year and is well on his way to 101 next month. Mom is physically hale and mentally as sharp as ever at 92, still writing a diary that I hope to read someday.

In recent years I have been able to see my brother Whitman and his dear wife, Annagreta Fife Morgan, with some frequency, as they both teach anthropology at the University of Hawaii, Manoa campus, only a short flight away for either of us. They remain actively involved in the Honolulu Natural Christian Church. I am grateful to have family members so close. When they were on the faculty at the University of Oregon, I saw them only at holiday visits. Their children, my nephew and niece, Mead Fife Morgan, born in 2012 and Macaskie Fife Morgan, born in 2014, are grown now and doing well living on the mainland.

Sometimes Elke and I go on floating expeditions with Whit and Annagreta, which is always wholesome fun. There are so many mystical places to explore on Oahu. Our favorite spots are Kaena Point (the westernmost tip of the island), Kolekole Pass in the Waianae Mountains, and the Ko'olau Range.

Whit is the only one of the Morgan kids, as we were known in childhood, to have been shortchanged in the sexuality department, being hopelessly straight. But he has never been one to complain, and he and Annagreta enjoy a deeply satisfying marriage.

My sister Darrow has become a nationally respected civil rights attorney. Since she now lives in New York City, we seldom cross paths, but she has written that she plans to be at the next Angel Nest family reunion, so I look forward to seeing her then.

Darrow had a number of love affairs with interesting men and women over the years, but eventually she embraced a lesbian identity and in 2011 married a multimedia artist, Vera Archer, after same-sex marriage became legal in New York. In 2013, she bore a child by the same anonymous sperm donor I had used. Darrow's daughter, Maddow Person Morgan, therefore is both cousin and sister to my son K. P. and aunt to his daughter Athena.

For a reason I never understood, Darrow rejected a bisexual identity. First came her relationships with men only and then the switch to women only. I much prefer my pattern of switching back and forth and even combining them. But Darrow is quite happy with her life, so what I prefer doesn't matter.

My children, K. P. and Harbinger, are healthy adults with interesting and challenging lives, as is my granddaughter Athena. I fully expect that each will be the subject of noteworthy biographical studies at some juncture. But that is not for me to tell.

From time to time, ignorant people have mischaracterized me as cold and uncaring. I have been described as a coolly rational academic. But I well know the laughing fervency that swirls inside me and have tried to reveal some of that in this tale. If, on the other hand, I have described my antagonists in this essay as two-dimensional or stereotypes, it's because that is how I experienced them at the time. For all I know, Thirel Messer may be a complex person with a nuanced personality, but I never saw it.

What I trenchantly believe is that, for the most part, my life has unfolded in beneficent ways, and what I think and feel have always been closely attuned. Thinking and feeling are so intimately entwined in my mind that separating them serves no ultimate purpose.

Yet I am able to name certain singular feelings that provide memorable texture to my life. Rising out of my body and gazing fixedly at the midday sun with no harm to my eyes is one example. Sight when out-of-body involves a form of perception not requiring physical organs. I find the sun to be a more splendid object for meditative wonder than the moon, although both fill my soul with light that warms but does not burn.

Whenever I have been out floating, the first moment after returning to my physical body is one of exquisite sensate pleasure that is pure feeling without conscious thought and which makes going back always an alluring prospect.

Opening a new book with an intriguing title provides intellectual stimulation but also a distinct feeling of anticipation, impatience, and yearning for emotional satisfaction. When approaching books, I am a thoroughgoing romantic.

As for living intimately with two different hominid species, I feel privileged and blessed at the opportunities to have done so. Since my introduction to Sojourner came at an early age, moving back and forth between human and Merven communities has seemed ever a natural and matter-of-fact occurrence. Learning the Merven language, however, has greatly shaped my conceptual patterns. Until I studied Merven, I had been thinking in sequentially connecting angles and lines. Now I think in spirals where past, present, and future often coincide in different places at the same time.

IV
A BRIGHTER GARDEN

All prophets are more or less fussy.
Samuel Butler

You can't teach an old dogma new tricks.
Dorothy Parker

Here is a little forest, whose leaf is ever green,
Here is a brighter garden where not a frost has
been.
Emily Dickinson

CHAPTER TWENTY-FIVE
DISCOVERING DAD, EDITING MOM

Sadness permeated my senses when I deposited two manuscripts of my autobiography (Merven and English) in the Merven Library. Following Polyglot's suggestion, I kept duplicate copies in each language for my personal library. Despite the optimism I had felt while I was actually writing, once the task was done, I felt sad. Completing the task that Key had given me now seemed to signify that little of significance remained for me in the years ahead. At 67, I was physically fit, internally healthy, and enjoyed the face and body of someone about 42. But the important milestones, including my academic career, were in the past.

And yet, I never should have worried about the future. There is more to report, though the pace of activities has slowed considerably. The garden still brings forth beautiful flowers, perhaps all the brighter because I pay them more attention now. I no longer feel the need to fill each day with multiple tasks, and not every thing I do must have significance beyond personal enjoyment.

Earlier in my life I ate mostly for nourishment and secondarily for enjoyment. Now Elke and I can spend days in the kitchen preparing gourmet meals and taking all the time we want to savor them.

Although at an earlier time Elke and I had decided not to entangle our lives with a legal marriage, when we reached 70, we changed our minds. We were both in stellar health but recognized that tragic accidents could happen to anyone. In addition to wills, we wanted to make sure that the survivor had unrestricted control over our respective estates, especially literary works and other intellectual property. We had been living together in ***Anela Punana*** for more than two decades, as it had made no financial sense to maintain two residences within walking distance. So on my father's one-hundred-fourth birthday, November 1, 2047, we got married. Neither of my parents was able to attend, and Elke would not have invited any of her Danish relatives even if they were still living. We had a brief, simple ceremony at home officiated by the young pastor of the new NCC congregation on Maui and witnessed by Athena and K. P.

My dad died peacefully in 2048. My mom followed him in 2053. Of course I grieved their passings, but each had made it into triple digits, and both had led exciting and satisfying lives. Their departures merely opened the way for my siblings and me to represent the senior generation of the Angel nest clan.

Key never told me the name of K. P's biological father, and Polyglot, who had access to Merven documents containing that information, refused to open them on my behalf. Nevertheless, now well into my seventies, I decided to conduct an intentional search for him, relying primarily on observation and intuition. Since I knew that the sperm donor had connections with the Angel Nest community, and was therefore a kindred spirit of sorts, I began to think of the man not as an unknown donor but as Key Person's mysterious dad.

Whenever physically present at the Sedona Angel Nest, I paid attention to the extra-sensory behavior and commentary of males within a decade of my age in either direction. Those who shared close genealogical roots with me were eliminated from consideration.

At the reunion in 2055, I overheard Isaac Nabi talking about his bi-sexual twins. "Geniuses can be difficult to relate to," he said. "They inhabit their peculiar worlds to which mere mortals are barred from entry."

"But you have a genius IQ yourself," my brother Whitman responded to Isaac.

"Perhaps, but Benjamin and Rebekah take whatever intellect I possess to a geometrically higher level," Isaac said. "But it's not only that. They also talk to one another and their spouses, carrying on lengthy conversations, telepathically. Have you ever tried to join in a telepathic conversation? I feel completely ignorant. And I swear, they can alter their complexions at will, becoming lighter or darker as they wish. Where did that evolutionary trait come from?"

"Complexion doesn't have anything to do with intellect," Whit said. "But the ability to change skin color is a recent evolutionary development. The adaptation from darker to lighter skin is only about 8000 years old, roughly within historical times. Because of the climate, people living in Northern Europe had less exposure to sunlight. The absence of sun on their skin led to vitamin deficiencies. A mutation for lighter skin spread quickly in the population, aiding the survival of those who had it. Lighter colored skin absorbs more sunlight. In sunnier climes, darker skin color prevents too much sun. It was an evolutionary balancing act. The bottom line is that so-called white people are a recent development and not normative for humankind as a whole. It's not a marker of superiority but of choosing to live in places with lousy weather."

Isaac laughed. "Yeah, but my kids insist on having it both ways. They alter their skin color to suit the environment they're in. But they have to be careful when traveling, because their passport photos don't change color. They've both been hassled at ports of entry because their faces were significantly darker or lighter than their photos, depending on where they'd been. One time Ben quickly lightened his face to match the passport while the control officer was staring at the photo. The officer was startled to look up and see the face now matched the photo. He seemed suspicious, but my son planted the notion in his head that a passing shadow had been responsible for the difference. Bekah's even better at planting ideas in peoples' brains than Ben is."

I had to interrupt. "Pardon me, Isaac, could I have a word with you - privately? Whit, would you mind?"

"What is so important that your brother can't hear it?" Whit said.

"Perhaps nothing," I replied. "But please indulge your older sister for a moment. I suspect that you will hear of it soon enough."

Whit excused himself and I looked Isaac in the eyes. "Have you ever donated to a sperm bank?"

He blushed and said, "That's an extremely personal and intrusive question that doesn't deserve an answer."

"OK," I said. "You don't need to answer it aloud, because I just read the answer in your mind."

Isaac knew that this was true.

"Another question; were you influenced by Sojourner to donate?"

"Yes," he admitted.

"Would you like to meet your other son? And by the way, you have another daughter too, as well as a granddaughter."

The look on his face was a mixture of bewilderment and joy. At his age, there would be no question of parental responsibility for them. Isaac was not the type to measure such things financially, but he has always been one who devoted much quality time to child rearing.

"I have more children?" he whispered. "Somehow in my mind I never connected sperm donation with parenthood. I knew it was possible but honestly thought no one would ever choose mine. Apparently two women did."

"Unnecessarily modest as ever," I said. "The other woman is Darrow. Neither of us knew it was your sperm when we made use of it, but I learned later from a Merven source that the donor had a connection to Angel Nest. So, I've been keeping my ears and eyes open, and you provided a major clue when you mentioned Ben and Bekah altering their skin color. K. P. can do that too."

"I've always been fond of K. P. There's something about him I find very appealing," Isaac said. "I had no idea you used artificial insemination. I assumed K. P. came from a dalliance while you were at Stanford."

"That rumor made the rounds," I said. "I didn't start it but did nothing to quash it. However, I never confirmed it, because that would have been a lie."

Thus, K. P. and Maddow met their biological father and Athena her grandfather. All of them were pleased.

The next day, I telepathically advised Polyglot that I had discovered the identity of K. P.'s dad.

"Key was confident that you would figure it out on your own," Polyglot said. "It is much more satisfying that way."

"It is indeed," I replied and sent along a telepathic smile of satisfaction.

<><><>

In her will, Mom bequeathed to me what had become a succession of handwritten journals. Some were blank books and others were bound note pads. She had not made entries daily or in any disciplined pattern following the calendar but wrote at kairos moments. She was consistent, however, in dating what she wrote.

As soon as I had them in hand, I read through all of them, enjoying a wonderful journey through Mom's life. I was struck by the fact that she had invented a pronoun for use with references to Merven. I could have made use of that, if she'd ever told me about it. On the other hand, I had ample opportunity to do the same but never thought of it. Mom used the word *fam* as an intersexual pronoun, which she developed from the initials of "female and male."

Elke read the diaries, too, and said that others in my family would want the chance to do the same. She suggested I edit them and put them in a format for publication so as to make copies available to the rest of the family. Though I recognized that she was right, for a reason I don't understand, I procrastinated and set them aside.

After discovering the identity of K. P's biological father, however, I felt a burst of energy connected with the task of editing the series. Though it was a time consuming task, I completed the job and arranged for it to be privately published in one large volume entitled *Terp's Diary*.

To be honest, her writing did not need much editing. The major issue was organizing the material and transferring it to an electronic file. In several places I changed the word hermaphrodite to intersexual, recognizing that I was making an anachronism, but by that time, I had mellowed about such matters. In the years since she began writing, the term hermaphrodite had fallen into disfavor, so I deliberately chose to replace it with a preferable word. At the time Mom used it, however, hermaphrodite was the commonly used word. It did not become mildly offensive until much later.

Since I had derived great joy from reading what my mom had chronicled over the course of her adult life, I made it possible for all my siblings and their offspring to do the same. Indeed, this volume has enjoyed great favor among multiple generations of the Angel Nest family.

With regard to anachronisms, it now seems to me that a deliberate anachronism, one that the writer or creator is aware of, can make an artful juxtaposition or fine joke. During the brief time I was on Facebook, a frequently posted meme depicted a quote to the effect that not everything on the Internet is true, attributed to Abraham Lincoln.

CHAPTER TWENTY-SIX
SIDE EFFECTS OF AGING
SLOWLY

Soon after my hundredth birthday, I received an inquiry from the Social Security Administration as to whether I was still alive. I wrote back with assurances that not only were my wife and I still among the living but noted that both my parents had survived into triple digits. Elke also received such a letter and responded similarly, except that her parents had died much earlier than mine, so she could not boast about them as I had.

Thereafter, it seemed that Social Security and my pension plan displayed ghoulish interest in the state of my health, including demands for periodic proof that I still drew breath.

More troublesome than these bureaucratic inconveniences, however, were the questions and comments from people in our community. How could I explain that I was aging very little compared with virtually everyone else? To say that I was manipulating my DNA would sound crazy, though it was true. I fell into the habit of laughing it off by saying it was due to excellent genes and adding that my parents were centenarians.

But it was becoming increasingly difficult to explain away the issue. When we married at 70, Elke and I looked extremely youthful for that age. The county clerk assumed there had been typos in our dates of birth and only reluctantly accepted our applications as submitted. And so, when we reached 90, Elke and I made the difficult decision to leave our beloved Maui and move to Angel Nest in Arizona. There, at least, we could live in a community where we would be sheltered from suspicious questions and where the truth would be believed.

Life back in Sedona was bittersweet because of the absences of so many people I had grown up with and loved. Being the last survivor of one's generation can bring on a peculiar form of depression, and I already had a history with that ailment. But I experienced more joy than sorrow. Elke and I still floated regularly. It was great fun to guide her to the many places in Central Arizona that had meant so much to me in my formative years. I kept mentally active and in time became a mentor to Angel Nest children more than a century younger than I. They delighted in hearing my stories about what life was like in the olden days of the Wild West, especially descriptions about the primitive technology we employed. They were aghast to learn that public nudity was illegal during my childhood and many people considered it immoral. In turn, I delighted to see the evolution that Key had predicted actually unfolding in these subsequent generations.

In the year that Elke and I turned 105, the Social Security Administration sent an investigator to meet with us in person in order to confirm that we were still alive. The agent, Dylan Stearns, hated people defrauding the government, and his investigative efforts had resulted in millions of dollars returned to the SSA.

It was a common practice for adult children to hold power of attorney and joint ownership of the banking accounts of elderly parents. Sometimes, those adults failed to notify the SSA when a parent died, and the monthly benefits continued to be deposited directly into those accounts. This was only one of the ways the system was bilked, and Agent Stearns was justifiably indignant at the fraud and proud of his recovery efforts.

When Dylan Stearns met with Elke and me, we were clad in the standard Angel Nest uniform of khaki shorts and white tee shirts. He seemed a little nervous.

"Is this your first time in a naturist residence?" I asked.

"It is," he answered. "I didn't know if you would be dressed. I'm glad you are."

"It is a matter of etiquette when meeting with textiles," Elke said. "Fair warning, however. Not everyone here has covered up for your visit."

He shrugged and diplomatically said, "Can you tell me the secret of your longevity?"

I responded, "Have you ever read *Lost Horizon*?"

"No, but I've seen the movie," he replied. "I'm a bit of a classic film buff."

"Which one, the 1937 film or the 1973 musical version?" Elke asked.

"Neither," he replied. "I saw the 2057 remake."

"Do you remember the High Lama?" I said.

"Of course," Dylan said. "Rupert Grint won an Oscar for that role."

"Well, Angel Nest is a kind of Shangri-La hidden in plain view," I explained. "Similar to the High Lama, Elke and I make use of arcane techniques for life extension. We learned them from someone who grew up in Tibet. We could easily live three or four more decades."

He looked skeptical, so I reinforced the story with a telepathic suggestion that it was indeed true, and he seemed to relax. As if on cue, a group of naked children gamboled through the room, giggling as they went. Dylan turned to watch them for a few seconds and then returned his attention to us.

"That reminds me a number of scenes in *Lost Horizon*," he said. "This really must be Shangri-La."

"Is there nudity in the 2057 version?" Elke asked.

"Quite a bit, actually," he said. "Not the High Lama, of course, but various residents of the place skinny dip or go horseback riding or do gardening in the nude."

"It would be even better if the High Lama were nude. That would be worth watching," I said.

"We should watch it anyway," Elke commented to me.

"Let's do that. I imagine the church library has a copy. But first we have business with Mr. Stearns," I said. "Many years ago, I was falsely arrested. I was quickly released, and the subsequent trial of my accuser is well documented. But in the course of my arrest, I was fingerprinted. I am willing to be fingerprinted again to prove that I am who I am."

"We don't do that anymore," Dylan said. "The practice is antiquated."

Elke then said, "How about DNA samples? We'd be happy to provide those."

"I was just about to ask for that," said Agent Stearns. "Have either of you provided DNA samples to any government entity in the past?"

"Not that I know of," I replied.

"Well then, the samples won't help in confirming past identities, but will provide a basis for future confirmation," he said. "I think we have enough documentation to continue benefits for the present. In all likelihood, you will be asked to submit DNA material every five years."

Apparently, Dylan had taken a liking to us, because a few weeks later, Elke and I received an unofficial note from him, saying that DNA tests confirmed that both of us had genetic markers for exceptional longevity. He wrote, "The techs in the lab were floored by the lengths of your telomeres, both of you. Normally the telomeres protecting the ends of chromatids shorten as people age, as I'm sure you know. In both your cases, your telomeres are longer than those of a 50-year old."

Our telomeres retained their lengths for the retest when we reached 110, and only slightly shortened in subsequent checks.

In future decades, Elke and I became the two oldest people in the Social Security system. Since Elke is three months (to the day) older than I, she wins the prize for being the oldest (human) person in this country and probably the world. Within that arcane bureaucratic world of government benefits, we became celebrities. Over the years, we received unauthorized communications from many administration employees who admired us and wished us many more years. Our cases were monitored closely, of course, and rumors came to us that various officials had made bets relating to when we would croak. So far, all the bettors have been disappointed.

I still run, making circuits around the Angel Nest property and longer runs on the NCC campus, usually naked. Sometimes I itch to run in regional Ten-Ks. I would be guaranteed first place, because there would be no one else in my age group. However, that would draw attention to my age and give me unwanted publicity as well as raise intrusive questions about my longevity. Elke said I would probably be accused of cheating or witchcraft. Were it not for floating expeditions, I would feel as if I were under house arrest.

Elke and I spend time each week tutoring young Angel Nesters in the techniques of ***doomoo leeekaadzg*** and ***dzjing*** [rising sigh], as well as the Merven language. They don't need to be taught how to float, converse telepathically, change skin color, or control aging, for they were born knowing these things.

Teaching youngsters is a new experience for me, as my professional career was spent with graduate students, and I find it very satisfying. These young ones are not competitive the way grad students are, and they eagerly soak up the subjects. At the end of one morning session, a happy student proclaimed, "Professor E and Professor Z, you are the best. Between the two of you, learning is EZ."

That put a glow in the rest of our day. It feels good to be productive and still count for something.

CHAPTER TWENTY-SEVEN
THE ANTI-MOSES

As I write this, dawn has come on April Fools Day of 2130. I am 152 years old and very near the end of my life. Biblical literalists believe that in Deuteronomy 34, Moses described his own death and the events following it. As anyone reading this knows well, I am not a literalist, and I am not so filled with hubris as to make predictions about how long people will mourn for me or whether anyone will weep at all. My siblings and my age cohorts in the Angel Nest community are long dead, for half a century more or less.

Sojourner died of natural causes last year. So did Elke. A week before she passed away, she joined the church by anointing with oil, rather than baptism. I loved them both and still ache at not hearing their voices except in my imagination.

And yet, I am able to hear the much younger voice of Elke, from a time decades before I met her. The technology for screening her old films is long outmoded, but last week, with the help of a great grandchild, I managed to dig up an ancient DVD player so that I could watch some of them. She was such a beauty in those days, so innocent and unaffected. Her face radiated a wholesome eagerness that made her look like she was having good clean fun, the kind a mother would approve. Ironically, in this case Elke's mother did approve. I cried and cried and loved every minute of seeing her young and bursting with sexual fun.

Pilgrim, Quester, and Polyglot are still alive, and they visit me from time to time. So too do Athena, Harbinger, and K. P. These will weep for me when I die, I imagine, but not excessively. I've had a longer run than any human they know, although absent any unforeseen catastrophes, their runs should be longer and their offspring longer yet.

Chief Librarian Key once suggested that I might be the Eve of a new hominid species. This is a label I must reject. Too many other women and men have contributed to the evolutionary vanguard of what is emerging. I am more like an Anti-Moses. I did not lead a slave revolt and guide a disgruntled band through the wilderness but rather have cooperatively played a key part in a genetic revolution. Pun intended.

My will specifies cremation and that my ashes be scattered from the air over the Red Rock-Secret Mountain Wilderness. Like Moses, then, the exact location of my remains will be unknown to history. Unlike Moses, however, I have been denied nothing. Not only have I seen the Promised Land but have been privileged to live in it. I have loved many people and have been infatuated with so many more. I have loved many places and have become infatuated with even more. I have loved animals and books and music and ideas and have been infatuated with simply being alive. And that love has been reciprocated so fully that I am overwhelmed with gratitude. Now I am eager to pass into the unknown, whether it be to embrace another adventure or oblivion.

Editorial Note:

Zara Person Morgan died on her half-birthday, April 7, 2130. Her children, grandchildren, and three more generations of her family keenly mourned her passing and have endeavored to keep her memory alive.

K. P. inherited her intellectual property, which included Elke's books and films, because his mother had gained those when Elke died. However, K. P. turned over those items to Athena, so that he could concentrate on serving as executor for his mother's literary estate. Zara's unpublished papers, along with those of Elke, were donated to the Merven Library in Uluru. The books that Zara and Elke had co-written were entrusted to Athena's care. K. P. privately published the epic poem Zara had written while in college, *The Third Song of Creation*, and it has found a place of esteem among the Angel Nest community equal to the work of Zara's mother, *Terp's Diary*

This edition of Zara's autobiography differs from the one she submitted in two installments to the Merven library at Uluru. The last part was entrusted to Harbinger a few days before her death. For this version, K. P. rearranged the beginning and ending places of some chapters and renumbered them. He also wrote all of the chapter titles, including those in the sections marked with Roman numerals. Zara created the first four of these sections and selected the quotes at the beginning of each but did not name them. K. P. added section V.

At the time of her death, Zara had been listening to music on a sound projector that sensed when she was no longer listening and stopped playing. Thus, we know the last earthly song she heard before passing from this realm of existence. It was a love duet from the Broadway musical *Kismet*, sung by Alfred Drake and Doretta Morrow, and based on the work of composer Alexander Borodin, with lyrics and musical adaptation by Robert Wright and George Forrest.

The reader may wonder whom she was remembering as she listened to this final song. Knowing his mother's nature, K. P. was certain she had images of two lovers in mind as she savored "And This Is My Beloved."

V
THE THIRD SONG OF CREATION

*Millions of spiritual creatures walk the earth
unseen, both when we wake and when we sleep.*
John Milton

The Third Song of Creation

a myth in five seasons

Zara Person Morgan

Contents

Summer: The Garth

I

The day that humans count as sixth was not an equal
Day in spring. It was Midsummer's Eve, a solstice day
When God the Androgyne -in gravid mood- was ruminating.
"I will make two lovers fit for me -two limber,
Sensuous and cerebrating creatures suitable for dancing
And for adding charm and entertainment to my seasoned garth."
And through the brevity of night God labored, pushing,
Panting, so at sunrise, moist with dew the two soft
Lovers stretched their arms and legs into the longest
Interval of sun the year could give. They knew not then
Each day that they would live would end a little sooner
That the one before, until at half a year their shivers
Would induce them into wearing woven fiber coats.
But it was balmy when the breath of God condensed
Into that dream which bonded with saliva, soil
And summer fruit to form a female and a male.
"Oh see how very good we are," God said. "The curves
And skin and nerves within encasing the magnetic force
Of twins, together recreating my imagination. See
How beautiful they are, I am." God laughed delightedly.

II

"I see," the angel said, "but what of me?
What's happened to the wind we used to make
To stir the seas and tease the life forms to emerge?
Do you expect to purge the heavens
Of incestuous, angelic love and bid me die?"
"Do I expect? My intersex offspring,
I am expecting much, yet not to purge but merge.
Have patience, holy one. I urge you search for beauty
In my earthy work of art, and I will seek
A time in all of this for you to play a part."

III

The setting for the incubation of the twins was broad,
With corners in Arcadia and Upper Egypt, Ur and Asshur:
Marsh and desert, cedar forest, seacoast sand and fertile land
With curving paths to roam and beds of leaves for rest,
And figs and dates to eat and grapes for fermentation.
Only in the sight of God was this a garden.
It was more than adequate for him and her, from where they
Were that day when they were blown full grown
Out of the mouth of God into an orchard wild and ripe.
They stretched their bodies side by side supine and languished
In the summer shade, titillated by a riant breeze, nipples erect,
Limbs absentmindedly relaxed, breathing slowly, welcoming
The odors of the earth. As soon as they were able to distinguish
Phosphenes from the sun-illumined shafts of dust surrounding them,
They focused eyes on one another's skin
And reached across caressingly with twenty fingers,
Curious and playful. Then their tongues began exploring

Lips and mouths and necks and breasts, and deeper feelings
Grew within these two, and so they knew each other,
Entering, receiving, wet and breathing, parallel and even.

IV

Afterward, at peace in union, tucked contentedly in one another's folds,
She felt a glimpse phosgenic in intensity pass through her mind:
A premonition of the future lit itself and died, taking with it
Conscious memory and leaving sadness without reason.
And she said, "We are I think how men and women ought to be together."
Then she cried and so did he, for he had felt the light pulse
In her brain and knew an omen had been dealt. Now wet
With tears and sexual secretions, warm with sweat, they moved
In unison, joined once again at hips, each giving and receiving
While their voices lowered into laughter, and the moon arose.

V

As summer lumbered on, the woman and the man
Ingeniously discovered one another, learned to play
With all their senses, eagerly initiating waves of pleasure,
Plushing through a thousand places in and on their bodies,
Rident faces brushing one another, cheek to navel,
Tongue to toe, trying every sybaritic way to know
Their corresponding selves. And just before the moon
Made yet another course, a course of blood
Began to flow from her. A cleansing stream
Poured forth, a rich, dark offering returned now to the soil
With thankfulness. A blessing's worth of fertile fluid
Was the gift she gave to earth on this occasion,
And again and yet again through lunar cycles,

Till the wind grew cold and daylight short.
But all that summer he gave white to her and she gave
Red to earth. And they were dancers in the tepid showers,
Crowned themselves with summer flowers, ate the passion fruit
And turned the water into wine with great delight
And gustatory flair. They bathed in sun and slept in shade
And laughed and gloried in the love they made.

VI

He asked, "How does it feel for me to be in you?"
She pulled him near and kissed his face, arching to his mouth,
And pushing with her tongue she slipped beyond his teeth deep
Into his cavern, swept its dimpled sides, pushing, probing
With her tongue. He felt an echo sound between his testicles
And anus, faint and slight, a sense of penetration,
Just enough to cause his tongue to stretch into her mouth
In recognition of her answer. So they spent an hour of the day,
Then two, then three with tongues and lips discovering
Their oral folds and ridges, bumps and tips, taste and aftertaste.

VII

The autumn came; mysterious decay grew up around their bed.
They burrowed into piles of leaves and felt a novel hunger,
Felt a tightening within that was not frightening
But fascinating, calm. Determination rose in them as they
Decided time had come for them to wander far beyond
Their nest in search of other fruits and edibles.
They happened on a wounded deer, and knowing naught
To help, they watched it die. The male thought meat might satisfy
Their hunger, so they cut and dressed the flesh and gorged

On roasted venison, which made them sick to vomiting.
The female said their teeth were better fit for vegetables,
But thought deer hide would do for robes to mitigate the wind.
As winter solstice came they found a cave in which to sleep
And curl together warmly through extended nights.
And strangely, as the moon progressed, her gift of blood
Did not. It ceased, replaced by **mal de mer** from tides within.
And yet she rose with him to search for succulents and nuts
And gather wood to burn. The smoke and scent of roasted nuts
Enfolded them, and seeped inside the granite crevices,
Enhancing appetites for snug and rocky kitchens safe from snow.

VIII

With spring the robes came off, their breathing damp,
The icy dryness gone. The swelling trees were mimicking
Her swollen abdomen, and full of wonder, side by side
They wandered through the yellow fields of grain
And borderlands and forests green, walking naked
Through a world which was re-clothing after months of cold exposure,
Walking to the sea, drawn on by memory and scent.
"It's time," he said, "that you and I should have a name beyond
My Other Self. I name thee Ocean." "I then name thee Shore,"
She said, "for who can tell where ocean ends and shore begins?"

IX

Shore and Ocean sensed their kinship with the universe,
But lacked abstractions for theologizing. Once, when decorating
One another, putting poppies in their pubic hair
And braiding daisies into wreaths, a sense of stimulating peace
Spread evenly between and through them, radiating

Into limbs and hollows, warmly isometric in effect.
"There must be words for this," she said. "The wind of God
Rubs softly as it circles us," he said, inventing language
Out of intuition. "Yes," she said, "yes, yes, the breath of God
Brings pleasure with its air of wet perfume. Shore,
We are part of some enchantment brought to life by God."
"And there are hints of it, dear Ocean, things that we can know
When we are deep in one another. Pleasures of the spirit
Are the same as all the pleasures of anatomy."
Each with half a body, whole together; each with half a soul,
Complete in circling moments, in their knowing one another,
Seeking without knowing why the re-creation of the God
Who made them demigods. "See how they flow together,
Float apart and flow again together," chortled God,
"Connected always by the cord I laced between them."

X

The angel left the chamber not at all amused by God's delight
And sought a corner of the welkin night in which to brood.
"And now they talk of pleasures of the spirit, realizing not
How close they are to consummating their creation. God
Adores them so and leaves me much too often to myself.
My God, my God, have you forsaken me? And just because
I know you well, do you prefer to give attention
To your other arts? Well, after labor day I'll travel to your garden
Studio, interpreting for them the pain in pleasure and the contrasts
In the earth they see but do not understand. They will."

XI

Shore and Ocean spent their birthday on the beach,
Smelling, watching, listening to the ancient sea.
She lay in the sand, content to let it warm her back.
He rose up from swimming, legs and arms remaining in the water,
Back in air, enjoying waves that splashed against his rump.
He crawled to her, arriving at her feet coincidental with the tide
Which washed her heels as he with tongue caressed her toes.
As the waves progressed, lapped up her legs, he too progressed
Until he moved inside her as the tide arose and covered
Both of them, retreating to allow them intervals to breathe,
Re-covering in motions parallel but slower than the holy
Movements they were making. Later, as they lay
Relaxed and motionless, their hearts in rhythmic unison,
His navel over hers, they felt the movements in her womb.
The gentle kicking made them laugh. They knew that life
Was there inside and someday she would open up
To let it out. She thought how painful
That must be but kept this notion to herself. He thought
About attending her, a helpmate in her labor needing
To be calm and reassuring but kept this to himself.

XII

Twins were born in autumn. Shore attended well,
Though labor was prolonged, the pain intense. And Ocean had
The sense that she had wronged the earth somehow to suffer so.
Yet quicker than she thought she healed from all the bursting stress
And nursed her boy and girl while Shore wove wool
To cover him and her. Eight days past giving birth
Shore bathed the girl and swaddled her for warmth

While Ocean said, "I name thee Moon." As soon as that was done
She bathed the boy and also swaddled him
While Shore declared, "I name thee Meteor." Down went the sun.

XIII

God was ruminating, muttering into the Godhead, undelighted
With a certain angel. "I shall have to see how Shore and Ocean
Take to interference from another godly creature. Not that I
Approve of interference, but that feature of free will
Is still the boldest stroke of artistry I've drawn
For either kind. I am resigned to conflict for the sake
Of art, yet I will pray that they will wrestle skillfully
With this or any other angel they encounter."
Presently the angel found a biding place on earth, not far
From Shore and Ocean's cave, and when they ventured out
For food and fuel, the wingy thing accosted them
And asked if they'd been eating from a certain tree.
"Not recently," they said. So angel said, "I wonder if
God's angry with your way of life. For half a year
You practice nudity quite unashamed, two *Akte* acting
Innocent. I wonder if God's blamed you for enjoying
Far too casually the fruit God labored hard to make.
For heaven's sake, you must have given some offense
To God, who gave you life but soon may take it back."
"We've seen no evidence of God's displeasure," Ocean said.

XIV

"And yet your measure is imperfect," said the angel. "Let me
Offer my suggestions. Hasn't earth grown cold not once
But twice? Has not the ice burned fingers, faces, toes?

Was not the pain extraordinary in the throes
Of childbirth? God must certainly be angry to create
Such hindrances to paradise. You must concede my evidence
Is strong. But I can bring amelioration to your wrong."
Just then a serpent slithered from a hole beneath a rock
And curled into a circle, head upon its tail, and chuckled,
"Angels can be clever fibbing. This one's giving you a ribbing."

XV

Then the serpent disappeared. And blushing now, the angel
Rummaged in a duffel kit, pretending nothing had been said
Of any serpentine suspicion. "Now, your sin has brought
To cold fruition all the wrath of God, but I have gifts
For you which I suspect will soon correct the painful
Situation. Here are aprons, breeches, muumuus, hair shirts,
Many garments fit to wear to cover nakedness. But never
Wear them for adornment or protection from the elements.
Just wear them to protect your eyes from one another
Lest you see too much and be entranced by images
Of your Creator. Hide yourselves that you may live.
Now give me some assurance of good faith and I
Will take my leave." "Do you think we will die?" Shore asked.
"I grieve it may be so," the angel said (while thinking:
Yes, I've sown a doubt. This fruit may spoil before it's ripe).
The clothes were stuffed into their arms and then
The angel lifted off against the wind and sailed away.
"What did the serpent say? I am confused," she said.
"And so am I," said he, and older, how much older
In a single day I've grown. The day seems colder."

XVI

Out of gratitude for spring they wore their aprons,
Seeking to determine if offenses had been given and forgiven
And if spring and summer would remain the only seasons
Inexhaustibly. But even with the aprons, supple bodies
Called to one another in repose or movement, so they shed
Their clothes as often as they might and kept them off
At night. And neither flax nor fig leaves could suppress
The kinesthetic charm these lovers felt by force of incarnation.
Therefore, guilty explanations were the harvest offerings they made
When autumn came. God smiled wistfully and for their spirits prayed.

Autumn: Red Wine and Wind

XVII

The angel came to garth again when Moon and Meteor
Had passed successfully through puberty. When they had gained
Those contours reminiscent of their parents in the early days,
The angel thought the time fortuitous for telling them
Some stories of rebelling hosts in heaven, caused
By God's continuing preoccupation with the progeny of earth.
Since Ocean had just given birth again, the children numbered
Seven, and the Androgyne had pollinating plans for tucking
Other full-grown humans into fertile corners of the garden
So that geometric reproduction could begin. "Oh, grin
You rutting creatures, if you must," the angel said. "But I
Will turn your lust for finding God in one another into
Something fearsome, something cultural, repressed at best."
The being shuddered quite theatrically but absent of an audience.
At autumn equinox the angel sailed to earth to find
The twins and found them ingleside upon the beach, engrossed
In roasting apples and in beeking in the glow of flames
Which warmed the salty air now that the sun was once again
Relinquishing superior position. "Oh, God's heart!"
The angel swore, "How beautiful they are."

XVIII

With voyeur's eyes the angel watched them for a while before
Intruding on their naked nonchalance. Streaks of firelight splashed
Against their tans. Their desultory conversation seemed sufficient
For their quiet motions. Meteor stared into flames while Moon arose
With fluid grace, grazed fingers on his face and found a sandy rest
Behind him where she rubbed his neck, massaged his shoulders, swaying
As her fingers kneaded, crooning with her hips, all while her knees
Pressed deeper into warm, receptive sand. She set her face into his neck,
Her legs around his hips, and pressed her breasts into his back.
Moon sent her hands to pleasant mooring in his lap, then sighed.

XIX

The angel's punctuation of their reverie was less dramatic
Than the visitor had hoped. Their xenodochiality caused
Angel's voice to falter for a time, but soon enough the preplanned
Attitude adjusting lecture made its way to speech. "The news,
Dear Twins, is that the residents of heaven now are flapping mad
Because of human impropriety. God worries so about your deeds,
Neglecting to take care of higher things (with wings).
Why don't you two grow up and spare God wounds. Moon,
You're a hoyden, Meteor a wimp. And just because the One
Who made you is an Androgyne, don't think that imprint
Has effect on you. My heavenly advice is go your separate ways.
Seek out the differences in sex and prophesy that men are men
And women women. Never should they fully meet lest
In that meeting they presume to be as whole as God.
And now, before I go, these things you ought to know:
Freikorperkultur and your viticulture are lapsarian pursuits
Which you should shun. And furthermore [and this

The angel had some doubt about but said it anyway]
Beware the innocence of incest, for a limping ampersand
Is likely to result." And with these words the angel fled.

XX

The psychic impress of this verbal apparition made them draw apart.
Neither said a word. And Meteor, by dawn, was westward gone,
In search of one of God's new women, whom he'd meet sunbathing
On a riverbank surrounded by papyrus plants. Her hair
Was black, her nipples, eyes, and skin more dark than any he had yet
To see. "I prayed to Ra for you," she said and stretched one leg
And stroked her calf along his thigh. Then he lay down beside her
For an interval of exploration of her skin with fingers, lips, until
She turned and arched up like a cat and he pressed into her, the tandem
Lovers dancing till their rhythm burst, spilling them into the Nile.

XXI

Moon pursued the eastern coast until she found a man asleep
Beside a pit of china clay. His hands and arms showed chalky patches
From his work, his tablets strewn about the place.
Nude upon a cotton mat he lay, as Moon in silence sat beside him,
Gently teasing him from sleep with fingering along his length.
When he was fully roused, she straddled him and took
His rising sign into her depths, swallowing his sun into the welcome
Darkness of her body. All that day they played, while Meteor
Across the world went on his way. And Moon with morning left the man
Of clay. Each twin moved on to search and know as many as they met.
Yet every quart of knowledge each consumed, though slaking
For the nonce, left aching aftertastes, sharp reminiscences
Of manna neither one had ever known. Moon dreamed of being

Filled by Meteor, her brother groom, and he, in mind, was penetrating
Her, his sister bride, while moving inside every other lover. Drawn, at last,
By inner knowledge of the place, they met inside a garden laced
With ferns and all the greens of early May. They folded into one another,
Kissed in every way they'd learned and rolled onto the fertile
Carpet, making love with every orifice and digit, shouting,
Laughing, letting go so fully that the flora and the fauna surely heard.

XXII

The child that they conceived was born in early February,
Fine and healthy, yet with a quiddity of strangeness,
Something intangibly golden in his face that drew the others
To him with desire and anxiety. They named him Vintager
And set him as he grew to tending vines and making wines.
At seventeen he was a man with female breasts, a slender man
Without a beard, but searing eyes, cerulean in hue, a man
Of intuition who could heal a withered bush or cause a fig
To grow by touch or voice, whenever he would choose. Sometimes
He would refuse. And Vintager was lonely, wanting more than vegetation.

XXIII

The angel came again, expecting to inspect this double creature
Born of twinly incest. Vintager was happy for the visit,
Not at all embarrassed by angelic curiosity. The day was hot,
So Vintager pulled off his tunic as he tended vines and chatted
With his guest. Those angel eyes dilated at the sight of breasts
Which glistened in the sunlight filtered through a tan
Of dust and perspiration. Angel asked and asked about the earth,
While Vintager became aware of rising need for intimate connection
With celestiality. "What is your name?" he asked. The angel

Answered, "Zero." "Well, I want to touch you, Zero." Now the angel
Quivered, pleased yet fearful, since this human was so beautiful,
Magnetic. Vintager caressed a fragile wing and gently with his tongue
Invaded Zero's lips without protest. The angel acquiesced to skillful
Hands which probed electrically for tender places, hungry cavities
Concealed and waiting for affection. Zero's apprehensive fingers stroked
Those fascinating breasts and slipped across the tip and down the sides
Of Vintager's erection. Vintager now found the space he sought
And penetrated deep into a moistness hidden by a skirt of fleshy feathers.
Zero felt the searching semen, cringed, yet lacked the will to counteract
The fluid's work. "I love you, Vintager, though payment be our death."

XXIV

Zero found a cave in heaven for a period of gestation,
Then returned to earth for giving birth. Beside a spring,
With Vintager attending, came into the world a girl appearing
Fully human. Zero said, "I name thee Zephyr, and I give you
To the charge of Vintager, yet I shall watch you grow. And now
I go to God." As Zephyr grew to womanhood her hair and eyebrows
Turned to golden red, with fine white feathers interspersed,
And downy, auburn feathers spread across her mount of Venus.
Zephyr's eyes were turquoise bright, her breasts were slight,
Her arms and legs were slim, but she was ageless in her ripe maturity.

XXV

For seven years past menarche she tended to her parent's vines,
But she was restless, lured by mental images of something
She must find. And each succeeding year the urge grew stronger
For the pilgrimage that she must make to find an unfound place
Which was to be. The call that Zephyr felt increasingly was for

A grand and slippery something which she knew most clearly
When the wind blew lightly on her skin and made her muscles squeeze
With pleasant ache. One day she donned a robe that matched her eyes
And left the fields and wandered to a cliff above the sea.
Two men were arguing about a pregnant woman who was resting
On the beach below. They stopped to look at Zephyr, who approached
Them silently. She reached down to her hem and raised her robe
Precisely over slender legs, above her navel, over breasts and off
Her body. "Now, before you kill for what you feel, take me.
Cast lots for first and promise only that no violence will occur."
The saffron-shirted man was first to slither through her pubic feathers,
Laughing as his fountain burst. The purple-shirted man observed,
Then Zephyr took him into her with captivating gulps of labia,
Deep down into her warm but barren cave. And then she left
While they, now spent, more placidly resumed their argument.

XXVI

A dozen lovers later, Zephyr hiked into a desert, walking leagues
Before a palm oasis rose from a perpetual mirage. And there
She found Simoom, a roughly chiseled man who tolerated trees
For shade but loved to rampage through the shifting dunes.
She thought, "This is a man I do not care to love yet who many teach
Me much about the earth." Without her robe she walked into the water,
Relishing the cool of it. He leaped into the pool, still wrapped in dirty
Bolts of wool, and lifted her into the muddy bank and sank
His staff into her –forcibly– for she was dry despite the swim.
He smothered her with wrath, then left. She cried and took another bath.

XXVII

Zephyr washed away the venom of Simoom and told herself
This pain served as inoculation for experiences to come.
She left the desert, sought the mountains, found a waterfall
That poured into a quartz and mica basin. There she lolled
In solitude for months, until another seeker wandered in to bathe
Away accumulated forest loam. Favonius he called himself.
He wore an undyed cotton sash around his waist, a red silk band
Upon his head, accentuating red-blond hair and beard, which also
Grew profuse and fine across his chest. He asked if he might rest
And trade her stories full of time and curiosity, and she said yes.
Their stories, crafted out of pain and laughter, led to touching,
Running fingers over faces, necks; it led to kissing, licking,
Then undoing garments, lying naked by the basin's edge
And making love so gracefully that neither knew whose motion
Gave or took. They flowed; she bowed her hips toward him,
He lilted into her and out and in; she wrapped her legs in his
And they remained in union forty days and forty nights,
Content to let the world creak on while they restored their souls.
And yet, this foretaste of the end of time was not their end,
And they agreed to roam together and apart in seasons and in space.

XXVIII

Shore and Ocean ceded ground to gravity's relentless aging
Of their bodies, growing slower, thicker, yet their sensate
Needs remained. They never failed to stroke each other,
Finding comfort and the force of life in nerves and skin.
Stretched and scarred and loosening, their tired frames
Gave in to entropy, and yet their spirits were reborn
With each caress, each kiss, each gentle penetration,

Each reception. Every night they lay together, side by side,
Still parallel and even, rocking in the loving rhythm
They perfected over years of being good to one anther.

XXIX

Zephyr wandered home to see the vines and Vintager, and while
Enjoying early, bitter grapes, Simoom appeared, far out of place,
And sought to smother her. But Vintager swept in between them,
Freezing all the strength Simoom could bring and using holy hands
To drive the desert mutilator out to sea. Yet Vintager inhaled
Such sandy draughts that suffocation stole his breath,
And Zero swooped from some invisible redoubt to lift this lover
Up into a cloud of oxygen. Swiftly up they flew, while Zero chanted,
"Prana, prana, fill his lungs!" Then Zero reached the limit
Of angelic muscular control, and for an endless instant
Both peculiar creatures hung in space, with neither breathing.
Then they plunged, wrapped up in one another, to the sea and down
As far as they could sink into an underwater dune that covered
Them, as if to prove they never had disturbed the depths.
Shore and Ocean, Moon and Meteor, and Zephyr made a raft
And sailed it out to sea, and spread the surface of the waves
With wine and grape leaves, feathers, and their salty tears.
In time the fluids sank and sifted over hidden, shifting biers,
And leaves and feathers washed upon the beach within the reach
Of children, who would set them into walls inside a city made of sand.

XXX

Six years had passed since Moon and Meteor had been together.
Each had circled after other lovers, gaining knowledge and experience,
Neither generating any other children. Vintager had seemed sufficient

Praise and folly for a dozen incarnations. Now that he was dead,
They sought each other in a secret lea. The moon was new,
And in her sorrow Moon slipped out of her burnoose, removed
Her muslin sheath, unbuttoned her chemise, let drop accumulations
Of apparel, while the moon -absolved from time- now quartered,
Halved, grew full with her unburdening. Her twin in turn, undressed,
And they took grief to bed, remaining, making love for all that year.

XXXI

Seven years of searching after reasons for her pain brought Zephyr
Empty answered to a riverbank she must have walked upon
Some years before (or else someone she'd known had left
An aromatic memory) because her feathers stood erect
In recognition of the place. The newly risen morning brought her
Warmth and sunly clarity as partners for her meditation.
Thus arose the thought to stay, to cease her wandering and let
The answers come to her. She built a booth of reeds and waited
For a messenger she sensed would come. And soon the angel
Ebenezer came and said, "A fair wind blows this way, a wind
Who knows from intimate rapport the calling you must heed.
This wind will serve your need." A league away, the moment
Ebenezer spoke, Favonius abruptly, without thinking, altered course
A quarter turn, and so within an hour danced into the booth.
Pulling off his cassock, she her shawl, and naked in the shade,
The two embraced to form a synergistic bond. And Zephyr said,
"This river's edge shall be a place for seekers to abide in quest
Without the need of wandering." Favonius said, "I must then
Be wanderer at your behest to set such news in motion."
Yet he stayed a month, and then set out to search for Shore and Ocean.

XXXII

A flock of pilgrims gathered on the bank. Some knelt,
Some stood, some wrapped in linen head and limb, some naked.
Zephyr sang a song she had composed for the occasion:
"This shall be Urania, a city where enchanted dreams
And charms may be expressed and questions asked and inwit
Shared and outwit spoken. This shall be a nexus never broken,
Where all evidence is heard with discipline apart from law.
I pray the grace of God shall permeate Urania, Urania the free."
Then Shore and Ocean, Meteor and Moon, Favonius and Zephyr
And the other charter seekers drank a cask of Vintager's best wine.

Winter: The City

XXXIII

Ebenezer came to Zephyr, who was meditating in a terra cotta tub,
To tell her that her barrenness had been revoked by act of God.
"You proved to be so fertile mentally that God decided not to waste
Your genes," the angel said. "Indeed, you're pregnant now."
"Favonius?" she asked. The angel smiled and whispered, "Yes,
And please remember that your son will be a quarter angel."
Now Urania grew more complex, increasing population, swelling
With these pilgrims who sought places for the waiting they must do.
And Zephyr's belly swelled in concert with the building of her city.
Labor came: Favonius attended her and wrapped their newborn son
Inside a linen sail, a remnant from a river craft abandoned
By a seeker who had settled in the city. Eight days later,
Zephyr and Favonius went wading with their son into a shallow
Corner of the stream, and there the naked three embraced the water
With their arms, the silken mud with feet and rumps. The parents
Chanted, "Thou art Corposant, whose living body pleases us.
O let this water and this silt be playground, home, and school
To thee. And may this river and this city of your birth be
Mental food for thee as long as earth remains ensconced within
The artist-mind of God. We thank our artful God for thee."

241

XXXIV

So slight was Corposant, so lightly boned that breezes often
Challenged him to fly. When walking or when running, he seemed
Always on the verge of being airborne. When he laughed
His body rose then slipped again to earth. But he could
Fasten down by focusing his turquoise eyes (brighter even than
His mother's) onto any face he chose. And he could heal with touch
Or spit or words such living things as came to him, without discretion,
Like and unlike Vintager, his grandpapa. He liked especially
To touch the maidens whom he met in secret places near the river,
And to have them feel the vestiges of feathers on his chest and legs.

XXXV

Favonius believed the city needed artists who would paint its lines
And faces, oil and canvas images to circulate throughout the Garden,
Vivid signs and lures for seekers. Thus he left Urania in search
Of such. Each night away he dreamed of lying next to Zephyr
In their city bed. He longed to stroke her head and hips. One dusk
He found a covert fit for sleeping, at a place where woods
And grassland met, where he could stare into the darkness of the trees
Then turn and gaze across the rolling green savannah. Lying there alone
He spit into his palm and nursed himself erect with thoughts of Zephyr,
Pumping till he spurted his fertility onto the soil. Now Zephyr missed
Favonius as well, and lay in bed that night imagining his odor,
Touch and taste. She took a virgin candle in her hand
And gently pushed it in her, moving in and out, remembering
The rhythm of Favonius. At dawn she put the candle in a basket.
Weeks elapsed, until Favonius returned with Chrome, an artist
Eager for the work. And Corposant escorted Chrome around Urania,
While Zephyr set out apples, cheese and wine, undid her hair and slipped

Out of her robe. Favonius undressed as Zephyr lifted out her candle,
Lit it, let its earthy fragrance burn as they united. After food, he spit
On fingers, snuffed the flame, and curled into her arms and legs and slept.

XXXVI

Chrome had no intention of remaining in Urania.
She came with a commission to create some works of art
And then return to Murex, mate to her for twenty years.
He traded purple shells and other rarities, and so
They lived adjacent to the sea, where she grew intimate
With sand and brine. Her hair was reddish dark sometimes
And sometimes reddish gold. Though two score years, her frame
Was girlish and her face a decade younger than her age.
While Corposant, one half her years, was setting city scenes for her,
She sensed the most compelling scene was he, and he must pose.

XXXVII

Corposant was not demure when asked to pose.
Without request he stripped himself of clothes, declaring,
"Paintings of Uranians should show the nakedness inherent
In an urban seeker's life." Across the river on a barren bank she led
Him through a series of positions –standing, hands on hips and legs
Apart; reclining, rising on his elbows, one leg bent, one straight.
His patience for display was long as artist sketched and painted
All that afternoon, until the rain began, its soft drops washing
Down her skin and soaking through her dress, which she removed.
And so, the artist and the model danced around the muddy bank,
And splashed through newly forming puddles, sliding down
Into the warm, demulcent earth and rolling into one another's arms
And making love in concert with the rising rhythm

Of the bursting clouds. And as the downpour reached
Its culmination, so did they. That evening Chrome decided
She would stay and paint as many aspects of the city
As she could before a summons home could not be set aside.
She worked intensely, drawing from her palette death-denying colors
That she brushed into contrasting visions of Urania.
And all the while she painted she made love to Corposant.

XXXVIII

Murex had a client who appreciated purple shells beyond
Their trading value. Corinth felt the beauty of their swirling
Lines. He also felt affection for the man who dealt in them.
One night, the two were acting melancholy over wine,
And Corinth quietly confessed his love for Murex. Murex,
Not surprised, began to stroke the blushing cheek of Corinth
And proposed a consummation, which ensued with fumbling
Honesty and latent guilt. Thereafter, when their economic
Interests coincided, they found ways and places where their love
Could be requited. Yet in secret was this manly marriage built.

XXXIX

Watching as the garden grew increasingly complex
Inebriated God. The Androgyne Creator laughed
Without reserve because the humans dared to live
With relativity. "How long," God wondered, "will it take them
Till they recognize the universe is running down
While they are running up? Will anyone suspect
Their end will not extend into the end of time?
Their consummation will be unexpected at the middle,
When and where and with a crossing of the cosmic wax and wane.

But till that instant when I suck them back into my lungs
I pray that they will have the courage to withstand the pain
Inherent in unfolding beauty. Maybe I should send
An angel to them, bearing hints, alluring bits
To keep them searching, keep them running up
Toward climax." God then summoned trusted Ebenezer
For this apostolic task and told the angel certain things,
Suggestive, incomplete and tempting thoughts to fill
The ears of those on earth who had the strength
To hear. Obeying, Ebenezer traveled to Urania,
Where Corposant and Chrome were linked in fertile passion.

XL

Chrome conceived, though she had not anticipated this, for she
Had never missed a monthly flow in thirty years. Her blossoming
Brought fears related to her body and her husband. Correspondence
From him told her he was trading on the isthmus, would be gone a year.
He need never see the child, yet marks, she knew, remained across
A woman's skin. Would he observe and know? She bore a girl and gave
The child to Zephyr and Favonius to raise. But first, however, Corposant
And Chrome went wading in the river where, with ritual solemnity,
They named the infant Vayu. Then the lovers made a pilgrimage
Into the mountains to assuage a call they'd heard to artless meditation.

XLI

Ebenezer's visit to the city coincided with Chrome's unbeknownst
Conception. Not by chance the angel met the lovers
As they lolled about their terrace after making more than love.
The haloed intersexual engaged them with celestial talk,
Enticed them with expansive speculation over what it was

God wanted of humanity. "The heights reveal some answers,"
Ebenezer said, "for those whose minds are open left and right
To depths." "Yet God seems in the midst," said Chrome, "of everything
I paint." "Can God be known?" asked Corposant. "Inside
Reflection of experience," said Ebenezer, "God is felt,
And yet interpretation often kills the sense. And in unseeking
Silence God is sometimes heard and yet dismissed as music too absurd."
Ebenezer sojourned in the city on extended apostolic mission,
And when Vayu started speaking sentences at six months old,
Favonius sought out the angel to be nurturer and tutor to the child.
For forty days –on trial- the angel led the infant through a realm
Of lore. For forty nights the angel wrestled with the implications
Of the task. "If I accept," thought Ebenezer, "choosing earth,
The entrances to heaven will be closed to me. And yet I do
Accept, for Vayu has beguiled me. Blindly I embrace Urania."

XLII

Chrome sat shivering beneath the unobstructed sun. The thinnest
Breeze swept past her naked body as she meditated on a granite
Ledge above the line where trees will grow. And yet it seemed
A gale to one unused to insufficient atmosphere. She saw
That Corposant, across the slope, was covering his shoulders
With a fur, but she preferred the penetrating coldness
On her skin to focus her attention to the choice she felt
Constrained to make. "The force of history directs me to return
To Murex, re-establish life beside the sea," she thought, and walked
To Corposant, who read her eyes and burrowed deeper in his fur.

XLIII

Corposant descended from the heights and wandered aimlessly
For weeks until his fasting frame could move no more. Unable now
To heal himself or any other living thing, he sat suspended
In a paralytic trance beneath a Bo tree, where
His weather chiseled mind at last released its grasp on anger.
"How can I diffuse the passion that I feel for Chrome, so I
Can live in harmony with others? Will some ever-changing,
Never-ending action scatter me enough to tame its tide?
Or must I meditate severely and by strength of will
Transcend the pulsing spirit, render impotent desire?
Resurrection seems unlikely either way. Perhaps,
Through concentration on a single aspect of this force
A channel can be shaped from which some satisfying beauty
Can emerge." This seeking of the tunnel of rebirth is what
He chose, and so with undiluted pain he rose, returning to Urania.
The paintings Chrome had made were stored unseen. Favonius
Asked Corposant to put them on display throughout the Garden.
This he did with melancholy joy and while engaged in showing
Works of art continued to imagine ways that he might turn
The unrenounced attachments of his heart to philharmonic wine.

XLIV

Vayu's skin was dusky, deeper hued than either parent. Dark blue eyes
With crystal whites around them added contrasts to her countenance,
As did the blood-red teardrop birthmark in the center of her forehead.
She was drawn into the minds of people and conversed in subtle ways,
So even strangers told her more about their inner lives
Than they had known themselves. With Ebenezer's tutelage she gained
A passion for the power lodged in symbols and devised a system

For expressing words with lines and curves. She loved to run
Throughout Urania with messages she'd written down, delivering with joy
The words she reproduced from dreams and observations.

XLV

Murex never mentioned Chrome's few stretch marks, never consciously
Took notice of them, nor did he ever speak of Corinth.
In the months that followed Chrome's return their conversation
Broadened but grew shallower and much was left unsaid by each.
Chrome devoted great imagination to redecorating rooms within
Their home, and Murex worked the landscape with inspired vigor.
Anyone could see their home was artfully arranged within, without,
And this brought satisfaction honestly to both. And each
In silence acquiesced to the sufficiency of living well aesthetically.
In passion they were friendly, kind, but sometimes inattentive,
Lost in fantasies. But life was adequate. The trade in shells
Was good, and Chrome produced a painting now and then.
A clean, perceptive painting of a shell brought tears to Murex,
But he could not tell her why. On summer evenings
They would entertain their friends from up and down the beach.
The wine was poured with generosity and yet conviviality
At intervals was punctuated by remembrances of other lovers.
Chrome and Murex had the perfect marriage, all their
Neighbors said, except they had no children. Chrome
Dreamed often of her daughter, dreamed of holding her again.

XLVI

The energy that Corposant was dissipating through his
Wanderings and speculations now had focus. He had found
A task in which his passion and his wits could be

Combined: the composition of *The Saga of Urania.* The prelude
To the poem would be the *Song of Zephyr.* Corposant would
Celebrate in verse the city's bliss and pain. And as he
Formed the words he knew the inspiration for his verse was
Chrome, who lived within his mind, a muse most intimate, and he
Derived from this, their only intercourse, the strength to love
The world. Yet when he saw Chrome's smile on Vayu's face he cried.

XLVII

The studio where Ebenezer tutored Vayu radiated warmth,
In contrast to the early February cold outside. Aromas from
The fireplace combining with the scent of angel stirred emotions
In the student, who now recognized how much she loved her teacher.
She was fascinated also with the angel's sexual sufficiency.
Her great grandfather Vintager, according to the family legend,
Had seduced an angel. Why not she? She reached across
The table and with fingers traced a downward curve
On Ebenezer's feathered chest in desultory quest
Of what might rise for her. With anxious grace the angel
Murmured, "Dear one, are you sure?" Unbuttoning her shirt,
She said, "I am." Unfastening her skirt, she said,
"And so are you." They lay together, teenage woman, ageless
Angel, near the hearth, with skin and feathers and the furry
Rug beneath them all contributing erotic sense and smell.
And Vayu felt dilation of her soul as Ebenezer covered her
And filled her, overflowing fluid, overflowing motion,
Overflowing fate. They were inseparable from that day on,
And they took deep delight considering for months
What symbol name to give to that which was conceived in her.

XLVIII

Vayu hurt throughout her pregnancy. The child she held
Within created havoc with her body. Who was this
Who twisted and refused to grant her rest? In autumn
When contractions came, the pain grew worse. Her labor carried on
Three days, and as the infant's head emerged into the air,
The life of Vayu waned. Before she ever saw the child
She died. And Ebenezer groaned so deeply resonations
Could be heard for leagues. The child, a woman helping Ebenezer
During labor later said, was neither girl nor boy. But no one really
Knew, for Ebenezer bundled up the infant carefully and disappeared.

Spring: The Avatars

XLIX

Drained of every purpose for his life except to share his grief
With Chrome, Corposant walked to the sea in search of her.
He found her on the beach, absorbed in sketching naked children
As they played in sand and water. Chrome was shaken by his lined
And haunted face. "Our daughter's dead," he said. When Corposant
Had finished telling her this tale of death and disappearance, Chrome
Went wading in the sea, her tears in dark communion with the waves.
Corposant stood watching her, starving for an hour of transcendence:
He and she embracing, making love, escaping from their grief
For any brief, enlightened moment that might break the hold
Of night. But each pronounced self-judgment, taking blame,
And Corposant went home alone, and Chrome fell into deep depression.
After months of watching Chrome in agony he could not ken,
Her mate knew he must leave. So Murex went to live with Corinth,
Openly, without apology. Abandoned now, the rage she'd buried
Over years came bursting forth, and on a sleepless dawn she climbed
A bluff and dove into the rocks below. And as her body
Smashed and broke, her soul whooshed free from all the years
Of psychic pain. Now Corposant returned to beg her to come home,
But when he found her dead, he also climbed the bluff and leapt.

251

L

God was stung. Absorbing all the earthly wounds from love and death,
God groaned. "I never thought the plot would move this far.
The scenes were meant to be endurable. And yet the players
Freely took the racking possibilities to levels I did not anticipate.
My glee has been annealed, my brightness dimmed by visions
Bending through their pessimistic prisms. Should I strike the set
And start again? Or simply interfere with certain actors to reduce
The agony? I do not cherish ache, yet ache from them is part of me.
I know I shall -I will- alleviate their plight somehow.
As much for them as me; as much for me as them. Amen."

LI

The sun had been in Scorpio when Vayu's child was born
And was in Scorpio again when Ebenezer reached the mountain
Village suitable to raise this male and female entity.
The highest mountains of the earth surrounded them. The winds
Were uncaressing, cold, and life was daily filled with clarity,
The contrasts clean and insights unobstructed. Here, a year
Beyond the death and birth day Ebenezer wrapped the child
In layered woolen cloths and climbed with the angelic babe
Up to a lesser peak and faced the solar dawn and sang,
"From sorrow came thy birth, and yet thy life may bring
To earth a healing breath in answer to the deaths we grieve.
Thy name is Ruach. May thy life relieve the anguish waiting
In the world's tomorrow." Ebenezer tutored Ruach with the aid
Of mystic monks and nuns who lived in mountain caves,
As well as the prolific villagers who framed and crafted
Precious wooden artifacts. For generations Ruach meditated
And absorbed the wisdom of the highest places, till the sun

Crossed into Scorpio the ten times seventh time since Vayu
Died. And then this aging woman-man began a pilgrimage
Of preaching, down the mountain, past the plain, into Urania.

LII

The city had become a place of fierce and bitter striving.
Brutal, angry acts were commonplace and thievery the norm
For merchants, clerics, and officials. Ruach wandered through
Cloacal alleys searching after eyes which had abandoned
Hope, the faces of surrendered souls, and then as he-she
Gathered twelve or so with promises of wine or morphia,
Proceeded to unfold a story of the future. "Time will come
When two return to earth, arriving with the kindest winds,
And each forsaken, Styx-embracing one of you will know rebirth.
No longer wait politely for your death but watch for two as one."

LIII

A single, piercing voice arose to challenge Ruach, soon becoming
Two, then four, and then the masses' voice: "Who is this thing,
This bearded hag, who tells us not to wait for death?"
They gathered stones and turds. "Be gone!" they yelled
And flung their missiles at the prophet's cheeks and chest
Till Ruach staggered, dripping blood and dung, away and toward
The river, finding stinging silence and relief from angry
Arms within a darkened shoal. The reeds and muck were
Welcome medicine for Ruach's wounds, and after seven days
Of healing in the waters at the city's edge, this daughter-son
Of Vayu and an exiled angel climbed up from the river, meditated
In the drying sun, then walked across the quiet waves and east
Into the barren hills. Precarious atop a finely chiseled tor,

With arms extended wide the prophet dove into the wind
And in descent observed the city atalene yet shining
As a perfect gem. Then lifted by the thermal hand of God,
This demi-angel glided toward the oriental north. For fifty
Sunsets Ruach fasted in the air while sailing upward
To the Himalayan toft, the place of nurture, education,
Peace, acceptance, home to Ebenezer, home to grace.

LIV

"I must retrieve those humans whom I dreamed and then exhaled
Full grown to earth," God said, conversing with the sparsest
Space in which God sought creative thought. "My Shore and Ocean,
Meditating now in charming limbo, shall return incarnate. Maybe
They can sway enough of humankind toward loving and accepting
Incarnation as a calling to poetic sense. Those two were
Near to knowing my intent. Perhaps they may influence multitudes."
And thus the temporary dwelling place for souls at rest but not
Yet merged was searched, and Shore and Ocean, elegant and wise,
Were plucked and shifted into newborn bodies on the earth.

LV

Dark in woodlands in the middle of a northern island
Ka was born and raised, the only child of ancient parents
Who conversed with rocks and trees and kept a buried crock
Of secret knowledge given by an eidolonic breeze (or so they said).
She grew in solitude and innocence of men. In winter she wore
Fur and skins and other seasons her own fur and skin sufficed.
Blonde and flowing hair would rise above her head and ride
The wind when Ka ran circuits round her sea bound land
In search of sunny spaces. She identified as holy certain

Fetching places where the forest and the water met and formed
A bond with stone and sand. At twenty she received from God
A silent and beguiling call to search the continents
For some man she would recognize though never having seen
His countenance before. She took a winter robe, a summer belt
Of cowrie shells and father's wooden crook and sailed alone
To find the largest mass of land on which to walk. Within
A moon Ka moored inside a western harbor and set off
On expedition. She told island tales and parables to gatherings
Along the way, for bread and meat and mead. She wandered
South and east and scrutinized each face for corresponding need.

LVI

Ebenezer sat in stupor, molting out of season, fasting
Without reason and rejecting inquiries of care from villagers.
Penitential anger kept the angel's thinning frame erect.
"I willed myself to earth with full awareness that these
Demi-holy humans must relate to one another to relate to God.
No intermediaries did I need to gaze at the Creator till I
Chose to love a planetary *objet d'art*. Should I have stayed
Among the stars? No matter; I am here, and I have loved
And grieved as if I were a human. God, forgive me for the pain
That I set loose. Now let me disengage from Terra. Let me die."

LVII

People of the canyon, male and female, wore their straight and fine
Black hair in braids to signify their twining with the One
Who carved their rainbow colored gorge and placed a warm
And muddy river in its bottom. They were mystics yet were mystified
When Supai, fourteen years and virgin, bore a son with blazing

Copper hair and lighter skin than any in the clan. The shaman claimed
The Sun as father, then induced an ecstasy to find a name beyond
The language of the canyon for the infant boy. The name Elysium
Accordingly was chosen, and at twenty this fair stranger
To the tribe heard voices calling him to climb the narrow pathway
Up and out and leave to find a woman he had never known,
A woman who would be alone, as alien as he had always been.
And so he traveled north and west, against the press of peoples
Who were searching south and east. Elysium crossed tiny islands,
Turning south and west and wandered over desert, mountain ranges,
Crossing seas and rivers, finding food and shelter on the trek
By reading faces and revealing to his benefactors secrets
Of their lives. He looked into the eyes of every woman
On his way. With questioning authority he stared, absorbing
Sadness, curiosity, and wisdom, yet he failed to see the stranger.

LVIII

Ruach sailed into the village, slipped in silence to the side
Of Ebenezer, stroked the feathered head with stiff and frozen
Fingers. "I will die before the equinox," said Ebenezer. "I will
Care for you until that day," said Ruach. So these wounded
Holy creatures lived in wordless symbiosis, Ruach tending Ebenezer
Till the eve of spring. That day a bolt of energy struck deep within
The parent's brain. The angel's body jerked and died and Ruach cried
With atavistic resonance. The first tears of the prophet's life
Now flowed as Ebenezer's soul was hurtled through a tunnel, dark
Yet light, increasingly familiar, summoned to an interview with God.

LIX

Ebenezer felt the boundless glow of God which did not burn or blind.
"Please speak your anger, angel," God invited. "Why,
O Androgyne, did you impose such pain on humankind?" "I
Did not do it," God intoned. "I gave them possibilities,
And they imposed the pain upon themselves. They made up rules,
Interpreting their flaws from seasons, and from hints of jealous
Angels, and mistook their guilt for love." "But what
Did you expect?" the angel asked. "With all the chaos
In the world that you created, what can they create
Except interpretations from ambiguous events? They blame
Themselves and seek relief from you. I did the same as I
Became more human in the midst of them." Now God
Released a melancholy breath and said, "They do not know
That I experience every erg of pain they generate. I have
No vested interest in continuing their hurt. Yet even I
Have limits set upon myself. My interference must suggest,
Not force. And I have set in motion something to alleviate
Distress –I hope. Your daughter-son has played a part in this
And will again, for Ruach has a channel of prophetic intuition
Which is agent for my godly influential ***modus operandi.***

LX

Losing Ebenezer caused disquietude to linger in the mind
Of Ruach. Sleepless months ensued, and meditation was impossible.
At autumn equinox a thought of awesome clarity came overriding
The exhaustion of the prophet's brain: Return now to Urania
And speak to any who will listen for the godly possibilities
Inherent in each life. Then Ruach slept with holy soundness
Forty days, then rose and ate and traveled to that place. No stones

Were slung this time, though most inhabitants dismissed
The prophet as eccentric. He-she tended bees and sold the honey
For a living and continued to tell tales of two to come as one.

LXI

Word of Ka, the island storyteller, spread throughout the region
Of Urania. Midsummer's Eve upon a hill that overlooked the town,
She stood, clad only in a simple string of cowrie shells about her waist,
Prepared to string with words the rapt imaginations of the crowd,
That numbered more than seven thousand. Naked from his
Warming hike, Elysium arrived and stared into the eyes of Ka.
Gold sweat poured down his face and chest, his breath hung still
Within his lungs, and every feature, every other person faded from
Awareness. Ka stood fixed in time and rapt within a corresponding
Line of sight. They met. She traced the angles of his face
With startled fingers as he stroked her braided hair and followed
Gently the circumference of her breasts. Without exchanging
Words of any language, known or otherwise, they kissed
And fell into a trance wherein the dance of sexual
Communication swirled around them. Ka leaned backward, braced
Her hands and arms against a boulder, faced Elysium,
Unaware of multitudes of eyes recording images for mythic
Recollection. Ka-Elysium in union saw a flash of previous
Existence, knew as one that they had been on earth before.

LXII

Chrome expected nothingness as payment for her death. Instead,
She was surrounded by an atmospheric sense of being loved
Without regard to karmic debt. Neither were apology nor praise
A part of limbo. Here acceptance of the truth without affixing

Blame to self or any other being was the only law. Her sense of self
Was clustered with familiar souls, and she was not surprised
When Corposant's identity came rushing into hers, and there
They bided time, not one, but overlapping, touching, knowing
Peace, aware of indications for the future. Further incarnations
Would be needed to advance the course of earth and theirs as well.

LXIII

Elysium and Ka explored the land and found a long neglected
Garth that satisfied the sensibilities of each. Their smitten
Bodies and their limerant minds found frequent opportunities
To touch, to play with genitalia, tongues, and hair and
Hands. Their glands, at last, awake from hibernation, galloped
With abandon. Now at last, they also knew that they must find
Within their union wisdom for some purpose which they failed
As yet to see. What news could they –as two in one– provide
To humankind that each alone could not? The bond they felt
Was strong apart from sex, and yet it deepened, opened
Other spheres of understanding in the midst of intercourse.
So they exulted in their carnal love, and talked, exchanging
Myths and allegories from their natal homes. And in the course
Of time they understood how humans seek to know the One,
To track the ways of God, to fix their places in the universal
Scheme. "We must describe the Deity we know," said Ka.
"The One who grants us momentary glimpses of the unity of all
Creation," said Elysium, though either could have said
The other thought. And so they wandered through the world
To share the new and ancient stories of the God within the two in one.

LXIV

God relaxed and murmured, "Pain will still define the human work
Of art, but there are tinctured sweeps of joy as well. I am
Content to know I have created deep resilience in the figures,
More than I was thinking of initially. And influential souls will
Reinterpret images of hope from me, recurrently. So I
Will let humanity create, substantially, its own design,
Though I'm considering withholding certain options as I may
Delight in interjecting now and then with *ex cathedra* rhyme.
But mostly now I'll watch and listen, laugh and cringe,
And pray for everyone as earth moves toward the eye of time.

Ananda: The Fifth Season

LXV

Millennia experienced their durations, burning high or cooling down
In turn, and men and women flowed through time in various
Configurations, loving, losing, dying, living, bound in pairs
And double pairs and singly and in triangles, each being taking
Whatsoever sense there be in maleness or in femaleness in tune
With all the incarnations given seriatim. Woman, man,
Man, man, woman, woman, woman, man, and androgyne. And then
The sucking started. Now began a gentle pull that lifted
Bodies up, away from earth, surrounding each with cosmic,
Warm saliva, melting each into a consciousness of shared
Delight in male and female unity. Their feeling was well-being
In the floating in an upward stream of breath toward God.
And it was very good. And one by one the blind could see,
The deaf could hear, the impotent and cold began to feel.
All senses brightened and intensified. The smell and taste
Of distant heaven teased their faculties. The middle
Had been reached. And now a kundalinic knowledge
Spread in even waves throughout the human host.
All souls approached the pre-orgasmic plane where they
Remained without impatience, held in pleasant tension,
Now prolonged in erogenic state, and knowing self and other
As complete. And there was light and darkness unified, and there

261

Was recognition by the host that God was in this intercourse.
A day, a billion years elapsed in peace and confidence,
In pulsing beauty, as the sentient art of God experienced
The arrest of time and the fruition of desire. So the choir
Sang –libidinal and intimate the song- in four part unison.
Andromorph and gynomorph and God and angel lost and found
In miscible adagio. The Self emerged discernible at last
Without relationship to time or place, a curving, calm
Awareness, never sated, satisfied and innocent and immanent.
And yet eternity was not eternal. Imperceptibly at first, the light
Grew lighter, music stronger, senses fuller, penetrating past
The balanced unity, receiving now that unexperienced, unrefracted
Fraction of the soul of God, until the choral union knew
That love must burst into perfection and release. And burst
It did in grand and potent, glowing climax staying
Bright for centuries. And then the light began to dim,
The senses trembling at the height of limitation faded rapidly.
The universe and God contracted into spheric density and paused.

Commentary

Androgyny is a mental rather than corporal phenomenon, and thus an androgyne is one who unifies masculine and feminine elements within the mind. This is distinctly different from the physical state of an intersexual (previously referred to as a hermaphrodite), whose body contains both male and female sex organs.

Angels, according to *The Third Song of Creation,* are both male and female. That is they are intersexuals, unlike Pauline Christians, who are neither male nor female. These beings represent an unsuccessful experiment by God to create divine entities who have complete free will but who are constrained to desire only the good.

The earliest forms of worshiping God remain appropriate today, namely dance, singing, sex, and thinking. Other forms of human art are also suitable. Genesis reports that humans were made in the image of God. This Deity who imagines both male and female must therefore be Androgyne as well as Creative Artist. .

The first song of Creation is Genesis 1:1-2:4a. The second song is Genesis 2:4b-25. If taken literally, the inescapable fate of the offspring of the first man and first woman must be children born of incest. If taken figuratively, other possibilities abound. *The Third Song of Creation* can be read at multiple levels and subject to many methods of interpretation, except the factual and historical.

There is a legend that an ancient holy poet produced a scroll bearing *The Saga of Urania,* then sealed it in a stone jar and hid it in a cave in an arid mountain zone. Perhaps a shepherd or an archaeologist will discover it someday.

About the Author

Kenneth Alan Moe was born in Phoenix, where from an early age he experienced mystical events. At age ten he began writing poetry. His working life has included service in the U. S. Army as a prisoner of war interrogator, in the corporate world as an insurance investigator, and as a mainline Protestant minister.

Consistently underscoring it all, for more than half a century he has practiced the vocation of writer, evolving through pencil, pen, manual and electric typewriter, and computer to produce reams of fiction, non-fiction, and poetry. Moe's novels reflect his staunch advocacy for feminist and gay rights issues.

About Strange Angel Press

Strange Angel Press is a consortium of writers who act as editors, advisors, and cheerleaders for one another. We pool our collective experiences and talents to help participating writers with the art, craft, and discipline of fully telling the stories that have inspired us to put words to paper.

Visit our websites:
strangeangelpress.com
facebook.com/StrangeAngelPress
facebook.com/HereticsInOccupiedEden

NO SUCH THING AS COINCIDENCE...

The Rider had chosen him. The knot of darkness would billow out of his chest like a mist of writhing tentacles, to feed, flay and kill. Its goal, its need... its passion bled through his dreams as he slept. Salvation would only come once he brought the Rider to its desire.

Now bound to the deadly spirit, Evan Michael's only chance for survival lay with two witches from the Order of Magdalene: women who could bind the Rider to prevent it from feeding and help him avoid the authorities.

If they failed, he would be executed in front of a live television audience.

But, the Rider's passion was to kill the Abbess, the leader of the Order of Magdalene.

If they succeeded...

Available in Paper and Kindle editions on Amazon.com

STRANGE ANGEL PRESS